Ides of March

TIME PATROL

Cool Gus Publishing

Cool Gus Publishing
coolgus.com

http://coolgus.com

This is a work of fiction. Names, characters, places, and incidents either are the product of the author's imagination or are used fictitiously, and any resemblance to actual persons living or dead, business establishments, events, or locales is entirely coincidental.

Ides of March (Time Patrol) by Bob Mayer
COPYRIGHT © 2016 by Bob Mayer

ISBN: 978-1621252726

Ides of March

TIME PATROL

BOB MAYER

"Who controls the past controls the future; who controls the present controls the past." George Orwell: *1984*

Dedication

For
Haydn Riker Cavanaugh

Where The Time Patrol Ended Up This Particular Day: 15 March

"The vicissitudes of fortune, which spares neither man nor the proudest of his works, which buries empires and cities in a common grave."
Edward Gibbon. The History of the Decline and Fall of the Roman Empire.

Rome, Roman Empire, 44 B.C.

MOMS HELD A WARM LIVER ABOVE her head in supplication, dark blood oozing around her fingers, running down her arms into her armpits.

It tickled.

She wasn't sure for whom or why she was holding it up.

Moms remained still, but her eyes darted about, checking out the immediate situation, her ears attuned for any noise. Distant, muffled sounds, nothing specific. She sniffed? Death, which was to be expected, given the fresh blood. She was inside a dark chamber, the

1

only light coming from a round opening in the ceiling. A sheep, the source of the smell and blood, was on a dais in front of her. A knife was stuck in the opening carved in its side. A woman stood on the other side of the carcass. Her white robe trimmed with gold was splattered with blood. She was staring intently at the liver, head leaning to the side, pale blue eyes unblinking. She had pure white hair and a face lined with age, with very pale skin.

Moms figured such rapt attention meant she should keep her position. The blood finished draining. It was slowly drying on her skin, not quite ticklish any more, rather a bit bothersome, especially as it drew forth memories for Moms. Of performing triage on soldiers, comrades, who'd been wounded in battle, desperately trying to keep them alive for medevac. Often succeeding, but failing too often. Once is too often.

"Put it down, Amata," the woman snapped, pulling Moms out of her dark memories, which were yet to be made in terms of the planet's timeline, but she couldn't dwell on that, because down that path lay madness.

Amata? Then it was there, in her consciousness. Not her name, but a label: a woman in training to be a Vestal Virgin. *A bit late on that,* Moms thought, although Mac had found it hilarious during the mission briefing, until Scout had cut that short.

It is 44 B.C. The world's population is roughly 160 million humans. It is the year of the consulship of Caesar and Antony; Pharaoh Ptolemy XIV of Egypt dies; the first of Cicero's Philippics attacking Marc Antony is published.

Moms had blood on her hands.

Some things change; some don't.

Moms placed the liver on a silver tray. The old woman walked around the dais, leaning heavily on a cane.

She leaned over and poked at the liver with a finger. "See that?"

"Yes," Moms said, seeing only liver.

"Ah!" the woman hissed. "I told Caesar to beware the Ides. But this? This is different."

Spurinna. Moms knew the woman's name, except history had recorded the seer who warned Caesar as a man, not a woman.

Such is history's presumptive misogyny, Moms thought.

"Different how, Spurinna?" Moms asked.

The old woman didn't look up from the liver, continuing to poke and prod. "Marc Antony. He must do his duty and save mighty Caesar today, since I fear my warning will not be heeded. It is Antony's destiny. He must be told." She gazed into Moms' eyes. "And you are not an Amata."

Spurinna snatched the sacrificial knife and held it to Moms' throat.

Petrograd, Russia, 1917 A.D.

"PLEASE DON'T!" DOC PLEADED.

The Tsarina was startled by Doc's shout. "How dare you enter my chambers!"

It was not phrased as a question, but an admonition from someone who was used to having her every word obeyed from the moment she could speak.

Her four girls were kneeling, their heads bowed, and lips moving in silent prayer to the mixture of orthodoxy and subsequent mysticism that had consumed their mother. The Tsarina held her frail boy in her arms. While one hand cradled his head, the other clenched a small knife, the point pressed against her son's forearm. Prince Alexei's eyes were closed and he wasn't reacting to the pressure.

It is 1917. The world's population is roughly one billion, eight hundred and sixty million, although the First World War, the War to End All Wars, is taking a chunk out of that, well on its way to totaling twenty million dead; J.R.R. Tolkien begins writing The Book of Lost Tales; in the U.S. imprisoned suffragettes from the Silent Sentinels are beaten in what became known as the Night of Terror; the first Pulitzer prizes are awarded; Mata Hari is arrested for spying; John F. Kennedy is born; a race riot in St. Louis leaves 250 dead.

This was Doc's first Time Patrol mission and it wasn't looking good.

Some things change; some don't.

"Don't do it, Tsarina." Doc attempted a calmer tone, realizing he was speaking Russian, not exactly the greatest revelation at the moment.

"I must," Alexandra said. "For all of Russia. Only then, will my dear Nicholas listen and the people understand. It is what Rasputin prophesied." She nicked her son's skin and blood flowed.

More blood than Doc had ever seen from such a simple cut, but this was the curse of the Royal Disease.

Palos de la Frontera, Spain, 1493 A.D.

"WHERE'S THE BAND? THE KING? THE QUEEN? The Sons of Italy?" Mac muttered. He was watching a small ship riding its anchor chain in the muddy backwash of an estuary formed by the confluence of two rivers.

The names of the ships that had left here on a voyage of discovery the previous year ran through his brain, echoing from the historical rhyme of his childhood: The *Nina* and the *Pinta* and the *Santa Maria*.

But there was only one ship here: the *Nina*.

His download confirmed that the *Santa Maria* had run aground off Haiti on Columbus' journey. The *Pinta*? It would arrive shortly; if history remained true.

Mac couldn't believe men traveled in such small ships across the ocean. He was standing just above the mud flats on the south bank of the estuary. Behind him were a number of low buildings. To his right, on a low rocky bluff overlooking the merging of the two rivers, was a friary, a watchtower poking above the walls. To his left, the estuary opened to the Atlantic Ocean.

"Devotio Moderna?"

Mac turned. The man who'd addressed him was dressed in a plain brown robe, with a rope cinched around the waist. A small wooden cross dangled from it. Given that was exactly the way Mac was dressed, it wasn't much of a leap on the other's part.

"Yes. *Devotio Moderna*."

"I am Geert. From Belgium. Welcome to Palos de la Frontera."

"I'm Mac."

Geert cocked his head. "'Mac'? That is all?"

"That is all."

Geert had thinning blond hair and was several inches shorter than Mac, his face scarred from smallpox. He was slight of build, lost inside his monk's robe. "They should give a better name before they send you back. Welcome to my time."

Mac relaxed. But only slightly, remembering Scout's debriefing that the first supposed Time Patrol agent in her last mission had worked for the Shadow and tried to kill her. Along with the second supposed agent. *They'd really had it in for her*, Mac thought. He hoped

4

her trip this time was smoother. "It's only for twenty-four hours. My name is not important."

"True," Geert acknowledged. He nodded at the ship. "Columbus arrived from Lisbon an hour ago. It is odd he went to Portugal first. Many are speaking of it, considering Ferdinand and Isabella financed his journey, not King John."

It is 1493 A.D. The world's population is roughly 425 million humans; there had been 450 million 150 years ago, but the Black Death had done some damage and the world still hadn't recovered; England imposes sanctions on Burgundy for supporting a pretender to the English throne; Maximilian I succeeds his father, Frederick III, as Holy Roman Emperor; Russian Prince Andrey Bolshoy dies; Spain, having issued the Edict of Alhambra the previous year which demanded all Jews convert or be expelled, begins to suffer economically without many of it most successful and influential citizens.

"Why am I here?" Mac asked. His head was throbbing, not just from the knowledge downloaded before coming back, but also from a tremendous hangover.

Some things change; some don't.

"*You* know what is supposed to happen," Geert said. "I only know what has happened and a little of what is happening. Columbus is on board the *Nina*. He has allowed no one to disembark yet, which is strange because a number of the crew are from the town."

That explained the group of women and children who were gathered at a small quay, talking angrily and peering at the ship.

"Why has no one come ashore?" Mac asked.

"I have no clue," Geert said. "There are people visible on deck, but otherwise—" he shrugged. "And there is also that." Geert looked past Mac.

Fifty meters away, six men clad in black doublets and hose were seated at a wood table outside a shabby building that appeared to be an inn, bar and eating establishment.

The men weren't sleeping, drinking, or eating. They were gazing at the ship. They had rapiers sheathed at their waists and a demeanor Mac was familiar with, being one himself: Soldiers. Killers who knew their business; one who has served in an elite unit can always tell the difference.

"Who are they?" Mac asked.

"They're from the *Cent Suisses*," Geert said.

"The Hundred Swiss?" Through the fog of receding alcohol, the pertinent information materialized.

"Swiss mercenaries," Geert said. "They fight for whatever Crown will pay them. These particular ones? They've been sent by Rome."

"Why are they here?"

Geert spread his hands. "Who knows? Protect Columbus, perhaps?"

"From who?"

Geert looked at him. "Perhaps from us? You tell me. In your history, does he die today? Or does he live? Are *we* to help him live or let him die? Or kill him ourselves?" His hand strayed inside a slit in his robe to show Mac the hilt of a dagger. "Life or death. Just let me know what it is to be."

Thermopylae, Greece, 480 B.C.

"IF THE WORDS OF YOUR ORACLE are true, this is my final night." The speaker, without any apparent concern in his tone about their grave situation, was clad in armor that was battered, bent, and freshly splattered with blood. He was lying on his back, looking up at the stars, a rolled up red cloak acting as an expedient pillow. His helmet was on the ground next to him, as ordinary as any other warrior's, except for the stiff brush of horse hair indicating his rank: King.

Scout could smell the death. Worse, she could sense it, all around them. She was sitting on a stone, her dark cloak wrapped tight, one hand holding a Naga staff. On the narrow pass between the mountain and the cliff overlooking the Malian Gulf, small groups of warriors were gathered round fires, conversing softly. A wall composed of bodies and stones hastily piled together, blocked the way to the north. A handful of Spartans stood watch on the grisly bulwark.

There had been three hundred Spartans when this fight began several days ago.

Not many were left standing.

Scout realized King Leonidas was staring at her. "What say you, priestess of the Oracle of Delphi? What of the prophecy?"

"The words are true," Scout said, but didn't add: *If my mission today succeeds.* Which naturally led to the next thought: *Of course, it would be nice to know exactly what the mission was.*

"The way you paused," Leonidas said. "It almost gave me hope. But it's strange. Before every battle, I have felt fear. Of being maimed. Killed. Most of all defeated. But no matter how dire the fight appeared, or how terrible the odds, I always believed deep inside that none of those would happen." He sat up and looked at his soldiers. "We all know we'll die one day. Everyone does. In battle or of disease or inevitably of old age. But it's always in the future. Not today."

Leonidas reminded Scout of Nada. Despite what the king was saying and the circumstances, there was calmness surrounding him, a steadiness that inspired confidence. It was reflected by the remaining Spartans. Even though they'd all experienced enough battles to know what awaited them in the morning, prophecy, or no prophecy, they were poised. There was no sense of panic. Military reality dictated they were at the breaking point; as their number dwindled with each death, King Xerxes of Persia had an endless supply of warriors to throw against them.

The Spartans were speaking in subdued tones, no bragging. Having conversations that only the prospect of imminent death could unlock from deep within a man's soul.

"When you take this map," Leonidas said, "will you stay with it or do you deliver it somewhere?"

"I will know when I have it." *So, this was about a map,* Scout thought. *Dane had been vague in the briefing, but that went to the essence of this battle against the Shadow's attempts to change the timeline.*

"And after you fulfill whatever task has been laid on you, will you go back to the Oracle?"

"I don't know my fate." That, at least, was true.

"If you survive somehow and stay in Greece, will you do me a favor?"

"Yes, if it is within my power."

Leonidas smiled. "I believe it is indeed within your power. Go to my home. Tell my wife how I died."

"I can do that," Scout lied.

"I'm not done yet," Leonidas said. "I have grown to admire you during our journey here from the Oracle. I want you to teach my daughter."

Scout had no clue what had happened on that journey. "What would you like me to teach her?"

"To be like you."

Scout hated this next lie. "I will."

It is 480 B.C. The world's population is roughly 100 million humans. Troops from Rome, far from being an Empire yet, march against the Vientes, the richest Etruscan tribe; Zhong You, a disciple of Confucius dies; the Imperial Treasury at the Persepolis Palace in Persia is completed after three decades of work; artists begin the detail 'Musicians and Dancers' on the wall paintings in the Tomb of the Lionesses in Tarquinia, Italy; it will be completed a decade later.

Scout sensed a presence. She got to her feet.

Some things change; some don't.

"What is it?" Leonidas was up, putting his helmet on. "The Persians come in the dark?"

"No." Scout took a step toward the grisly barricade of Persian bodies and stones. "Someone like me."

"The Sibyl Pandora that the Oracle spoke of?" Leonidas asked.

Scout shivered and realized the danger she faced was not Xerxes, or his troops, or even the pending battle. The Shadow had sent one with the Sight against her: Pandora.

Newburgh, New York, 1783 A.D.

THE WHIP RIPPING INTO flesh made a distinctive sound. Eagle was jolted by the sound and the immediate scream of agony. He lunged forward, made two steps, and was tripped. He sprawled face down into straw covered dirt, hearing the whip strike home once more.

"Easy," a deep voice hissed. "Easy."

A hand was on Eagle's back, not keeping him down, but slowing him from jumping up, forcing him to take in his situation. The hand belonged to an older black man, who was now kneeling next to Eagle, shaking his head ever so slightly.

Behind them were four other black men, standing shoulder to shoulder. They were inside a barn, the horses skittish in their bays. The other slaves glanced askance at him, before returning their attention to the lesson being inflicted.

The source of the scream was a young black woman, her wrist shackles hooked on a spike high enough over her head to put her on her toes and keep her in place. She was twisting and cringing, as much as she could, but the mark for the man holding the whip was impossible to miss: her naked back.

Which was crisscrossed with old scars, now being torn asunder once more.

The source of the whip was a short, squat redheaded man who was doing this with the nonchalance of someone performing a task he'd done countless times before. His face was blank, and a corncob pipe dangled from one side of his mouth. He took a puff between each stroke.

It is 1783 A.D. The world's population is roughly 900 million, of which only 3.6 million are part of the fledgling United States, announced seven years ago on the 4th of July; even though fighting with Britain had stopped, the war was technically not over on the 15th of March; that would happen in September with the Treaty of Paris; Catherine the Great of the Russian Empire annexes the Crimean Khanate, finishing off the final remnant of the Mongol Golden Horde; the last celebration of Massacre Day is held in Boston; the first public demonstration of a parachute jump is done in France by a man leaping from an observatory; the 1783 Great Meteor passes over the North Sea, Great Britain and France prompting fear and scientific speculation; the Cedula of Population is made into law in Spain, allowing any who swears fealty to Spain and the Catholic Church to settle in Trinidad and Tobago.

Eagle was in a place he had no desire to be.

Some things change; some don't.

"I do not take pleasure from this," another man said. The early afternoon sun streaming through the barn door silhouetted his tall figure, easily over six feet. "It is the law and we must respect the law. It is what makes us a nation. You all know this is only a last resort. But she did not just attempt to run away. She tried to go to the British carrying some of my correspondence. That is treason and I have had white men executed for less. I am being merciful."

The man was keeping his distance, as if by doing so, he distanced himself from the act of his overseer. "That's enough," he ordered after the whip struck home once more. The overseer wiped blood off the twisted leather braids with a dirty rag, then coiled it. He hung it on a hook on the side of his belt.

The man giving the orders stepped into the barn and Eagle recognized him. Dressed in a blue uniform, brocaded with gold trimming: George Washington.

Ravenna, Capitol of the Remains of the Western Roman Empire, 493 A.D.

ROLAND SLIPPED IN THE MUD AND BLOOD, which saved his life as the spear struck his chest armor obliquely.

The Goth didn't get a second chance as Roland took his head off with a single swipe of the sword, the decapitated body tumbling to join three others corpses.

They really had to get better with the timing on this time travel thing, Roland thought as he spun about, ready for more enemies. Twenty feet away, a fifth person, a woman wearing a long black robe, took a step back and vanished into a black Gate. It was gone a second later.

That was different, Roland mused. Now there was no one on the cart path other than four bodies. He checked the forest to either side, not taking the time to ponder the vanishing woman or even the bodies, focusing on staying alive for the moment.

"Centurion!" Several soldiers came running around a bend in the path, swords drawn. Roland went on guard, but recognized they were equipped with the same uniform and armor he wore, and not that of the bodies, which Nada would have said didn't prove they were on the same side. So, Roland lowered the tip of his sword a little less than an inch, until he could be certain they meant no harm. While one checked the bodies, the others spread out, providing security, which he took as a friendly sign.

It is 493 A.D. The world's population is roughly 190 million humans; in China, Emperor Xiaowen of Northern Wei begins his campaigns against Southern Qi, which culminates against the opposing Emperor Ming; Patrick, who would become the patron saint of Ireland, dies; the Byzantine Empire, once known as the Eastern Roman Empire, besieges and captures Cappadocia under the command of General John the Hunchback; Christianity has spread far beyond its start point in the Middle East; Buddhism reaches Burma and Indonesia.

And here on a muddy road in the middle of forest, Roland had once more killed.

Some things change; some don't.

Thirteen riders came around the bend. Astride a warhorse in the midst of them was a man wearing a purple robe over his shiny, for-show armor, which indicated he was some big muckety-muck, since Roland knew the type from his time in the army. Remembering the briefing, Roland realized this guy was probably *the* big muckety-muck. The reason he was here.

Unless Dane and the Time Patrol had made a big mistake, which Roland didn't rule out, and Nada would have expected.

But Nada was dead.

Odoacer, First King of Italy, sometimes calling himself Emperor of the Western Roman Empire, although technically he'd overthrown the last one, history just didn't know it yet, leaned forward in the saddle. "Did you kill all four, Centurion?"

"Yes, sir," Roland said, figuring he, whoever he was before he, Roland, became aware of being here, had taken out the other three. Mac would have been impressed with that leap of logic on Roland's part. But Mac was elsewhere; same day, different year. Doc would have been astounded at Roland's instant ability to accept an improbable, yet logical, concept, but Doc was also, well, same deal.

Roland didn't think it would be smart to mention the disappearing woman. Another person, traveling back in time and suddenly appearing in the midst of a fight for their lives might have doubted what they saw, but Roland never doubted what he saw. It was one of his strengths.

"I need a man like you close to me. A killer. Especially this day." Odoacer raised his right hand, while he pointed with his left at Roland. "You are now one of my twelve; a Protector." He gestured imperiously, which Kings actually get to do, at one of the riders around him. "Give him your horse."

The guy didn't look thrilled, but dismounted.

Roland liked the sound of that title, Protector, as his mind processed the implanted data: it meant he was still the equivalent of a centurion, but in the King/Emperor's personal guard, the *Palatini*. Of course, like every army, it meant more responsibility, but the same pay; Then again, he was going to get to ride instead of walk, so that was something. Upgraded from the Infantry to the Cavalry; *why walk when you can ride?* was a rule of thumb in every army. *Why ride when you can fly?* was still quite a few centuries off. And the faux promotion meant he was a soldier on his way up in rank, except Roland's future here was limited to 24 hours; and the First King of Italy, who had taken power from the last true Emperor of Rome, Romulus Augustus, in 476 A.D., had even less time than that.

But *BEFORE* the Ides of March and *AFTER* they came back from Black Tuesday

Andes Mountains, Argentina

IT HAD TAKEN MOMS FIVE DAYS of her leave to make it up to this altitude, battling snow and weather the entire way. The effort had called upon all her cold-weather training and experience in the military. Going uphill in snow was battling a vicious combination of gravity and the elements.

But she was finally here.

In a flat piece of terrain, about a hundred meters from where the plane wreckage had been there was a stone pile with a makeshift iron cross. Pieces of the wreckage were also mixed with the stones.

Most of the wreckage of Uruguayan Flight 571 was gone, burned by a search party that had buried the human remains.

The remains of the people from the plane. Moms was here for someone else. She read the inscription on a metal plaque, automatically translating the Spanish:

The World to its Uruguayan brothers. Close, oh God, to you.

Appropriate, Moms thought. She moved two hundred meters away to a large boulder. She pulled out her snow shovel, unfolded it, and began to dig into a drift piled against the rock.

It took a while. How long, Moms didn't care. What was time after all? A variable.

Until you ran out of it.

She reached the corpse, well preserved from the cold, altitude, snow, and ice covering it since 1972. The body was missing a hand, the stub still covered by Moms' bandage. She gently brushed snow and ice from the face.

"Pablo, I buried your dog tags at your lover's grave. I thought it's what you would have wanted."

She sat down in the snow.

She recited the prayer they'd shared just before he died. *"Ave Maria, gratia plena, Dominus tecum. Benedicta tu in mulieribus, et benedictus fructus ventris tui, Iesus. Sancta Maria, Mater Dei, ora pro nobis peccatoribus, nunc, et in hora mortis nostrae. Amen."*

Moms didn't believe in prayer; her mother had prayed all the time in their rundown house out in the middle of nowhere Kansas. And look how those had been answered?

But Pablo had and that was all that mattered. The dead had to be honored.

She repeated the prayer three times. Then she pulled off a glove and placed her hand on his frozen face. "I remember your name. Pablo Correa."

Then her satphone went off: *Send Lawyers, Guns and Money.*

Duty called.

Roland: Eastern Coast of England.

"THIS IS WHERE I LANDED with the Vikings," Roland told Neeley.

Surf pounded the beach, the waves riled by a storm offshore, somewhere between England and Scandinavia. There was no sign of civilization in either direction.

Neeley was a tall woman, almost six feet, with short dark hair, now with some grey. But Roland towered half a foot over her and while she was slender and lean, he was broad chested and well-muscled. They were both accomplished killers, which an observer might think was the attraction between the two, but it was really their differences that had drawn them together.

Roland was a simple man; not simple-minded, as his teammates sometimes joked, especially Mac, but it was more a case of having a direct and linear way of looking at life and dealing with situations. Perhaps it was a result of his large physique, but Roland went through things, physically, mentally, and emotionally.

Neeley, coopted by a terrorist cell as a teenager, saved by a covert operative when her terrorist boyfriend betrayed her, trained in the dark arts, then coopted by the Cellar to be an assassin, tended to be more circumspect. Each respected the difference in the other, and respect is the foundation of any relationship.

Roland recalled his bubble of time here in 999 AD. "It was foggy." He pointed inland, to the right. "Come."

The two strode across the beach and into the dunes, Roland narrating as calmly as if describing a pleasant vacation. "This is where the berserkers ambushed us. I took down two, but it was a ploy. One escaped to give word of the number of our party and capabilities."

"Look." Neeley pointed. There was a unnatural mist ahead. "Do you feel it?"

"It's chilly," Roland said, but he knew that wasn't what she was referring to.

"Reminds me of the Space Between," Neeley said, referring to the netherworld region where innumerable Earth timelines connected. "Very faint, though."

They continued toward a six-foot tall upright stone. There were more behind it, placed in a rough circle. In the center was a nine-foot stone, angled 45 degrees.

"I feel it now," Roland said as they entered the stone circle. "It's exactly what it was like a thousand years ago. Tam Nok, the seer, said this was built by the original people, the survivors of Atlantis."

Neeley was drawn to the angled stone. There were faint markings on it. "This looks like what you said they're using in the Possibility Palace. Hieroglyphics."

Roland reached past her and put his hands on the stone. "I had the vision here. Actually, Tam Nok gave me the vision from the stone. Of the nun who had to die and the possible futures if I failed in my mission that day."

Neeley put a hand on his back. "You didn't fail."

Roland let go of the stone. "Let's see if anything is left of the monastery."

They departed the standing stones and headed north. Cresting a small rise revealed the place where Roland's mission had concluded.

There was nothing to show of the monastery and the village. Even the stones were gone from where the chapel had stood. Grass and bushes struggled to grow, as if the ground was cursed.

"I don't like this place," Neeley said.

"Nothing good came out of that mission."

"Yeah," Neeley agreed. "But nothing bad either. And isn't that the point?"

Roland was about to say something when Neeley's satphone buzzed with a text message. She was reading it when the satphone every member of the Time Patrol had been issued by Dane prior to going on leave went off, playing a ring tone: *Roland the Headless Thompson Gunner.*

He pulled it out of his pocket and looked at the screen, then at Neeley. "You first."

"I've got to get someone, escort them back to the States. Chopper's inbound."

Roland nodded. "Same chopper's inbound to pick me up too. I've been Zevoned."

Scout: Arlington Cemetery. Section 60.

"I KISSED MY FIRST BOY and then I had to kill him," Scout whispered to the cold stone. She was on her knees in front of the marker, leaning forward, forehead touching the tombstone. "Actually, Nada, he wasn't a boy, he was a man, and he was trying to choke me to death, even while we were kissing. But still, he was young. And I killed him. Did just as you taught me, in the heart, then shredded it with a twist of the blade. And I thought he'd really cared about me, but it was just pretend. I thought he was my contact. And I know, you'd have warned me not to trust him. A Nada-Yada: *trust no one.* But *we,* you and I, trusted each other."

She was surrounded by the dead-before-their-time, although as a member of the Time Patrol, Scout was beginning to doubt the nature of time itself. All the coffins were under the same upright headstones, 42 inches high, 13 inches wide, and 4 inches thick, according to Department of Defense regulations. It made them seem the same, except for the words inscribed in the stones.

"Then I had to kill again, same day. Same way. And I thought *he* was there to protect me too, but it was also pretend. They came after me, Nada. Of the six of us who went back, I'm the one the Shadow deliberately went after." Scout pulled her head back and traced the letters and numbers with her fingers.

EDWARD MORENO

MSG   USA

29 OCTOBER 1969

28 JUNE 2005

OPERATION RED WINGS

DISTINGUISHED SERVICE CROSS

SILVER STAR

PURPLE HEART

Sparse words for a life. She hadn't even known Nada's real name until she'd seen this marker in a vision after joining the Time Patrol. She'd served with Nada in the Nightstalkers, but when they became the Time Patrol and were given a chance to go back and fix one thing in their past, Nada was the only one who'd chosen to go back. A decision that meant one was unfit for the Time Patrol.

But he'd had a very good reason to try to fix this particular problem. Several in fact.

He'd fixed it and this marker was the price he'd paid.

Scout looked to the side, down the row. There were no flowers in front of the distant marker; the reason Nada had gone back: to make sure the man under that marker died.

Then Scout focused on the other date; the date of Nada's birth. He'd been born on the day she'd been sent to on her last mission. Black Tuesday. Scout felt a chill slither around her.

There were no coincidences. All of time was a pattern, millions of streams, billions of lives, woven in the tapestry of history that made the present and led to the future. Looking down into the spiraling depths of the Possibility Palace convinced one of that.

What was going on with that date? What was she caught up in? What--

"Did you know my father?" a woman asked, startling Scout.

Nada wouldn't have approved of Scout allowing someone to get so close without being noticed, but he would definitely have approved of the person. The woman was just out of her teens, her thick hair framing a beautiful face and eyes that reminded Scout so much of Nada.

"Isabella," Scout said.

"How'd you know my name?" Nada's daughter asked.

"Na—your father spoke of you often." Scout was disoriented, looping back to her vision of this cemetery during retrieval from Black Tuesday, 1969. But that vision had been of the place in 2005, and now was now.

"You look too young to have served with my father."

Not even in high school yet, Scout thought, trying manage the numbers, the years. "My father served with him," she lied. She held out her hand. "I'm Scout."

"Isabella." Nada's daughter frowned. "You seem familiar. Have we met?"

Scout was at a loss how to answer that honestly. "I don't believe so."

"And your father?" Isabella asked.

"He passed away."

"So we share that," Isabella said. "I barely remember him," she added, nodding at the stone.

"Your mother?" Scout asked.

"She's fine. Did you know her too?"

"We never met. Is she also visiting?"

Scout regretted the question as soon as she asked it, but between the date on the marker and this apparition, she was completely off-kilter. She saw the dark shadow flit across Isabella's face. Scout sensed the long ago pain which caused that; not of Nada's death, but of his life, who'd he been and one of the reasons he went back: to spare his wife and daughter any more pain living with the raging, abusive alcoholic he'd been.

"She doesn't come here," Isabella said, without any further explanation.

Scout fumbled in her pocket, pushing aside the satphone Dane had issued, and pulled out her personal iPhone. "Let me give you my number. If you ever need anything, anything, call me." She rattled off her number and told Isabella to call her right now, to get her number in the memory.

Isabella checked it, glanced at the screen. "Scout is a strange name."

Your father gave it to me, as he gave you your name, Scout was tempted to say.

"He was a fine soldier," Scout said. "I'll leave you alone. Remember. Call me if you need anything."

Why today? Scout wondered as she walked away. Why had Isabella come here today, so many years later? The vagaries of the variables? She didn't believe it. She could sense Nada. He, his essence, was in a place between life and death. A place out of time. He'd lived in this timeline up until recently, but now this timeline was saying he'd died in 2005. What was in between?

Scout walked down the row. She paused at the marker for the man Nada had taken down at the cost of his own life:

CARL COYNE
OPERATION RED WINGS
28 JUNE 2005
BRONZE STAR
PURPLE HEART
US NAVY SEAL

Scout spared one last glance over her shoulder at Isabella standing as still as the stone she was looking at.

Then the sat-phone's ringtone interrupted and as she heard it, she began crying as she pulled it out, because it was *Keep Me In You Heart*.

She was being Zevoned and the text indicated an aircraft was just two minutes out to pick her and another member of the team up.

I'll always miss you, Nada.

She could feel the words, at the edge of her consciousness, where her 'Sight' resided: *I miss you too.*

Mac: Old Palace Yard, London

"GUY FAWKES WAS EXECUTED in the open space directly in front of you," an obnoxious American tour guide was saying with an over-abundance of semi-knowledge. "Drawn and quartered, a most horrible way to die. And Sir Walter Raleigh had his head chopped off in the same place."

Mac wanted to tell the guide that Guy Fawkes had fallen from the ladder leading up to the scaffold *before* being executed. The fall broke his neck; whether deliberately, if he were smart, or by accident, either way he'd saved himself a lot of pain. And Raleigh would almost *not* have been executed, if it hadn't been for Mac's intervention.

Mac tipped back the bottle in the brown paper bag and took a long, satisfying gulp, then had to struggle not to retch. He settled for a couple of belches. A couple of tourists standing near him moved a few steps away. It wasn't just the bottle in the bag; he hadn't shaved since coming back from the Possibility Palace to the Gate in New York City and from there to the airport to board a flight to England. He also hadn't bathed. His eyes were bloodshot and alcohol was oozing out of his pores after five days of nonstop indulgence. Before the binge, he'd looked like a younger version of Tom Cruise.

"Hey, fellow." Someone grabbed Mac's elbow and he reacted instinctually. Pulling his elbow out of the grip, spinning in the opposite direction and using the other elbow to hit the man in the side of the head, knocking him to the ground. Only then did Mac notice the 'bobby' hat rolling away and the man's uniform. The crowd dispersed, leaving Mac standing over the unconscious policeman. A half-dozen more coppers were running at him.

Mac jiggled the bottle, estimated he had time to drain it, and began to guzzle it down. He'd just finished when the first cop tackled him. The bag fell to the pavement, the bottle breaking. Two more cops piled on.

Mac didn't put up any resistance, actually glad to be done with the binge. Some time in a cell would do him a fair amount of good.

He was thrown on his stomach and cuffed, face pressed down, one cheek to the cold concrete. Mac wondered how far into the soil underneath the concrete remnants of Raleigh's blood might still exist.

There'd been a lot of it.

Two cops pulled Mac to his feet, his hands behind his back. They were hauling him toward a waiting van, when a voice of authority stopped them.

"Scotland Yard. He's ours."

The man wasn't wearing a Sherlock Holmes' deerstalker hat, but then again, that was fiction too. And Holmes hadn't been Scotland Yard; Mac vaguely remembered Eagle ranting about it one day in the team room back at the Ranch, located just outside Area 51. That seemed forever ago, a thought which caused Mac to laugh, because, really, time was relevant, wasn't it?

He knew that for a fact.

The Scotland Yard fellow had a hard look about him, someone who'd seen a lot of bad stuff. Mac could commiserate with that.

"Cuffs off," the man ordered. "And clear out."

"He assaulted—" one of the cops began, but didn't finish.

"Cuffs off and clear out. Take your man with you."

Grumbling, picking up their unconscious comrade, the cops retreated to their cars and vans.

"You're a bloody mess," the man said, folding his arms.

"Just had a bloody time recently," Mac said and then laughed once more at his own private pun. His satphone went off, playing *Werewolves of London*.

"You a funny guy?" the Scotland Yard detective asked.

"Someone is," Mac muttered. "Mind if I check?"

The man pointed past Mac, at a black helicopter coming in fast and low. "You can check once you're on board that. You're their problem. My job is to get you on that helly."

The chopper touched down, the side door slid open and Roland and Neeley hopped out.

Oh great, Mac thought. *The dynamic duo.*

And then it occurred to him they might be working for the Cellar at the moment, in which case they'd probably be tossing him out of the chopper once they got to altitude.

At the moment, that didn't seem like too bad of an idea.

Eglin Air Force Base, Florida

EAGLE BROUGHT THE SNAKE in fast, barely a foot above the trees, before abruptly rotating the jet engines up and bringing the tilt-jet aircraft to a hover. Typical Florida panhandle terrain. Flat, scrub brush, low trees, and swamp.

And a graveyard for the men who'd supported him here in his Black Tuesday 1980 mission. They were long gone, melting into the dank soil, becoming part of it. They'd been losers, outcasts, a form of Dirty Dozen who had, most of all, been expendable.

Wars always needed the expendable.

Eagle rotated the engines and went back to nap of the earth flying, then dropping down as he cleared the trees. He skimmed over one of Wagner Field's landing strips. A twitch of his hands on the controls and he was on the runway.

Eagle shut down the engines and dropped the back ramp. A black man with a rangy build, Eagle had scars scrolled on one side of his bald skull, the results of an IED explosion a long time ago (in relative terms), in a country far away. With Nada's passing, in life and from this timeline, Eagle was now the team sergeant for the Time Patrol. But since they didn't go on missions together, as they had as Nightstalkers, it meant a different role, one he was still new to.

They were all new to it after only one mission under the new paradigm.

Eglin Air Force Base was where Eagle had gone for his Black Tuesday mission, but it was also where he'd gotten his first true taste of leadership as a young soldier, while going through Ranger School.

A faint mark crossed the remains of a line painted across the runway. It was here, on this very field, that James Doolittle had trained his pilots to get a B-25 bomber airborne in the short distance they would have on the flight deck of the *USS Hornet*.

Eagle knelt. The line was a marker, still here after all these years, an indicator where the pilot had to lift off. He placed his hand on the black rubber scar cutting across it and closed his eyes.

He could hear the sound of bomber engines, the smell of fuel. An image flashed of a B-25 racing down the tarmac, pilots struggling to get it airborne.

Eagle shivered and opened his eyes. The airstrip was empty except for the Snake. Not a person in sight. But he knew what he'd sensed was real; almost a memory. Or a memory to come? Whatever it was, Eagle had no doubt traveling in time had an effect, a lingering one. Whether that was a good thing or a bad thing was--

His satphone came alive: *Accidently Like a Martyr.*

Eagle gritted his teeth, not amused with Dane's humor.

He checked the screen, read the text, and jogged back to the Snake. He fired up the engines and rotated them from the usual takeoff position of vertical to horizontal. Turned to face the length of the runway. He couldn't see the line, too faded at this distance, but he had a very good idea where it was.

Eagle powered the engines, but kept the brakes on, feeling the aircraft vibrate. He released the brakes, accelerating, faster and faster.

He saw the line, pulled back, and the Snake lifted a few feet short of the line. Eagle banked hard as he gained altitude. Then he flew over Wagner Field one last time, dipped his right wing in acknowledgement of the airmen who had practiced for such a dangerous mission and conducted it.

Arlington Cemetery

THE GRAVE WAS HALFWAY UP the hill to Arlington House, once the residence of Robert E. Lee. The house, and surrounding plantation at Arlington, had been appropriated by the Union during the Civil War and utilized for a very different purpose: burying Union war dead.

This one gravesite covered three acres. There were three others subsequently buried here, besides President John F. Kennedy: His wife, and two brothers, Robert and Edward.

Ivar felt a deep sense of accomplishment in preventing Meyer Lansky and Bugsy Seigal from wiping out the Kennedy family on Black Tuesday in 1929. Of course, he had lied in his after-action report and debriefing. He'd broken one of the key rules of the Time Patrol: he'd told Lansky something of the future. Enough to insure Lansky didn't put the hit on the Kennedy clan. At least that was his internal spin to justify breaking the rule to save his life when threatened by Lansky.

It hadn't worked. Lansky had sent Ivar to take a swim with the fishes in concrete boots; technically concrete around a cinder block, the movies seemed to get that one wrong. The bothersome thing about the Time Patrol was that Lansky's history before *and* after Ivar's mission was the same. So which begat what?

Ivar had been trying to wrap his brain around that ever since getting back. Then he'd decided it was simpler to accept: it is what it is. He'd saved them. Lansky and Seigal could have killed JFK and RFK as children in 1929, along with their father, Joe Kennedy, and then Edward Kennedy would never have been born in 1932. *That* certainly would have changed things.

Ivar knew he had to shut down thinking any further into the what if's, could have been's, maybe's, whatever.

It is what it is.

He was startled when his satphone activated. He didn't recognize the tune, although any of the other members could have told him: Warren Zevon's *Excitable Boy*. He was pulling the phone out when he saw Scout striding toward him; a young woman with a purpose.

For the slightest of moments, Ivar wondered whether she was here to whack him. That Dane, Moms, Eagle or somebody else had figured out he'd lied. But he realized that they'd send someone from the Cellar to handle that detail; most likely Roland's whack job girlfriend, Neeley. The redundancy of 'whack' caused a crazy smile along with a twitch. He'd never been quite right after the *Fun in North Carolina*. Sometimes the others wondered if he were the original Ivar or one of the copies. He occasionally wondered the same thing.

Ivar shuddered to think what Roland and Neeley were like when they were alone together. Discussing ballistics, which knife to use, how best to garrote someone?

He glanced down at the text message and relaxed when he read it.

"Chopper's inbound," Scout said, echoing the text, as she reached him. She pointed. "LZ is there."

She hadn't even gone to college, Ivar thought, as he obediently followed. Actually she hadn't even graduated high school, getting 'recruited' into the Nightstalkers before that. And she was what, like nineteen now? But there was something about her that he'd picked up the very first time he met her back during the *Fun in North Carolina*.

She was different.

"What do you think—" Ivar began, but she waved a hand, without even looking back, and that was enough to silence him.

"We've been Zevoned, Ivar. It means we're going back."

Assembling For The Missions

The Possibility Palace, Headquarters, Time Patrol
Where? Can't tell you. When? Can't tell you (or Neeley would
have to whack you)

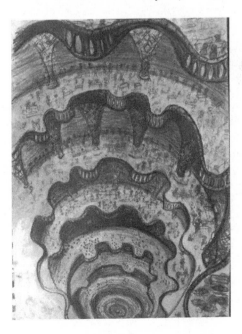

"WHAT'S GOING ON?" Doc asked.

He stood on the edge of a balcony, looking down into the massive pit that was, in essence, staring back into history. A wide spiral track ran counter-clockwise around the outside of the pit, descending into a vague, distant bottom; the beginning of recorded history. Almost a mile deep.

"Your team has been alerted," Dane said. "We have another attack on the timeline in progress."

"How can it be 'in progress'," Doc asked, "if it happened in the past?"

"You know better than to ask that," Dane replied. His once thick black hair was still thick, but streaked with grey. He was lean, perhaps too lean, and had a thin haze of grey beard, not as a 'look' but simply the result of not sparing the time to shave recently.

Dane, more than almost anyone, understood the value of not wasting time.

The descending spiral deck was of varying widths, depending on the importance of the spot in the timeline and the number of Time Patrol analysts assigned to that era. The analysts wore varying outfits and sat at bland grey desks, which appeared to be government issue, circa 1950. There were no computers, no phones. There were, however, lots and lots of filing cabinets stacked along the outer edge, against the stonewall. There were occasional zip lines going across and ladders here and there, going from one level to another, making direct connections between certain eras. It all looked rather disorganized.

Doc had learned, during his short time here, that it was anything but.

To their right, as the spiral ascended ever so slightly, the ramp faded into a gray mist: the future that was yet to unfold,. Above them, like a ceiling, was a deep grey cloud. The future. If that got hit by a Time Tsunami coming from below and turned black, then it would be over an instant later.

"See that?" Dane pointed across, and one spiral below, to the right. "Nineteen-ninety-six."

"Is that the mission?" Doc asked. "What are the others years? The date?"

"No, it's not the mission," Dane said. "See that fellow in the baggy pants and sweater?"

"With the long blonde hair?"

"Yes," Dane said. "He's dealing with a ripple from the last mission. Fixing it." Before Doc could ask, Dane explained. "Several men died on Eagle's Black Tuesday op. Turns out one of them had some minor importance. Not much, but enough to be noticed in the timeline. Actually, to be more exact, a son of his, who now was never born, had the importance. So our agent there is working on smoothing the ripple."

"This happen often?" Doc asked.

"Why do you think all these people are working here?" Dane asked. "They search for ripples. The Shadow's efforts cause us to respond. And while our response stops the Shadow from enacting the six Cascade Events leading to a time tsunami and wiping us out, our efforts have their own consequences."

"About that," Doc tested the reception.

Dane folded his arms. "Yes?"

"I've been going through the data. You know it would be easier if it was uploaded and catalogued and—"

"No computers," Dane said. "Learned that one the hard way."

"What happened?"

"Not important. Go on."

"There's a thing you say all the time. 'The vagaries of the variables.' Are you certain the Shadow has to succeed in all six Cascade attacks on the same day?"

"We're not certain of anything," Dane said. "Why?"

Doc pointed at the 1996 desk. "That's a ripple. Even though Eagle caused it. And your agent is—"

"Our agent," Dane interrupted.

"Our agent is dealing with it. But isn't that a win for the Shadow? What if *it's* a Cascade Event?"

"The other five missions had no ripples."

"I know," Doc said. "But what if it's a blind? What if the Shadow is launching six attacks on the same day, in different years, to distract us?"

"From what?"

"From the fact that while it would be great for the Shadow if they hit six for six on the same day, maybe another, more likely possibility, is to achieve at least one Cascade success per six attacks. Thus, the alternative goal is to get the right combination of six Cascade Attacks after so many assaults, so that they culminate before we can correct them and cause a Time Tsunami?"

"The Shadow is cunning," Dane allowed. He rubbed the stubble of his beard. "If that's the case, though, wouldn't they have to succeed in their goal on at least one of the attacks? That ripple," he pointed at 1996, "is from *our* success in stopping the attack. The Shadow's goal was to allow Operation Credible Sport to go forward and for the United States to try a second Iranian hostage rescue in 1980."

"Right now we're looking broadband; same day, six years." Doc gestured at the hum of activity in the Possibility Palace. "For most people, time is linear. I think the attacks are designed both ways. Broad and linear."

"Explain," Dane ordered.

"I'll show you, it's easier."

Doc opened one of the many doors along the top level of the balcony, which represented the present. The two men went inside to the Time Patrol's team room. Doc went up to a chalkboard and began drawing, starting with 29 Oct/Black Tuesday. Then he listed the six missions next to it.

"This is what we *think* is going on." Doc drew a horizontal line through all seven boxes. He turned to Dane. "Humor me. What's the date of the upcoming mission?"

"Fifteen March."

Doc whistled. "The Ides. Okay." He drew a box directly below the Black Tuesday box, labeling it 15 Mar/Ides. Then he wrote one through six. Then below he did the same beliw it labeling it Day 3. "I could keep drawing more days, but you get the idea."

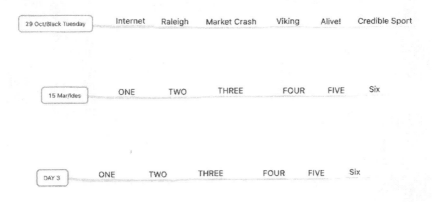

"What if the Shadow's goal," Doc said, "is to keep attacking, trying to succeed in all six on the same, but satisfied if it gets one or two. Because each one also goes linearly through time, in addition to sideways?"

Dane was nodding. "All right. You're saying each Cascade is possibly connected to a Cascade on another date."

"Right." Doc quickly drew an arrow from one box to another on the line below, then one to the third line, crossing some of the arrows. Then again, from first to second to third. "Now envision more dates. They have three-hundred-and-sixty-five to work with. All they need is the right combination of Cascades and they win."

Dane looked at the drawing in silence for a few moments. "It's possible you're right. All six are real attack, but not just connected to each other laterally but linearly to other dates."

Doc nodded. "Yes. Like a Turing Machine. They're dialing in attacks until they get six Cascades that line up. Maybe the Shadow doesn't even know what the right combination is." Doc put the chalk down. "It's just a theory."

"True," Dane said. "And the more likely possibility, and more imminent threat, is if they succeed on all six missions on one date."

"Let's assume the probability of winning or losing is even," Doc said, "between our Team and the Shadow. Fifty-fifty. Mathematically, it's like flipping a coin. This is why Turing used zeroes and ones to break Enigma. Fifty-fifty chance, multiplied out. The odds of six heads, or tails, in a row, six wins, is point five times point five, six times. Which comes out to less than one percent. Point zero-seven-eight percent, to be exact."

"The odds of us succeeding on all six were the same," Dane noted.

"That's the odd thing," Doc said. "The data from Black Tuesday means the odds are in our favor on every one. Somehow."

"It's our timeline," Dane said. "Home field advantage."

"True."

"Or—" Dane paused. He shook his head. "Nothing."

Doc knew it wasn't noting but didn't press it. Dane was not a man to be pressed.

"If we do have the advantage," Doc said, "and the numbers indicate that is so, then the Shadow's odds are infinitely less to get six on a single date. But increase the number of dates and . . ." He left the rest unsaid.

"That's why this is called the Possibility Palace," Dane said. "But, again, our most immediate problem is to make sure the Shadow doesn't win *any* of the attacks they're making on *this* mission."

"I agree absolutely," Doc said. "But I think we need to build our own version of the Turing Machine. A Time Turing Machine. We need to research this further."

"Could you do that with what you have right now?" Dane asked.

"Of course not," Doc said. "I don't have anywhere enough data."

"You're going to get a chance to gather more data," Dane said.

"How so?"

"The best possible way," Dane said. "You're going back on this next mission."

New York City, The Present

AS WAS HER HABIT, AND SHE was a woman of habit, Edith Frobish halted briefly at Cleopatra's Needle, located in Central Park, right behind the Metropolitan Museum of Art. A psychiatrist might have told her that the needle was her subconscious anchor in the present. Since she dealt with history for the Time Patrol and actually traveled to the Possibility Palace as required, she needed an anchor, since her brain, never mind her body, was rarely in the present.

But she could never tell a psychiatrist about the Time Patrol, because that would entail a visit from the Cellar, which would entail the end of *her* timeline. And the psychiatrist's.

Not that doing such a thing would ever occur to Edith Frobish. It would be like cheating on her taxes or jaywalking. Some things just aren't done.

The Time Patrol actually had a psychiatrist, but he scared Edith and she doubted very much that his job was to help untangle the psyches of the members.

Edith was a tall woman, with a long beautiful neck and figure, elegant enough to be a fashion model, something else she couldn't imagine.

Besides being a psychological anchor, the Needle served a practical purpose for Edith. She was an art historian The Patrol had realized early on that art is one of the best recorders of human history. If the art changed, whether it be a sculpture, a painting, a novel, a play, etchings on a cave wall, a clay pot, etc. it meant the timeline had changed.

As Edith perused the very faded hieroglyphics, moving from one side to the next, it looked the same as it always did, to Edith's relief. Secretly her fear, what a shrink would never quite understand unless they knew her job, was that some day she'd walk by and it would simply be gone.

The shrink would probably want to put her in the loony bin, not understanding such a possibility was real.

It did bother her that it was called 'Cleopatra's' when that particular hussy had had little to do with it. It had been carved long before Cleopatra's time. Only after her demise had Augustus, who'd caused her death and her lover's, Marc Antony, well, lover after Caesar's death, and Edith was sure there'd been one or two more in between, she was quite disapproving of such dalliances. Edith forgot for a moment her train of disapproval, as the image of Cleopatra shagging Caesar and then Marc Antony caused some quaint disturbance in her body. Ah, yes, she got on board the train: After Cleopatra had her date with a snake, Augustus had the Needle moved it to Alexandria to a temple he built and dedicated to himself.

Men.

Edith made it to the fourth side, ready to move on the job, when she gasped.

It was smooth.

This was not good. Not good at all.

The art had changed.

Thus, the history had changed.

She barely heard the helicopter landing in Central Park behind her and certainly didn't register it consciously.

With both hands, she clutched her old leather satchel tight to her chest, trying to get her rapid breathing under control.

"Are you all right, miss?"

Edith almost dropped the satchel. It was a New York City policeman.

She was so discombobulated, she pointed. "Do you see?"

The cop looked at the Needle. "Yeah?"

"It's blank! There should be hieroglyphics on it."

"There *are* markings on it."

"This side," Edith said, taking a step closer to the Needle and shaking her finger. "It's blank."

"No," the cop said. "It's not." The cop stared at her, then at the Needle, then back at her, his eyes narrowing with suspicion. "What's in the case?"

Was she losing her mind? Edith re-grouped. She saw it. He didn't. "I work in the Museum," she said, nodding toward the massive building. "I'm carrying very important material."

"'Material'?" the cop asked, taking a step toward her. "Mind if I take a look?"

"I do mind," Edith said, vaguely remembering something in the news about 'stop and frisk' being done away with. Which meant this might be something different? And one side of the Needle was blank, but he said it wasn't. The cop might be someone different, which meant--

"She's with us," a woman's voice came from behind Edith.

Neeley was standing there. Next to her, Roland had an arm around an inebriated Mac.

"What's wrong with your friend?" The cop asked, taking a step back, his hand edging toward his gun.

Neeley pulled out a wallet and flipped it open, revealing a badge and an I.D.. "CIA. We're escorting our friend, and Ms. Frobish, to the Museum. National Security matter."

"Let me see that," the cop said, indicating the I.D..

"They're with us," another voice said, and the cop turned, facing Eagle and Moms.

Moms had her own I.D. out. "National Security Agency. We're on a Task Force. At the museum."

Eagle went to Roland and looped Mac's other arm over his shoulder.

The cop took two steps back. "What's going on? Who are you people?"

Another voice: "Let's all chill out."

The cop turned the other way. Scout was standing there, looking much older than she had when they'd all departed on leave. Ivar was behind her.

"And *who* are you with?" the cop demanded. His one hand was on the butt of his pistol, the other ready to press transmit on his radio.

Scout spread her arms wide and smiled as she stared at him. "I'm peace and love, man. No one here means you or your city any harm. We just need to go into the museum. Do you dig it?"

The cop blinked. The hand fell from the radio. The other from the weapon. He nodded. "Sure," he said vaguely, not sure at all. "Sure. I dig it. You folks have a nice day." And then he walked off, a little unsteadily.

"What the hell was that?" Moms demanded of Scout.

But Edith Frobish was too excited. "The Needle!"

They all turned to her.

"What?" Eagle asked.

"This side! It's blank. Someone chiseled the hieroglyphics off."

"I guess that's bad?" Roland said.

"Duh." Mac wasn't that far gone to ignore an obvious Roland dig. Edith grabbed Roland's shirt with one hand. "You see it, right?"

"Sure," Roland said, smiling reassuringly. "I see it."

Edith let go. "But the policeman didn't."

"Curious," Ivar said. "We all see it being blank, but you say he saw the markings the way they should be?"

"Yes!" Edith was relieved that she wasn't crazy.

"Everyone see blank?" Moms checked.

She got a positive from every team member. "Well, that's certainly interesting," she said. "Let's find out with this is all about."

Without another word, they trooped over to the south side of the Met. With more force than usual, Edith shoved open a metal door labeled: 'Authorized Personnel Only'.

The Security Guard barely looked up, but Edith showed her badge anyway.

The rest of the team didn't bother, but Edith was big on routine.

The guard knew better than to ask questions of anyone who came in with Edith. She led the way down a hall, then turned right into a dimly lit corridor marked: 'Closed For Construction.'

Still not a word.

They got on an old freight elevator, ignoring its 'Out Of Order' sign.

Edith pressed a spot, allowing her fingerprint to be scanned, then pushed the 'Fire Department Use Only' key opening. The elevator descended six hundred feet, deep into the bedrock that was Manhattan, deeper than any of the myriad of man-made tunnels below the streets of the City the Never Sleeps.

Six hundred feet of bedrock was enough for the place to survive a direct nuclear strike.

The doors opened to a brick-lined, narrow corridor. They took a left. A guard clad in black body armor, and the deadly accouterments of his trade, had his automatic rifle trained on them. He never said a word to Edith. Never acknowledged her in any way.

But he nodded as the team went by, recognizing kindred souls lost in the wilderness of violence from their past, and pending violence in their future.

Eagle, as team sergeant, nodded back, soldier to soldier.

Edith pressed her face to the eye scanner, got green, and a steel door slid open. The team piled in the space between it and the next steel door. The first slid down. Edith put her hand over the next 'key', her skin was pricked, her DNA was scanned, and the second door opened.

A spotlight was focused on the HUB, in the middle of large, otherwise empty cavern in the bedrock.

Since no one seemed very talkative, Edith didn't ask if they were ready, as she usually asked those who passed through. She had a feeling they were always ready. They went up the ramp toward the pitch-black circle.

Moms went past Edith, because now it was her turn to lead, and stepped into the darkness. She'd always been first to have boots on the ground for every Nightstalker mission.

Just as Eagle and Roland were about to haul Mac through, he broke the silence.

"Hold on."

With everyone else backed up behind them, they did so.

Whereupon, Mac puked all over them.

The Possibility Palace
Where? Can't tell you. When? Can't tell you. (Or it might be Roland who visits)

"THE PROBABILITY IS HIGH ONE won't be coming back," Dane said.

"Why do you say that?" Frasier, the Nightstalker and Time Patrol psychologist, asked. He had seven folders on the table in front of him.

"Because they all made it back the last time. Doc's been lecturing me on statistics. He does have some valid points."

Frasier snorted. "Doc. More curious than he is cautious. Almost got him killed several times with the Nightstalkers. Almost got all of them killed, except Nada preferred to shot first, ask questions later."

They were in a bland, off-white room, a door in the center of each wall. Dane and Frasier sat on opposite sides of an old wooden table.

"Doc gets one of the missions," Dane said.

Frasier raised the remains of an eyebrow, his left one, revealing a solid black orb, an implant surrounded by scar tissue, which, apparently, could still mimic raising an eyebrow. It wasn't the only part of him that was no longer flesh and blood. "Thought he was doing research for you. Didn't like his lecture?"

"Actually, he might be on to something."

"Then—"

"He needs first-hand experience," Dane said. "He's theorizing. Theories get people killed. Experience keeps them alive."

"Sounds like a Nada-Yada."

"Nada was a good man," Dane said.

"At least on missions and at the very end," Frasier said. "With his family before—"

"Never speak ill of the dead," Dane said. "How is Scout?"

"Different," Frasier said. "But we already knew that."

"Did she go back to UCLA, her Black Tuesday scene, like the others?" Dane asked.

"No. She went to Arlington."

"To Nada."

Frasier didn't answer the obvious. "She came back on the same chopper with Ivar."

"*He* stays this time," Dane said.

"Because of the trauma of his last mission?"

It was Dane's turn to lift an eyebrow. "Is that a factor I should be concerned with? He's the other scientist. And he had a unique experience in North Carolina. I want him to keep digging into Doc's findings. Get his take on it."

Frasier pulled one of the files and slid it to the left. "Down to six agents for six missions."

Dane waited.

"The missions this time . . ." Frasier began, but didn't finish the sentence.

"Yes?" Dane finally asked.

"Last time some seemed a bit mundane. This time, though. There's some heavy stuff going down. One Emperor, the last Tsar, a future President, two Kings. And the guy who discovered America."

"And?" Dane pushed.

"Maybe the Shadow is going for it all?"

"That's not your concern," Dane said. "Who goes when is what we have to decide. Remember, like Ivar's mission to Black Tuesday, or Scout's to UCLA, what appears to be the mission sometimes isn't." Before Frasier could speak, Dane raised a finger. "There's another reason I'm holding Ivar back."

Before he could continue, Frasier supplied the answer. "Because he lied in debriefing." Frasier pointed at his prosthetic eye. "I can see things others can't. Body temperature through thermal, pulse by the pace of the carotid, breathing via chest movement. There was something hinky about his story."

"Yes. I think he lied about what he told Meyer Lansky during the interrogation when the two of them were alone."

Frasier nodded. "I doubt someone like Ivar could stand up to a psychopath like Lansky."

"Which makes for some interesting historical possibilities," Dane said.

"Are you going to call the Cellar on him?"

"We only have so many bodies. We need him. For now." Then Dane shrugged. "And this is a case of it is what it is. None of the desks had an alert on a ripple coming out of 1929 forward. I had them double-check, with a focus on Lansky. Nothing out of the norm. What Ivar said didn't change the history that was in place before he went back, so his role, whether it affected things or not, played out like it should have. But we need to keep an eye on Ivar. No offense intended," Dane added.

"None taken."

"However, combine that lie with North Carolina and Ivar might not be what he appears to be."

"Even Ivar has some issues with that," Frasier said. "It was a traumatic event for him."

"We've all had trauma," Dane said.

"Not like his. Imagine being surrounded by multiple copies of yourself? You start to doubt who you are. Almost getting killed by Lansky's goons didn't help." Frasier waited for any more on Ivar. Then he grabbed the top file. "Mac is in bad shape."

"He was in bad shape before he went," Dane said. "I was rather surprised he didn't go back and save his brother when given the option."

"He had no love for his brother or his family," Frasier said.

"Sometimes it's not about love," Dane said. "You should know. A pathological need can drive someone to do things that don't make sense."

"True." Frasier said. "I propose we give Mac the year least fraught with danger. Apparent danger at least. Columbus."

"All right."

Frasier scrawled the year on the cover and Mac's file went to the right.

Before Frasier could continue, Dane reached out and pulled a file out of the stack. "Scout goes to Leonidas."

"Why?"

"Because it is what it is." Dane wrote the year and tossed the file on top of Mac's.

"Roland," Frasier said. "Odoacer."

"That fits. Murder and mayhem, his forte. And Moms gets Caesar."

"Why? I was thinking—"

"Because Moms and Roland have a bond," Dane said. "Both going to the Roman Empire, even five hundred years apart, will affect them positively. Especially Roland."

"Moms bond for Roland is as deep as his is for her," Frasier said. "She saved his life a long time ago, before they became Nightstalkers, but he's saved her ass a number of times since then. He's her personal pit bull."

"He's smarter than a pit bull," Dane said. "People underestimate him. The fact Neeley's hooked up with him says a lot."

Frasier nodded. "Neeley is brilliant. Flawed, but brilliant. You know, she'd be a good addition to—"

"The Cellar needs her more than we do. For now."

Frasier slid two files out, wrote on them, and put them on the growing pile. "That leaves us Eagle and Doc." He paused.

"Yes?"

"Forgive my ignorance," Frasier said, "but there are aspects of these missions I don't understand. The mechanics of them."

"We don't know much about the mechanics," Dane said.

Frasier tapped the files. "Eagle is African-American."

"Yes?"

"When the members of the Time Patrol travel back, do they appear inside their bubble in time the same as they look here? We dress and equip them as if they do, so I assume that—"

"We assume the same," Dane said. "That they look the same."

"But, the people around them—"

"It is what it is," Dane said. "The time bubble isn't real in a sense."

"It's real enough that Ivar almost died," Frasier noted.

"I've explained as much as I can explain," Dane said.

Frasier thought that was a carefully worded sentence, but he knew better to push. "In that case, Eagle is a problem because—"

"He's black," Dane said. "Doesn't fit in Russia at that time, or even in the other times, does he?"

"He fits," Frasier said, "but only if he's a slave. There were free blacks, but a very low percentage. He'd draw more attention if he goes back as a free man. The problem is Eagle might not handle going back the other way well."

"He's a consummate professional," Dane said. "He'll do his duty."

"Then how does Doc's appearance fit into Russia?"

"They'll think he's from far Eastern Russia."

Frasier shoved the last two files to his right. "We're set."

*****

"That outfit doesn't take a rocket scientist to figure out," Mac observed as Roland joined him in their Time Patrol team room, another bland, non-descript square off the top balcony of the Possibility Palace. Roland was beaming, sword in hand, encased in armor that had seen better days, or, more accurately worse days, given the number of dents and scrapes in it. "Sure whoever wore it before you survived?"

Roland took a look at Mac and smiled. "Found God? Decided on a new path in life?"

Mac was dressed in a brown robe, with a wood cross dangling off a rope tied around his waist.

"Why didn't they shave your head?" Roland asked.

"I'm not that kind of monk," Mac said, although he had no idea what kind of monk he was. If shaving his head were necessary, shaved it would be. He held a cup of coffee in his hands, fingers cradled around it. The surface of the coffee was jiggling from Mac's shakes, but Roland didn't mention it.

Mac knew his teammate saw. "For a moment in London I thought you and Neeley were there to kill me."

"If we're sent to kill you," Roland said, rotating his arms, getting the feel of the armor, "you won't see it coming. Don't worry."

Mac rolled his eyes, knowing Roland said that to make him feel better. He wrinkled his nose. "Where did they get those clothes under that armor? From a re-enactor? Because they stink. Do they pick you for the year based on level of smell required to blend in?"

"You didn't smell too great on your last mission," Roland noted.

Which was true; Elizabethan England had been a bit odiferous.

One of the four doors opened and Doc came in, dressed for winter, some time ago. He removed a fur hat, put it on the table and took off a heavy, black woolen coat and draped it over a chair, before taking a seat. He squirmed, bothered by the rough cloth.

"Lucky you," Mac said. "Moms got to freeze last time. Look like it's your turn."

"I don't feel lucky," Doc said. "What's it like? Going through?"

"Lots of pain and suffering," Mac said. "Feels like your body is literally being ripped apart cell by cell for an eternity and then you're suddenly there. Horrible. Worst thing I've ever experienced in my life. And let's not even get into how bad it is coming back."

Roland stopped playing with his sword and frowned. "That wasn't what it was like for me. It was like, I went into the Gate, then bam, I was just there. And coming back was cool. Seeing all those possibilities I prevented."

"Geez, Roland," Mac said. "I was messing with him."

"He didn't know that," Roland said.

"Really?" Doc asked. "It's not bad?"

"Nah," Mac admitted. "Like Roland said, you're just there. The weird thing is, for the people around you when you arrive, it's like you've always been there."

"That's cause that day is a bubble in time," Roland said. "At least that's what Dane briefed us."

"But I don't understand the physics," Doc said, always a sticking point for the scientist.

"You didn't understand a lot of things we did as Nightstalkers," Roland noted. "But you're still alive."

"That's cause you tend to shot first," Mac said to Roland. "Or stab," he added, nodding at the sword. "I don't think Dane understands the physics either. I don't think anyone does."

Doc still wasn't happy. "I don't know why Dane wants me to go. I've got a lot of—"

Another door opened, cutting off his whine.

"Whoa!" Roland exclaimed.

Scout was dressed in a long white robe underneath a red cloak, wearing leather sandals. Her hair was bright red and cut tight to her skull. But what drew the exclamation from Roland was the Naga staff in her hand.

"Why don't they give me one of those?" Roland wondered out loud. "I mean, I like the sword and all, but that thing can cut through pretty much anything."

"I bet you're not going back to 1969," Doc said.

"Could be Woodstock," Mac offered.

"Not with the Naga staff," Roland said, a surprising observation from the big man.

Through the same door Roland had entered, came Eagle, his lips tight in anger.

"Whatever and wherever that is," Doc said, "it's not good."

Eagle wore homespun breeches and a shirt which looked like it had been stitched together from parts of three other shirts. He had rough leather shoes, the big toe poking through on the right foot. His hat was the only decent piece of clothing, black felt, with a wide brim, but heavily sweat-stained. Eagle took the hat off, tossed it on the table and sat down.

Then he looked around. A slight grin broke his anger as he saw Roland and his sword. "Rome. Late in the Empire judging by the weapon."

"Huh?" Roland said.

"It's not a *gladius*," Eagle said. "It's a *spatha*. Longer. The Roman Army adapted it in the Second Century."

"I like it," Roland said. "Not as nice as the axe last time, but, still. It feels right. Good balance."

"A rock would feel right to you," Mac said.

Eagle checked out Mac's outfit. "A monk? Stranger things have happened, I suppose."

Mac fingered the cross. "Never liked going to church much. My parents and brother..." but he fell silent.

The last member of the team, Moms, came in and it was Mac's turn to be surprised. "I can see your—"

"Shut up," Roland said. When Roland said something in that tone, it was advisable to one's health to listen, so Mac shut up.

Moms wore a sleeveless white tunic that went to her knees. It had a gold border on the hem and edge of the shoulders. A narrow girdle on the outside went right below her breasts, cinched tight. The fabric was sheer, leaving little to the imagination.

Moms surveyed the room and began to speak, more to distract them from her outfit than having something to say since they didn't know the missions yet. "All right, listen up. We—" she paused as Dane and Edith Frobish entered.

Dane went to the chalkboard. "Everyone take a seat. You'll get knowledge downloads for your mission after this mission briefing." He picked up a piece of chalk and moved to write something, when Eagle suddenly spoke up.

"That was BS."

Dane turned to him. "Go on."

"The ring tones. That was *our* tradition. The Nightstalkers. You programmed those satphones. Put those ring tones in. You want to Zevon us, do it right."

"Or don't do it all," Moms added.

Scout spoke up. "That song, the one you put on mine, that was between Nada and I. Personal. You intruded."

Dane's nostrils flared. Edith was next to him, giving him a glare, which for her was more like a school-marm sniff of disapproval. Dane didn't notice it anyway. But the team did.

Dane looked each member of the team in the eyes, before finally nodding. "You're right. That was wrong." He waited a beat. "Can we move on?"

Moms curtly nodded.

"You all know how this works now," Dane began.

"I don't," Doc said.

"That's why *you're* here," Dane said. "Following the Rule of Seven, where Six cascades can form a Time Tsunami, we're sending you back to the same date, in different years, to stop the Shadow from altering history in those six years."

"Get to the headline," Mac said. "I've got a headache."

"It could have been much worse than a headache for you," Dane said.

"The date," Eagle prompted.

"15 March."

Eagle looked at Moms. "Rome. 44 B.C.. When's *he* going?" he pointed at Roland.

"A bit later than that," Dane said. "One at a time and we'll start with the most obvious." He wrote on the board: *15 March 44 B.C.—ROME*

"As we all know," Dane began, "on that date—"

"Don't assume Roland knows," Mac said.

"Enough!" Dane said.

"Sucks to get poked, don't it?" Mac asked. "You poked us with the ring tones."

"I apologized," Dane said.

"Not exactly," Eagle said. "You said it was wrong. You didn't say you were sorry for doing it."

Moms walked up to Dane, inside his personal space, which made him even more uncomfortable the way she was dressed, or rather not dressed. "We have to trust you, Dane. You're sending us on these missions. Giving us this briefing. We've got to trust you have our backs. Someone who jerks our chain like you did with the ring tones; that gives us a moment of doubt. You were MACV-SOG in Vietnam. I'm sure you know what I'm talking about. So. Can we trust you?"

Dane took a deep breath, let it out. "Yes. I understand. Yes. I apologize."

Moms went back to the table and sat down. "All right. Let's move on. 44 B.C.. What am I? Some sort of courtesan?"

"The furthest thing from that," Dane said.

"A Vestal Virgin," Eagle said, earning a snort of surprise from Mac.

"Not exactly," Dane corrected. "An Amata. In training to be one."

Mac couldn't hold back. "How do you train to be a virgin?"

"Shut up, Mac," Scout said, and that startled everyone in the room. Moms looked at her, then over at Eagle. He shrugged and gave a slight shake of his head.

"44 B.C.," Dane said, tapping the piece of chalk on the board. "The day everyone remembers as *the* Ides of March. Caesar is assassinated. A critical juncture in history, to say the least. It led to civil war, then Antony and Cleopatra, and eventually Octavian becoming Emperor Augustus."

"And you have no idea what I'm supposed to do," Moms said, not a question.

"That's the way it is," Dane said. "You'll get all the possible information about that day and that event in your download."

Moms held up a hand. "Let's back up a little. On Black Tuesday, a Time Patrol agent from the era met four of us. Pablo Correa was there, waiting for me to show up. I assume he sent the report forward in time, somehow, here, so that you knew where to send me."

"They weren't all Time Patrol agents," Scout corrected. "The guy who I met worked for the Shadow. As did the second guy. And I think there was a third Shadow agent. I figure they killed the real Agent I was supposed to meet." She pointed at Roland. "And Ragnarok, the Viking on whose ship Roland came to, also worked for the Shadow. He didn't meet his Time Agent until later on. The Berserker."

"Halverd One-Eye," Roland said admiringly. "He was pretty bad ass."

"You thought Ragnarok was a bad ass when you met him," Mac pointed out.

"I'm sure they both were," Moms said, "but that's exactly the point. It was pretty hit or miss. Out of six of us, two met Time Patrol Agents who helped, two met Shadow Agents who betrayed us, and two of us didn't meet anyone from the Time Patrol or the Shadow. So what's the deal?"

Dane sighed and looked off into the nonexistent distance in the room, framing what he was going to say. "I've admitted that what we don't know about all this is a lot more than we know. We're working a lot with inherited technology from Atlantis. Ancient, but more advanced than the world outside of here has. This is all on a level we don't quite comprehend. We can break down the physics to a certain point, but then it falls apart."

"Quantum and general relativity," Doc said. "Physicists have been searching for a unified—

"Both are missing a piece," Scout interrupted.

Everyone turned to her.

She tapped her chest. "The spirit of humanity." She pointed at Moms. "None of the survivors of that plane crash that she kept from being killed by the Shadow have shaped world history. Except as Moms realized: they inspired hope. Think on that. The Shadow was attacking hope, not an event. Why would it do that?"

Silence reigned.

Surprisingly it was Roland who broke the quiet. "Maybe it's more than hope? Maybe it's, you know, spirit, or guts, or whatever it is, that makes people different? Makes us better? We've all seen it in combat. Where we're willing to put our lives on the line for each other. That's bigger than, well, bigger than . . ." and then he ran out of words.

"Roland's right," Moms said. "It's an intangible." She turned to Dane. "Back to the original question. Will there be Time Patrol agents meeting us?"

"Certainly, for some of you," Dane said. Before anyone could object, he continued. "We don't know. There should be an agent there, but as you've noted, sometimes the Shadow gets to them first. Sometimes, something happens to the agent that has nothing to do with all this. We try to get a message back to them, giving them what we know about where you'll end up. But you have to remember the main problem: these missions come to us inside a time bubble. A bubble that the Shadow creates. How? We have no idea. All we know is we've inherited the technology to send you back in time into that bubble. But it's not our bubble."

"So we're bursting their bubble?" Roland said.

Mac groaned, but Dane nodded. "In essence. Yes. The Agents we have in the past are from their era. They don't know how things are supposed to play out. They just know something isn't right. My advice, which you already know from listening to each other's debriefings, is to be leery of anyone who approaches you pretending to be an Agent. And some of you will undoubtedly be on your own."

"Hold on," Doc said. "When the Shadow invades our timeline with a bubble, it only lasts twenty-four hours, right?"

"We don't know," Dane said. "We know each of you will be back for a maximum of twenty-four hours. Based on the debriefing from Black Tuesday, some of you were snatched back faster than the full twenty-four hour cycle."

"Why?" Moms asked.

Dane shrugged. "In a way, the bubble doesn't exist in reality. It's an intrusion into our timeline. A timeline that has already been laid done. It's a false reality. You succeed, it's as if the bubble never happened."

"If we fail?" Moms asked.

"We try to fix the ripple," Dane said. "You haven't failed yet, so let's not start."

"But dead is dead," Eagle said. "Those men who died on my mission. They died. Right?"

Dane nodded. "Yes."

There was a pause, and this time it was Edith who filled the vacuum, speaking to Moms. "It should be thrilling for you to go to Rome at that time," Edith said, her face immediately turning red for her intrusion and because her blatant attempt at misdirection.

"It *will* be fascinating at least," Eagle said, throwing her a bone for giving Dane a dirty look about the ring tones. "I imagine a lot more than my mission." He indicated his clothes.

"Don't jump to conclusions," Dane quickly wrote on the board: *15 March 1783 A.D. NEWBURGH, NEW YORK*

Everyone on the team waited for Eagle to chime in with the event from his vast wealth of knowledge. Even Dane and Edith waited.

"General George Washington," Eagle finally said. "He had his headquarters there in 1783."

"Yes," Dane said. "The Battle of Yorktown was in 1781 and most people think the Revolutionary War was over there and then."

"Treat of Paris wasn't until fall, 1783," Eagle said. "That officially ended the war. After Yorktown there was a truce, but not actual peace."

"Correct," Dane said. "But in 1782, since the war pretty much appeared to be over, and peace negotiations were underway, the politicians started doing what politicians tend to do to the military when they don't need them at the moment."

"Screw 'em over," Roland said.

"Exactly," Dane said. He nodded at Edith to pick up the story.

"Since they didn't have the revenue from the states, Congress stopped paying the Army," Edith said. "There were a considerable number of disgruntled officers. On 10 March, an anonymous letter began making the rounds of Washington's camp at Newburgh. He was in that location, fifty miles up the Hudson, because the British still occupied New York City.

"Aware there were peace negotiations and that a treaty would soon be signed heightened tensions among the officers. They knew they were running out of time and leverage to get Congress to act. Once the treaty was completed and most of the officers cashiered out, they would have nothing they'd been promised for their service during the Revolution."

Edith reached into her satchel and pulled out a file. "You'll get this data in your download, but I think the original helps focus." She pulled out an old document encased in hard plastic. She handed it to Eagle as if passing a fragile golden egg. "That's the original letter written by Alexander Hamilton to George Washington asking him to 'take the direction' of the Army, particularly the officers. Hamilton was in Philadelphia getting the direction of the Congress."

Eagle looked at the letter. "He was asking if they were going to munity?"

"In essence," Edith said. "But there is more to Hamilton's letter than concern for the officer's welfare. He was implementing a clever political maneuver, using the threat of this mutiny, which had vast ramifications, to push for the formation of a stronger Federal government. He would use the threat to get Congress to enact the Articles of Confederation, which would eventually lead to the Constitution and the government as we know it."

Eagle frowned. "So it worked?"

"It wouldn't have worked if the officers had *actually* rebelled," Dane said. "It was a very dangerous situation. On 15 March, Washington gave a speech. The Newburgh Address. It stopped the mutiny."

"I've got the original transcript!" Edith's excitement filled the room. The transcript was encased in plastic and she handed it to Eagle. Everyone waited while he read it through.

"Intriguing wording," Eagle said when was done. "Quite brilliant." He handed the two documents back to Edith. "I see why this is so important. But am I going back as a freedman or a slave? If it's the latter, and the way I'm outfitted suggests that, then what could I possibly do?"

"You'll figure it out." Dane was already moving on, leaving Eagle fuming.

15 March 1493 A.D.—Palos de la Frontera, Spain

"Christopher Columbus arrives back in Spain," Dane said, "via a two week detour in Portugal, which was a matter of some concern, given King John of Portugal hadn't financed his expedition. On 15 March, he arrives at Palos de la Frontera, Spain, the small port town where he'd spent seven years trying to get the funding for the mission and from which he departed for the New World. That day he forwards his official report to Queen Isabella and King Ferdinand and the Pope. That is the document which sets in motion what will happen to the New World he's discovered. People all across Europe and especially the Vatican, used it as the prompt for the future."

"Thought the Vikings were there first," Roland said.

"The Vikings were like you," Mac said. "They didn't write a report."

"Actually," Edith said. "That's true. Knowledge that isn't disseminated dies with time. Columbus' report, especially after it was printed and widely read, opened the gate for European exploration and colonization of the Americas."

"Genocide of the indigenous population," Eagle said.

"Okay," Mac said. "And what could be the problem? Columbus already found the New World. He's back. Everyone on his ships knows where they went."

"That's what you have to find out," Dane said.

"Thanks," Mac muttered. Then he tapped his chest. "What's with the outfit?"

Edith answered. "*Devotio Modema.* Modern Devotion. A call for religious reform."

"So I'm a modern devoted monk?"

"Not exactly," Edith said. "*Devotio Modema* was actually a rather unique movement. On one hand, it wanted to go back to the basics. A life emphasizing humility, obedience and simplicity."

"Picked wrong guy for that," Roland said, scoring one for the Vikings.

Edith faltered, but then pressed on. "But it was also very progressive for its time. You're dressed as most monks were at the time, but the cross on your belt is different. Not a crucifix, not metal, just a simple wooden cross that each member made themselves. And lay people could be part of it. Men and women. Actually, it gave a space for women which was almost unprecedented at that era. And—"

"Enough." Dane cut her off. "He'll get all that information and more in the download." Dane began writing the fourth year on the chalkboard.

Moms and Eagle exchanged glances, concerned about Dane's abruptness.

15 March 493 A.D. RAVENNA, ITALY

Dane tapped the chalk on the line. "The last year for the first King of Italy, Odoacer. The man to whom the final Emperor of the Western Roman Empire, Romulus Augustus, surrendered his crown."

Edith spoke up. "By normal historical convention the end of the Roman Empire was that event between Odoacer and Romulus Augustus in 476. Odoacer negotiated with the Byzantium Emperor, Zeno, who granted him what remained of the Western Empire as his fiefdom. But when Odoacer didn't completely bend to Zeno's control, he sent the Ostrogoth King, Theoderic, to handle it. Legend is that Theoderic betrayed Odoacer at a banquet where they were to work out how to rule jointly, then cut him in half."

"That's symbolism," Eagle said.

"Nice guy," Roland said.

"That change of power was significant." Edith said. "Odoacer at least paid lip service to a Roman Empire. Theoderic shifted that emphasis to Italy. He also began consolidating all the various Goth tribes, including the Visigoths who had sacked Rome earlier."

"Okay," Roland said. "And?"

Dane spread his hands.

"Why am I going to this Ravenna place?" Roland asked. "Shouldn't it be Rome?"

Edith shook her head. "Odoacer moved his capitol to Ravenna. Interestingly," she added, looking at Moms, "that's the city where Caesar made his decision to cross the Rubicon half a century earlier."

"*The vicissitudes of fortune*" Eagle quoted, "*'which spares neither man nor the proudest of his works, which buries empires and cities in a common grave'.*"

"The Decline and Fall of the Roman Empire," Edith said admiringly. "Edward Gibbon."

"Love at first quote," Mac said, in a very low voice, but Scout still gave him a look.

Edith didn't notice. "Gibbon blamed Christianity a great deal for the fall of the Roman Empire. His major objection was its intolerance to other faiths, an implicit Roman policy that allowed their Empire to last so long and cover so many different cultures and faiths. Once Emperor Constantine converted to Christianity, the foundation of the Western Roman Empire began to erode. But he also established Constantinople, which would lead to the Empire splitting into east and west."

"Gibbon had a valid point," Eagle said. "Intolerance for those who worshipped differently began to spread. Anti-Semitism and—"

Dane cleared his throat. "Bottom line is that Theoderic had Ravenna under siege for three years and had the upper hand. He finished Odoacer on that day."

He added a fifth line.

15 March 1917 A.D. PETROGRAD, RUSSIA

"Edith," Dane nodded.

She reached into her satchel and brought out a small leather pouch, which she handled as if it were explosive. She walked to the table, opened the drawstrings, and gingerly deposited a single item onto the table in front of Doc.

He picked up the wooden icon. A hand-painted Virgin Mary on one side. On the other, five signatures in Russian. "What is it?"

"It's your key," Dane said.

"To what?"

"For getting close to the last Tsarina," Edith said. "Empress Consort Alexandra Feodorovna, wife of Tsar Nicholas the Second; the last Tsar." She pointed. "The signatures are her own and her daughter's, the duchesses. It's dated 11 December 1916. Only 19 days before Rasputin was killed. It was on his body at the time. The tale of what happened to his body is complex and you'll get that in your download." She gave a sideways glance at Dane, who gave a twitch of a smile in approval of her brevity. "It was reportedly stolen from Rasputin's corpse just before it was burned. The icon disappeared."

Doc looked up. "Then how did you find it?"

"That's her job," Dane said, "and she's the best in the world at it."

Edith flushed again, a deeper red than before.

"Sooo," Doc said, drawing the word out. "Rasputin is dead and I'm showing up with something stolen from his corpse?"

"You'll figure it out," Dane said.

"It will get the Tsarina's attention," Edith said. "She was utterly devoted to Rasputin. She believed he saved her son, Alexei's, life. He was heir to the throne but a hemophiliac. Also known as the Royal Disease. Many of the Royalty at the time were related and Queen Victoria, the Grandmother of Alexandra, passed it on to quite few of them. It only manifests in males—"

"I know what the disease is," Doc said.

"He has a lot of PhD's," Mac said. "He usually starts conversations with that."

"And I'm a physician," Doc added.

"Hence the Doc," Mac said.

"And once you get the data download," Dane said, "you'll know more about the entire era than anyone."

Doc looked at the others. "Is this the way Black Tuesday's briefing went?"

"Pretty much," Mac said.

"I can see why you were pissed," Doc said.

"We're giving you all we have," Dane said.

"So I'm meeting with the Tsarina," Doc said, putting the icon back in the leather pouch and then in his coat. "Why 15 March?"

Edith beat Eagle to the history. "On 15 March 1917 Tsar Nicholas II, Emperor and Autocrat of All the Russias, abdicated. It was the end of Russia under the Tsars. Technically, the first Tsar was Ivan IV Vasilyevich—"

"Better known as Ivan the Terrible," Eagle said, getting a historical jab back in.

"In 1533. That monarchy ended on 15 March 1917, ushering in what became the Soviet Union."

All Doc could do was nod as the implication sunk in.

"Why the Tsarina and not the Tsar?"

Dane gave Doc the look. Doc slumped back in his chair. He put the icon back in the pouch and held it out to Edith.

"You keep that," Edith said. "It's your key to getting the Tsarina's attention if you need it. The Tsarina, the duchesses, and Alexei, were holed up in the Alexander Palace just outside Petrograd, what we call St. Petersburg. The Tsar was there also."

"That's where you're going," Dane said. He pointed at Edith. "We've made a few adjustments in mission prep since Black Tuesday. The icon is one example. Where we can, we'll give you talismans to assist in the mission. Edith?"

She pulled a piece of cloth out of her satchel and handed it to Eagle. "That is the original Badge of Military Merit."

Eagle took it reverently. "The first Purple Heart."

"It's commonly known as that," Edith said, referring to something that was only commonly known to her and Eagle. "But actually, it was announced by Washington in 1782 as an award for exceptional bravery. It's considered the first time in modern military history where an award was designed for enlisted men. At the time, all awards went to officers and—"

"Figures," Mac said.

Edith was growing used to Mac and didn't miss a beat: "Washington came up with it not just for gallantry but for extraordinary service in any way. He said, and I quote: *'The road to glory in a Patriot Army and a free country is open to all'.*"

"That's pretty cool," Scout said.

Eagle nodded. "It is indeed. I keep this?"

"Yes," Dane said. "Use it if necessary to get Washington's attention."

"Do we all get something?" Roland asked, hoping perhaps for a better sword.

Dane pointed. "Scout has the Naga staff. Doc the icon. Eagle the Badge. We don't have anything specific to a key person on that day for the rest of you."

"But I've gone through all the downloads," Edith said. "I've supplemented them with some extra information you might find useful."

"We appreciate that," Moms said.

Dane slid the chalk across the board. "We're to the last year."

15 March 480 B.C. THERMOPYLAE, GREECE

"The Gates of Fire," Eagle said.

"That doesn't sound good," Scout said.

"The Three Hundred Spartans," Eagle added.

"Oh. I've seen the movie," Scout said. "Lots of bare-chested, muscular guys on steroids running around hacking at each other. But if I remember rightly, the ending isn't so great. For them at least."

"That's about the only part they got right," Dane said. "You're going on the last day of the battle."

"That sounds even worse," Scout said. "Which side am I on?"

"Our side," Dane answered. "The side of our timeline. The Spartans are defeated, but they slow the Persians enough so that eventually they are turned back."

"Saving what is known as Western Civilization," Edith added.

"Okay," Scout said. "Why do I have this?" She tapped the haft of the Naga staff. "Am I supposed to fight?"

Dane turned to Edith Frobish. "Thank you."

Edith took the hint and headed for the door. Before she could get out, Doc leaned over and tapped her arm. He whispered something to her. She nodded and departed.

"Your mission," Dane said to Scout, as soon as the door shut, "is, for lack of a better word, cloudy."

"They're all pretty cloudy," Moms said. "What's different about Scout's?"

"We received a report from Amelia Earhart out of the Space Between," Dane said. "There's been some unusual activity there. And it's directed at this time and place." He tapped the line at the bottom of the chalkboard.

"What kind of activity?" Moms asked.

"It appears that other Earth timelines besides the Shadow's are interested in it," Dane said.

"Don't they have their own Thermopylae?" Scout asked.

"Of course," Dane said. "But that date, that year, seems to be a key connecting point in some way between timelines. A strong one. What that means?" he asked, before any of the others could. "That this event, in our timeline, affects more than just us. It affects other timelines."

"Good or bad?" Scout asked.

"It depends on what you do," Dane said.

"Vague much?" Scout said.

"When we first me you in the Space Between," Moms said, "you told us you were the Administrator of the Time Patrol. Across multiple timelines, not just ours. You have to know more."

"Think on this," Dane said. "If we have to compartmentalize information for security purposes, don't you think we have to compartmentalize timelines for the same reason? On top of that, there's the *vagaries of the variables*. I know it sounds like a cheap catch-phrase, but it's the reality we all have to deal with. You know too little you screw things up. You know too much, you screw things up. That's the reason the iron-clad rule for the Time Patrol is that you can never disclose information about the future to someone you meet in the past. By doing so you can change the future."

"The first rule of Fight Club," Mac said. "And the second."

Scout indicated the Naga staff again. "Why do I have it? And where did you get it?"

"It's the one from the Valkyrie your team killed underneath the Met," Dane said.

"You think I'm going to run into a Valkyrie?"

"Hey, I ran into one on my mission," Roland complained, "and I didn't get the staffy thing."

"We don't know what you're going to run into," Dane said, "but if Earhart is concerned, then the Space Between is very close to this mission. Best to be prepared. And—" Dane paused.

"What?" Scout said. "Give me the bad news. I mean the bad news beyond the bad news you've already given me."

"Sin Fen said you had to be the one that went on this particular mission," Dane said, referring to the mystical woman they'd met in the Space Between and during the last debrief.

"Because I have the sight," Scout said.

"That would be most likely," Dane agreed.

"Where is she?" Scout asked.

"She's with Earhart," Dane said. "In the Space Between. Trying to figure out what's going on."

"And if she figures it out," Scout said, "will anyone tell me?"

"Once you go back, we can't reach you." Dane put the piece of chalk down. "I know all of you have an infinite number of questions, but that's it. Time to get your downloads, then go."

"You know," Roland said, "I just realized something."

Mac opened his mouth to say something, but Scout gave him a look that stopped it before it made air.

"My download from Black Tuesday," Roland said. "It's gone."

The other members, minus Doc, who'd gone on Black Tuesday missions were suddenly aware that theirs was too.

"That's weird," Eagle said. "I didn't even realize it."

"You didn't," Dane said, "because any information you didn't have before the download was time-coded for just a little over twenty-four hours. Don't ask me how it works, but be grateful. You don't have unlimited data storage in your brains."

Mac glanced at Scout, and then slumped back in the chair, not uttering another zinger at Roland.

"Where's Ivar?" Eagle asked.

"He's staying behind for this one," Dane said. "He's going to do some work here, pursuing a line of investigation that Doc initiated."

"Is there something wrong with him?" Moms asked. "He was pretty shaken up after what happened to him."

"He's fine," Dane said, a bit too quickly, causing Moms and Eagle to share another concerned look. "Everybody ready?"

"We need a moment," Moms said.

Dane understood. He departed, leaving the six of them alone.

Moms stood up and the rest followed suit. "We have to keep some of our traditions from the Nightstalker' days. Even though we go on these missions alone, we're still a team. We have to hold on to that. It's the base we need to stay grounded, especially given how crazy this whole thing is. Makes a Firefly in a killer rabbit look pretty normal."

That elicited a few chuckles from who'd participated in the *Fun Outside Tucson*.

Moms looked around the table, meeting each member of the team's gaze for a few seconds before moving to the next.

"All right," she said. "Why are we here? Because someone has to man the walls in the middle of the night. Someone has to man the walls between our world and other worlds that mean us harm. The walls between the innocents who go to sleep each night with only the troubles they see in their lives. Normal troubles. Not about Kings and Emperor's and Valkyries. But about their families. Their little piece of the world.

"The regular, ordinary people who know little of the dangers, the nightmares, surrounding our world. Who need people like us to stand watch over them. To protect them from the Shadow and the forces it sends against our timeline, trying to obliterate us and everyone we know, and everyone we love, from existence.

"We fight against things like the Valkyries and the kraken and double-agents and whatever else is sent against us. We defeated Fireflies and shut Rifts as Nightstalkers. We've stopped the folly of man destroying our own world with nuclear weapons."

She paused and looked at Eagle to finish, filling Nada's void.

He cleared his throat. "We are here because the best of intentions can go horribly awry and the worst of intentions can achieve exactly what it sets out to do. It is often the noblest scientific inquiry that can produce the end of us all. We are here because we are the last defense when the desire to do right turns into a wrong. We are here because mankind advances through trial and error. Because nothing man does is ever perfect. And we are ultimately here because there are things out there, beyond mankind's current knowledge level, which man must be guarded against until we can understand those things, as we finally understood the Rifts and the Fireflies and our role in that. We must remember this."

Moms finished. "Can we all live with that?"

The Missions Phase I

Rome, Roman Empire, 44 B.C.

MOMS WASN'T THERE AND THEN she was there, but she'd sort of always been there. It was the best way to explain how she arrived, becoming part of her current time and place without fanfare or excitement among those around her. She was in the bubble of this day, not before, and hopefully she wouldn't be here afterward.

Moms held a warm liver above her head in supplication, dark blood oozing around her fingers, running down her arms into her armpits.

She held it until given the order by the only other person in the chamber, an old woman.

"Put it down, Amata," the woman said.

It is 44 B.C. Pharaoh Cleopatra VII (yeah, that one) is hanging out in one of Caesar's country homes, causing a scandal; Comosicus succeeds Burebista as King of Dacia; duck decoys made of reeds are hidden in a cave in what would later become Lovelock, Nevada. Average life expectancy is thirty, but if a child made it to ten, then add another 37.5, making the expectancy 47.5.

Moms had blood on her hands.

Some things change; some don't.

Moms put the liver down on a silver tray. The old woman walked around the dais, leaning heavily on a cane.

She leaned over and poked at the liver with a finger. "See that?"

"Yes," Moms lied.

"Ah!" the old woman hissed. "I told Caesar to beware the Ides. But this? This is different."

"Different how, Spurinna?" Moms asked.

The old woman continued to poke and prod the liver. "Marc Antony. He must do his duty and save mighty Caesar today, since I fear my warning will not be heeded. It is Marc Antony's destiny. He must be told." And then she looked up, gazed into Moms' eyes. "And you are not an Amata."

Spurinna snatched the sacrificial knife and held it to Moms' throat.

That didn't take long, Moms thought, noting that the old woman's hand was shaking and there wasn't any strength behind the blade. She could disarm the old woman quite easily, as knife to throat counter-move was one of the first things taught in close quarters combat, but Moms wasn't sure what Spurinna's angle was and she needed to find out. If she were a Shadow agent, why didn't she try to cut? If she was a Time Patrol agent, she was being cautious. And if she were what she appeared to be, then what was going on?

"I am who I am," Moms said, opting for vague.

"I told them to send me someone," Spurinna said. "Someone pure. You are not pure."

She had a point there, Moms allowed. "I am supposed to be here. Now." More vague on top of vague, with a sprinkling of an opening if Spurinna were her contact. And the knife *was* bothering her, so she moved fast, snatching it out of Spurinna's hands before the old woman could react.

Moms twirled the blade. "Good balance." Then she tossed it on the sacrificial altar. "I am not a threat to you."

Spurinna frowned. "Why are you here?"

"To help."

"You did not flinch at the blade," Spurinna said. "I have never seen that in a woman. Soldiers, yes. The best are trained so. Gladiators live by the blade and they do not flinch."

"I am a soldier," Moms said.

"You could have used the blade on me once you took it."

"Why would I do that?"

Spurinna sighed. "Come." She led Moms out of the chamber, into a tunnel. Servants awaited in an antechamber. Spurinna pulled off her robe. She gingerly stepped down into a shallow pool. Water was poured over her wrinkled body, the blood scrubbed away by servants.

Moms followed suit, stripping, extremely uncomfortable with others touching her skin, forcing herself not to flinch at this, but impressed that the water was warm.

Once cleansed, Spurinna led the way up the pair of stairs on the far side where more servants slipped clean robes over their heads, cinching them. Sandals awaited.

Spurinna had not said another word and began shuffling down a corridor lit by flickering candles. Moms followed. They arrived in a chamber with walls made of large blocks of stone. No windows. Just one door in and out.

"Close it," Spurinna ordered.

Moms swung the heavy door shut.

A small blaze crackled in the fireplace, the smoke drawn out a narrow opening. A few candles gave insufficient light in addition to the fire.

Spurinna settled down with an irritated sigh of arthritis on a couch. She arranged the pillows until she was as comfortable as she could get. Moms remained standing. Mainly because there was no place to sit other than the couch.

"How can you help?" Spurinna asked. "You who are not what you pretend to be?"

"How do you know that?" Moms asked.

"Ah, woman. I am the great Seer of Rome. I know all."

"Then why don't you know who I am?"

"Because you are not of Rome," Spurinna said. "Are you from the Egyptian whore? I even asked her for assistance in this matter."

Moms puzzled over that. "Cleopatra?"

"Apparently not from her," Spurinna said, reading the question mark in Moms' tone. "She resides outside the city, in one of Caesar's villas. She is a large cause of the problem we now face. The scandal is all over the city. Caesar belittles Calpurnia with his antics."

Moms had not known that, but the download did. Cleopatra had arrived in Rome two years ago.

"How are you a soldier?" Spurinna asked.

"In my past," Moms said. "Why you sensed I am not pure."

Spurinna shifted positions, vainly trying to get more comfortable. "My bones ache. Very deep. The fire doesn't help much any more. Nor the potions the healers ply me with. There is no cure for being old, is there?" It was on the verge of being a real question, but

Spurinna didn't wait for an answer. "Someone tried to kill me this morning. Poisoned my breakfast. That was not good for my taster. If it were you, perhaps just finish the job here and now?" She indicated a dagger on the table next to her couch.

"I could have done that in the sacrificial chamber."

"I know."

"I didn't poison your food. Is your taster all right?"

"She's dead," Spurinna said. "That's what poison does."

"Why would someone try to poison you?"

Spurinna replied with her own question. "Why are you here?"

When Moms didn't reply, Spurinna continued. "I believe the answer to both questions is the same. That the future lies in the balance today. So tell me, since you aren't going to kill me, and you say you are here to help, how do we save mighty Caesar today?"

"Why do you believe Caesar must be saved?" Moms asked.

Spurinna snorted. "Because it will be Civil War again if he is assassinated."

"Didn't you see his death in a vision? Don't you have the Sight?"

Spurinna rolled her eyes. "My dear girl. My visions? Do you believe in visions? Do you have them?"

That, Moms thought, *was a very good question.* She knew Scout did. And Spurinna had just confirmed she knew who Moms was; at least what Moms was: a time traveler.

"If you don't have the sight, how do you know there is a plot against Caesar?" Moms asked.

Spurinna spread her hands. "One does not need to have visions to see the future. You think a conspiracy against Caesar by so many could be kept a secret? Rome is the easiest place in all of the Empire to gather information. One only has to pay the slaves. The nobles? They act as if the slaves don't exist. They could murder someone in front of fifty slaves, and believe there were no witnesses at all.

"Of course, a slave who speaks out of house, would face torture and death. It's why I have to transform what I learn from my network into prophecies. This protects my sources and it protects me. And makes it easier for the nobles to believe."

Spurinna shook her head. "It's not just the slaves. My best network is among the gladiators. Husbands tell their wives things. The wives? They have to talk to someone. Unlike you. Many noblewomen welcome gladiators into their chambers. They share pillow talk with the gladiators. The gladiators then share it with me for coin. Unfortunately, there's quite a bit of turnover in the gladiator ranks. But that also makes it easier for the wives to confide, knowing odds are the man won't be around for very long.

"So it all comes here, to Spurinna, the all-knowing Seer. In this instance, not only were the slaves in many noble households abuzz about the conspiracy, some of my gladiators didn't even have to bed a woman to learn a key piece of information. Decimus has hired ten swordsmen from the arena, ostensibly for games inside Pompey's Theater near the Senate later today, but they have already received instructions that their real task, and why they are being paid so handsomely, is in case their services are needed if the attempt on Caesar goes awry."

Decimus. Gladiators in Pompey Theater. The download confirmed all that.

"It is your task to gather information," Moms said. "And you have done an excellent job at it. But why do you think the future is that Caesar is to be saved?"

"I told you. Another Civil War looms if he dies. Even if that doesn't occur, do you know who rules alone if Caesar is gone? That buffoon Antony."

"But the future is not yours to shape," Moms said.

Spurinna sat up straight. "What do you mean?"

Moms asked a question in response. "What have you done, besides the prophecy, to save Caesar?" The prophecy, at least, was in the history books.

"I went to Calpurnia and told her she must inform Caesar she had a dream last night. She should have given it to him already."

That too was, while not confirmed by history, was a legend surrounding the event.

"You've done more than just those things, haven't you?"

Spurinna tilted her head. "We *are* to save Caesar, are we not?"

"Not."

Spurinna put her hand to her mouth. "Oh. That is not good. Then I might have made some mistakes."

Petrograd, Russia, 1917.

DOC WASN'T THERE AND THEN HE was there, but he'd sort of always been there. It was the best way to explain how he arrived, becoming part of his current time and place without fanfare or excitement among those around him. He was in the bubble of this day, not before, and hopefully he wouldn't be here afterward.

"Please don't!" Doc pleaded.

The Tsarina was startled by Doc's shout. "How dare you enter my chambers!"

Her four girls were kneeling, their heads bowed and their lips moving in silent prayer to the orthodoxy which had consumed their mother. The Tsarina held the frail boy in her arms. One hand clenched a knife, the point pressed against her son's wrist. The boy's eyes were closed and not reacting to the pressure, she was exerting. He was tall for his age, pale, with his skinny legs dangling to the floor.

It is 1917. The U.S. Ambassador is shown intercepted messages in which Germany promises to return the American Southwest to Mexico, if Mexico declares war on the United States; nearly half the French Army mutinies, refusing to attack any more after the disastrous Second Battle of Aisne and over one million killed so far in the war; the United States pays Denmark 25 million for the Danish West Indies which were renamed the U.S. Virgin Islands; the Russian Civil War begins and would end up holding the Guinness World Record for highest death toll at a million and a half combatants and almost nine million civilians; but even that pales in comparison to the Spanish Flu which is percolating among the hundred thousand members of the Chinese Labour Corps, used by the French and British for manual labor on the Western Front and would eventually claim anywhere from fifty to one hundred million lives in the next two years; Mata Hari refused a blindfold and is executed by firing squad; nine members of the Milwaukee police department are killed by a bomb, the largest loss of police in one event in the United States until Nine-Eleven.

This was Doc's first Time Patrol mission and it wasn't looking good.

Some things change; some don't.

"Don't do it, Tsarina." Doc attempted a calmer tone.

"I must," Alexandra said. "For all of Russia. Only then, will Nicholas listen to me and the people will understand. It is what Rasputin prophesied." And she nicked her son's skin and blood flowed.

More blood than Doc had ever seen from such a simple cut, but this was the curse of the Royal Disease. Queen Victoria's legacy passed via two of her five daughters to the royal families of not just Russia, but Spain and Germany as well. One of the drawbacks of monarchies; among others.

"What have you done?" Doc whispered, because even in this circumstance it seemed wrong to make loud noises in this beautiful, small room, which was filling with the smell of copper. It had changed in an instant from a sanctuary for a proud and noble family to a place of pending death.

The cut was small, a Band-Aid matter for anyone else. But not for this hemophiliac boy, whose disease was a contributing factor to this revolution that would eventually cause the deaths of tens of millions. Numbers which Stalin, writing his own history, would simply label a statistic.

Doc stepped forward, but the Tsarina placed the edge of the small dagger across the boy's throat. Alexei was awake now, whimpering, his eyes wide with fear. Terrified not just of the wound, knowing what it meant for him, but shock at the betrayal of the mother who'd spent her entire life worshipping at his feet, the future Tsar, after birthing those four girls to no acclaim or acknowledgement.

"Let me help," Doc said.

The Tsarina shook her head. "This is all that is left." Strangely, she smiled and looked at her four daughters, the Duchesses. "We will carry his body to the very step of the Duma and show the people what they have done. Have them rip up the abdication!"

Doc knew who she meant by *they*. The Bolsheviks who were willing to destroy a family to get their way and eventually destroy a country.

For a moment, as he watched the blood pool, Doc thought of the possibilities. He was standing on a page of history that he could simply allow to turn. If she accomplished what she had started, the people who had been brainwashed into hating her would forgive at the sight of her dead son. It would all change. The people would need their Tsar more than ever.

Doc had the choice; he could keep Russia from the infidels and murderers; from falling to the communists and wouldn't *that* change the next century!

She had a very valid point and a shocking, but brilliant plan.

Despite his Hippocratic instincts, and his Time Patrol mission, Doc remained still, the pool of blood widening. None of the Duchesses had opened their eyes, their lips still mouthing prayers to a God who had abandoned this family; if ever He'd had them in the palm of his hand.

But Doc held their fate in his hand. Now.

The fate of millions upon millions.

The boy's eyes had closed; his breathing shallower.

Doc estimated the pool of blood to be just under a liter. At this point passing through a Class II hemorrhage, roughly twenty percent of the boy's blood. If it got to forty percent, there was no stopping it.

It finally sunk into Doc how Godlike the Time Patrol was by protecting their present at the cost of the past. He knew if he did nothing, let the boy die, let her carry the body to the Duma, the family would survive and it would all be so different and Stalin would not graduate from small-time hoodlum.

But he remembered the choice they'd all been given in the Space Between. And how he'd chosen not to go back and redo his own past. He could not be certain the Tsarina's choice would turn out any better than the history that was already written. Maybe not Stalin, but someone else, would replace Nicholas II. And maybe not the Soviet Union would arise, but a weak Russia, easily defeated in the future past by Hitler and the Nazis, who could then turn their entire wrath on the West.

Doc pulled the icon out of his pocket. He held it up so she could see.

The Tsarina gasped, lowering the knife. "My dears!"

The Duchesses finally opened their eyes. The three oldest followed their mother's gaze and saw the icon. But the youngest, the Grand Duchess Anastasia Nikolaevna, saw her brother, saw the blood. She bunched the hem of her sleeping gown and pressed it against the wound, vainly trying to stop the bleeding.

Doc took the opening.

"It is God's will!" He snatched the knife out of the Tsarina's hand. He grabbed the boy, putting him on the floor, away from the blood. Opened the bag Edith had given him just after the mission briefing, fumbled around, pushing some things aside, until he felt what he had asked for. A 21st century cure for a 20th century certain death.

He slid the syringe underneath the icon. With both hands, he placed the icon, syringe hidden, just above the cut.

"I will save the Prince!" Doc said in a loud voice. "From the power passed to me by the Prophet Grigori Rasputin who was God's anointed!" Doc slid the needle into the skin and pressed the plunger. "The little one will not die. From my hands to his soul, I give all my power. All the power of Rasputin, through this icon, into the future Tsar!"

All four girls and their mother were staring at their brother, as rapt as when they had been praying.

The Tsarina gasped when the bleeding stopped. Doc withdrew the icon, and the needle. He dropped the syringe which had contained the most modern recombinant antihemophilic factor for the relatively rare hemophilia B, into the black bag. While they were still amazing over the cessation of blood, he took a quick glance inside. There was a grey case with a red cross and a post-it taped to it, a hand-written message in Edith's thin script: *If Class III use this second!*

He flipped the top open, revealing a second, larger syringe. He had no idea what it was. It bothered him briefly that Edith had access to medicines he wasn't aware of, and that she had obviously thought even further ahead on this mission that he had, but he pushed that aside.

He placed his hands once more on the boy and gave the second shot.

The porcelain skin began to gain color. No longer matching the cold, lifeless marble of the palace but a color that the living possessed.

The Tsarina slid off the lounge with great difficulty, painfully kneeling, unused to such discomfort. She was no longer the lithe and beautiful woman the newly crowned Tsar had married in November 1894, just five days after the funeral of his father. She was a large woman, who spent most of her time in bed or on the chaise lounge.

Her thyroid was off, Doc diagnosed just by looking at her. But thyroxin had only been isolated in 1914 and it would be decades before treatment was—Doc realized his own knowledge was now competing with the download for distractions.

The Tsarina cut through that. "You are the angel we have been praying for!"

She reached out and grabbed his legs, wrapping her arms around him.

Doc's heart twitched, because he was indeed their angel.

Their angel of death.

He gently unwrapped her arms and tried to avoid seeing the hope and awe in the Duchesses' faces. He knew the utter devotion that the Tsarina had bestowed on Rasputin was now shifted to him. The rapture that had unwittingly set this entire mess up to begin with. Yes, he knew there were other factors: Nicholas' failure to lead being the primary one, but this woman, his wife, she had been the Tsar's strength. His pillar. But when she turned to Rasputin, by proxy, the Tsar had turned too. Now the country was revolting against them, choosing the devil they didn't know, and would only understand when it was far too late, rather than the flawed monarchy corrupted by the devil they did know.

He checked the wound. The coagulant had sealed it.

Once more, it was Anastasia who did the next practical thing, tearing off a piece of her nightgown and wrapping it around the wound on her younger brother's arm. She looked up at Doc and her gaze was different. She smiled, but there was sadness mixed in it.

"Thank you."

Doc nodded, not trusting his voice and disturbed by the young girl's gaze.

Doc understood that the Tsarina loved the Russian people even more than her family, because she'd been willing to sacrifice her only son for them. He had to give her something more in return than this temporary reprieve. He had to give her peace of mind.

"Yes. I am an angel. God has sent me, as he sent the Prophet Rasputin, to save the Russian people. As God sacrificed his son for mankind and brought him back to life, you must protect your son, whom I have brought back to life, for Russia. He is not to be sacrificed. He is to live. He is the hope of Russia!"

They began to weep, but the anxiety was draining from their faces, replaced with the glow of the truly faithful. Doc felt a pang of jealousy that they could so easily have faith; something his powerful brain would never allow and he knew would dog him the rest of his years.

Except for Anastasia. She was staring at him with dark eyes.

He pressed on. "I have come to deliver God's words. The future of your people, of your family, Tsarina Alexandra Feodorovna, depends on the Prince remaining alive. He will be Tsar one day."

Alexandra made the sign of the cross.

Then Doc cursed them with the prophecy of future history: "Tsarina Alexandra Feodorovna, your husband's abdication becomes final today. You must not talk him out of it. You must not protest. You must not take any other action to prevent that from happening. You must not fear. You, your daughters, your husband, and most especially Alexei, are now cradled in the hand of God.

"You must have patience, for in two years time, the monarchy will be restored. It will be Alexei who will take the throne and lead Russia into future greatness."

Tsarina Alexandra Feodorovna threw her hands up in the air, weeping loudly with joy. Her daughters joined, and Doc realized he too was crying. Not from joy, but from the horror of his lies, that he had said too much, had given them hope when there was no hope.

"I did not know angels cried."

Doc looked at Anastasia, the only one with no tears. He abruptly left the bedchamber, knowing there would never be penance enough for him.

Palos de la Frontera, Spain, 1493 A.D.

MAC WASN'T THERE AND THEN HE was there, but he'd sort of always been there. It was the best way to explain how he arrived, becoming part of his current time and place without fanfare or excitement among those around him. He was in the bubble of this day, not before, and hopefully he wouldn't be here afterward.

He wished this damn hangover would go away more than anything else. Traveling through time seemed to have exacerbated it.

"Where's the band? The King? The Queen? The Sons of Italy?" Mac muttered as he looked at the tiny ship.

The download intruded: The *Nina* was roughly forty to fifty feet long and twenty feet in beam at the widest. One deck. The crew slept exposed to the elements. There was a partial second deck aft, where the ship's captain got to bunk down under some cover. *My dinghy is larger than your boat*, popped into Mac's brain from somewhere, probably one of Eagle's many book or movie quotes. Crew around 25 men.

Mac was standing just above the mud flats on the south bank of the estuary. The town of Palos de la Frontera was behind. To the right, on a low rocky bluff overlooking the confluence of two rivers, was La Rabida Friary, where Columbus had spent years planning his journey, consulting with the Franciscans who ran the place, and, most importantly, trying to get funding.

It was afternoon, a gray day, the sun hazed behind a sullen sky. The smell of salt water filled the air and Mac could hear seagulls calling.

"Devotio Moderna?"

Mac turned. The man who'd addressed him was dressed in a plain brown tunic, with a rope around his waist. He wore a similar, rough wood cross on his belt.

"Yes. *Devotio Moderna.*"

"I am Geert. From Belgium. Welcome to Palos de la Frontera." Geert didn't seem to think much of the town and Mac had to agree with the assessment. Population a few hundred people, making its living off the sea through fishing and trade.

"I'm Mac."

"'Mac'? That is all?"

"That is all."

"They should give a better name before they send you back. Welcome to my time."

"It's only for twenty-four hours," Mac said. "My name is not important."

"True," Geert acknowledged. He nodded at the ship. "Columbus arrived here from Lisbon an hour ago. It is odd that he went to Portugal first. Most strange and many are speaking of it, considering Ferdinand and Isabella financed his journey, not King John."

It is 1493 A.D. Under the Treaty of Barcelona, Charles VIII of France gives Cerdange and Roussillon back to the Ferdinand of Aragon; in the Papal Bull Inter Caetera based on Columbus' report on the New World (if he gets to make it) Pope Alexander VI decrees that all lands discovered 100 leagues or further west of the Azores are Spanish, those to the east are Portugese; Alexander VI follows that up with Inter Siquidem, further dividing the New World among the various Catholic Monarchs, the locals not having a say in the matter; England places sanctions on Burgundy for harboring Perkin Warbeck, a pretender to the English throne; Deodorant still hadn't been invented.

"Why am I here?" Mac asked.

Some things change; some don't.

"*You* know what is supposed to happen," Geert said. "I only know what has happened and a little of what is happening. Columbus is on board the *Nina*. He has allowed no one to disembark yet, which is strange because a number of the crew are from the town."

That explained the small group of women and children who were gathered at a small quay, talking quietly and peering at the ship.

"Why has no one come ashore?"

"I have no clue," Geert said. "There are people visible on deck, but otherwise—" he shrugged. "And there is also that."

Six men clad in black doublets and hose about fifty meters away were seated at a wood table.

"Who are they?" Mac asked.

"They're from the *Cent Suisses*," Geert said.

"The Hundred Swiss?"

"Swiss mercenaries. They fight for whatever Crown will pay them. These particular ones? They've been sent by Rome."

"Why are they here?"

Geert spread his hands. "Who knows? Protect Columbus, perhaps?"

"From who?"

Geert looked at him. "Perhaps from us? You tell me. In your history, does he die today? Or does he live? Are *we* to help him live or let him die? Or kill him ourselves?" His hand strayed inside his robe enough to show Mac the hilt of his dagger. "Life or death. Just let me know what it is to be."

"What makes you think someone wants to kill him?" Mac asked, although he was leaning toward life, since Columbus didn't die until, the download pushed the date through his hangover: 20 May 1506, after being ill for a number of years. From complications of Reiter's Syndrome, which was a—

Mac shut it down. All that mattered was Columbus didn't die today. Plus, for some reason, accessing the download made the hangover worse.

"Why did he go to Portugal first?" Geert asked. "I have heard that Columbus left the *Nina* in Lisbon and traveled to a town just outside the city to meet King John II. If this is true, then his life is in danger from Spain. Also, why are the Cente Suisse here? Why has no one disembarked? Something is not right."

According to the download, Columbus had disembarked in Lisbon and met King John II. Something historians had not found worthy of much mention, nor was there any information about what happened at that meeting. But Mac had enough of the big picture to make a decision for the immediate future.

"Let's go with life," Mac said.

Geert seemed relieved.

Thermopylae, Greece, 480 B.C.

SCOUT WASN'T THERE AND THEN SHE was there, but she'd sort of always been there. It was the best way to explain how she arrived, becoming part of her current time and place without fanfare or excitement among those around him. She was in the bubble of this day, not before, and hopefully she wouldn't be here afterward.

And she knew she wasn't Scout. Not completely. She felt the tendrils of the past, a lifetime before her, many lives before, part of her blood, her genes, creeping into her consciousness, from the present stretching into the past. A long, long way back, like the way the spiral of the Possibility Palace faded down, far down, into a distant haze.

All the way back to Atlantis, a dim golden beacon before the start of history as we know it.

Scout, who was immediately aware she was called Cyra in this time and place, knew if she remained Cyra long enough, she'd have it all: The history of her bloodline; memories of Atlantis. But if she remained here, past twenty-four hours, there would be no Scout to remember anything.

She would revert back to Cyra and Scout would no longer exist.

She almost gagged at the foul stench of death that filled the air; the tint of iron from massive amounts of spilled blood.

"If the words of your Oracle are true, this is my final night," Leonidas said. "What say you, priestess of the Oracle of Delphi? What of the prophecy?"

"The words are true," Scout replied.

"The way you paused," Leonidas said. "It almost gave me hope. But it's strange. Before every battle, I have felt fear. Of being maimed. Killed. Most of all defeated. But no matter how dire the fight appeared, or how terrible the odds, I always believed deep inside that none of those would happen." He sat up and looked at his soldiers. "We all know we'll die one day. Everyone does. In battle or of disease or inevitably of old age. But it's always in the future. Not today."

Scout felt an affinity, affection for Leonidas, a memory of what she'd felt for Nada. She could also sense darkness in him, the ability to kill. But there was another side to such darkness, the side that had allowed Nada to make the decision to go back and sacrifice his own life to make things right.

"When you take this map," Leonidas said, "will you stay with it or do you deliver it somewhere?"

"I will know when I have it." *So, this was about a map,* Scout thought. But she could sense it wasn't a typical map. It was special.

Of course, if it *wasn't* special, why would she be here in the first place?

Leonidas continued. "And after you fulfill whatever task has been laid on you, will you go back to the Oracle?"

"I don't know my fate." That, at least, was true.

"If you survive somehow and stay in Greece, will you do me a favor?"

"Yes, if it is within my power."

Leonidas smiled. "I believe it is indeed within your power. Go to my home. Tell my wife how I died."

"I can do that," Scout lied.

"I'm not done yet," Leonidas said. "I have grown to admire you during our journey here from the Oracle. I want you to teach my daughter."

"What would you like me to teach her?"

"To be like you."

Scout hated this next lie. "I will."

It is 480 B.C. The world's population is roughly 100 million humans. Soon to be less three hundred Spartans and quite a few Persians, along with troops sent by vassals of Persia and mercenaries paid by King Xerxes. The average life expectancy is twenty-eight but if a child made it to ten, then they had an average of another thirty years.

Scout sensed a presence. She got to her feet.

Some things change; some don't.

"What is it?" Leonidas was up, putting his helmet on. "The Persians come in the dark?"

"No." Scout took a step toward the grisly barricade of Persian bodies and stone the Spartans had erected. "Someone like me."

"The Sibyl Pandora that the Oracle spoke of?" Leonidas asked.

Scout shivered at the mention of that name and the connection she immediately felt to it.

"Perhaps. She is not a danger. Not right now." Scout had no idea if that were true or not, but she knew this Pandora was her problem, not the Spartan's.

"How does she fit into the Oracle's prophecy?" Leonidas asked.

Scout didn't know that either since she hadn't been there for the prophecy. "What do you remember of the prophecy?"

Leonidas gave her a strange look. "She told me I would gain much honor and fame. And that I would die. She said I was to save a sphere that was a map. That the fate of not just Greece but the entire world lay in the balance. That we must give the map to another warrior." He shook his head. "A warrior who is not yet alive, but alive. Of this world but not of this world. You people speak in riddles."

Scout's first thought was Nada. Did he exist in some time, some place between his death and his choice to go back?

Leonidas didn't let her dwell on that for long. He pointed toward the north. "I know who we fight there. I can see them. But fighting a Shadow? That I don't understand. And your Oracle couldn't tell me what this Shadow is. How to find it to defeat it."

"Prophecies can be taken many ways," Scout said.

"Yes," Leonidas said. "We all learned the lesson of Croesus, last of the Lydian Kings. He earned that title after he consulted the Oracle. She gave him a prophecy. That if he went to war against the Persians, he would destroy a great empire."

Scout dialed up the info. "He heard what he wanted to hear. That is not the Oracle's fault. He led his troops into war with Cyrus, King of Persia, grandfather of Xerxes who we now battle."

"And he did destroy an empire," Leonidas said. "His own. A good reason I should not trust you. Or the Oracle. I should trust this." He tapped the hilt of his sword. "It has always been reliable."

Scout focused on the King, staring into his eyes. "You can trust me."

A long pause, then Leonidas nodded. "I believe I can."

A weariness passed through Scout, a brief wave, then it was gone.

"I will check on the men," Leonidas said, leaving her be and heading for the nearest fire.

Scout knew of the name Pandora without the download. Part of Greek mythology. Something about opening a box. And then data flowed, a fire hydrant of information overwhelming Scout's sketchy schooling:

After Prometheus sided with the Gods in the epic battle against Cronus and his fellow Titans, he'd been tasked by Zeus to create man. But Prometheus, jealous of all that the Gods had, stole the secret of fire from Mount Olympus. Angered, Zeus ordered his son Hephaestus to create a woman. Thus, Pandora was formed by the Gods out of clay.

Pandora was blessed, or cursed, depending on your perspective, with both beauty and cunning. She was given to Prometheus' younger brother as a bride. Once she was inside his house, Pandora showed him the *pithos* (a jar not a box; someone in records had been anal on facts, Scout thought, then remembered Edith and that answered that), which Zeus had bequeathed her to give as a wedding present.

Prometheus had warned his brother against accepting any gifts from Zeus, but one given under the allure of Pandora could not be resisted. He opened it, releasing the evil spirits trapped within and thus unleashed them on mankind ever since: '*burdensome toil and sickness that brings death to men, diseases and a myriad of other pains*'.

In other words, Scout thought: *bad stuff.* Sort of what she felt right now.

It was legend, myth, probably embellished and twisted over the course of time, but Scout knew at the core of every legend there was truth. Because reality was much stranger than the average person knew. The members of her team had run into many myths, legends, and unbelievably twisted science, that they'd learn to expect anything. Yet, they were still surprised at times.

Of course, as in many legends and stories, men liked to lay the cause of all ills at a woman's feet. From Eve to Pandora. And men wrote the history.

As if a man would listen to a woman.

Scout was startled as an affiliated piece of data flashed through her consciousness: the only thing left behind in Pandora's box was *Elpis.* Hope.

Hope. Sometimes it was all humans had in the face of overwhelming odds.

But Pandora had shut the lid, locking hope inside. Only evil had come forth from her jar, *pithos*, box, whatever.

Scout felt the echoes of the past, along with pulses reverberating back from the future. Even when there was no hope, mankind still persevered. She observed as Leonidas went from campfire to campfire, talking in a low voice, putting a comforting hand on a Spartan's shoulder, giving them hope in a hopeless situation.

Something came out of all of this, Scout realized. Some power. A power that pushed back the Shadow. She didn't know how, but it was affirmed by the faint presence of the real Cyra, outside the bubble of this day. It was as if she were out there, hovering, waiting to resume her role in her time and place and Scout was just a visitor that Cyra had allowed in for this brief, but critical time.

Lightning flashed to the east, over the water, followed by the rumble of thunder. A storm was approaching. Scout slowly walked to the barricade of dead flesh and rock. There were sentries, of course. Scout remembered the encounter with police officer near Cleopatra's needle. She'd just acted, knowing they needed the cop gone without incident and that Moms and Neeley pulling badges were just making him more interested in trying to figure out what was going on.

Instinct. Drawing on something, she'd always had but not been aware of. It was a strength, a power, that Nada had sensed during the *Fun in North Carolina*, which seemed a lifetime ago.

She'd done it again, just now, with Leonidas. And for that, she felt guilty. Trust was something to be earned, not conjured. But there was no time.

Scout halted just behind the wall. There was a sentry to her left and one to her right, both peering down the pass toward the distant plain where the Persian army was massed. The fires ahead were so many they lit the northern sky like a false dawn. It was only the narrowness of the pass that had allowed the Spartans to hold the line this long as Xerxes was only able to send a limited number of soldiers against them at one time.

Scout closed her eyes. Concentrated. Opened them and climbed up.

Her foot slipped on viscera, falling forward, her forehead striking a stone. A trickle of blood flowed. Scout continued up, to the top, and then over.

Neither sentry gave the alarm.

The narrow pass continued for about fifty meters, before widening and descending. Scout swallowed hard. It would be impossible for her to go forward without walking on top of a macabre carpet. The bottom layer were Egyptian corpses, who had attacked on the first day. Then the Immortals on the second day. Xerxes' elite corps of soldiers, 10,000 strong. And despite the dead who littered this battlefield, Scout knew from her download that there were exactly 10,000 Immortals this evening as every man lost was immediately replaced. She wondered if Xerxes even counted the dead if the living in his Immortals were always 10,000? On top, from the fighting yesterday, Scythians, from Eurasia, part of an ongoing tribute given by their country to Persia after Xerxes father had invaded their country. Many of the Scythians had arrows in their backs and Scout knew, from the vague part of her that had Cyra's memories, that Xerxes, had, in frustration, ordered his archers to continue to fire as his troops closed on the Spartans.

Scout fell several times, feet slipping on blood, flesh and exposed internal organs. She realized the best footing was to step from helmet and armor to helmet and armor.

Despite being ready, Scout was startled as a woman's voice floated out of the darkness from ahead.

"I can see you."

Scout stopped and looked up, about. Just darkness and the bright glow of the Persian camp.

"But you can't see me." Pandora was surprised. Her voice was low, but one that reached far; not just distance, but into the mind. "Strange. I can sense the Sight in you but you cannot see."

There was nothing for a few moments and Scout remained still, each foot on a helmet.

"Ah! They send but a girl. Should that be an insult? Or a sign of desperation? Or is it something else?"

"Show yourself," Scout said.

"I have, but you can't see. You're not Cyra. She would be able to see me."

"You are Pandora," Scout said.

"Not a difficult guess since all have heard of me. What is your name?"

"My name is my own."

The laughter was louder than the voice. "You have a point. It is not a name anyone will remember. My name, though, is legend. All have heard of me. I assume that is still true in whatever time you come from."

And then Scout saw her in a flash of lightning. A tall, willowy figure that didn't seem quite solid, coming out of the darkness, walking over the bodies as if her feet were barely touching.

In the next flash, Scout could see that Pandora had thick black hair with a shocking, single streak of white flowing from above her left eye, all the way down to the end over her left shoulder. Pandora had a Naga staff in her hand. Not in threatening manner; in fact, she put the seven-headed snake end on the ground and leaned on it. She cocked her head, peering at Scout. A half-smile creased her lips. "You are quite pretty. And quite flawed. Like this," she indicated the streak in her hair, "except the flaw is inside you. A weakness you'll never overcome. It will destroy you, sooner or later. I have a strong suspicion it will be sooner. Now. Your name?"

"Scout."

"Scout? What a strange name to be given at birth."

"I was given it long after my birth." Scout remembered Nada bequeathing her team name in North Carolina, putting it to the vote and the entire team accepting her.

The first group that had ever accepted her into their ranks.

Scout tried to look past Pandora, but could see little in the dark; just the glow of thousands of camp fires from the Persians.

"We are out of bow range of both the Spartans and the Persians," Pandora said. "They do not fight at night. It is difficult to discern friend or foe in the dark. The Persians are not afraid of a Spartan attack." She gave a low laugh. "They are correct in that one assumption at least. Although I believe that if Leonidas had more men he would dare to do just that; try to cut his way through the camp and kill Xerxes and end this. But even three hundred Spartans cannot defeat this many. And then there are the ten thousand Immortals surrounding Xerxes tent."

"Why are we meeting?" Scout asked. "Why did you reach out to me?"

"Time is short," Pandora said. She laughed. Even her laughter was enticing, eliciting a pull inside Scout. Motherly.

Then Scout remembered her mother and that feeling was squelched.

"That's not going to work," Scout said.

Pandora was still. "True. True. We've only just met. But time is indeed short. I've been whispering that in Xerxes' ear for months now, pushing him to get here in time. But he is just a man, despite all his titles." She intoned them: "King Xerxes, son of Darius, King of Medea and Persia, ruler of Libya, Arabia, Egypt, Palestine, Ethiopia, Elam, Syria, Assyria, Cyprus, Babylonia, Chaldea, Cilicia, Thrace and Cappadocia, and most blessed of God Ahurumazda. All that for just one man. Such is the pride of the ignorant."

"Why is time short?" Scout asked.

"Is it not for you?" Pandora asked. "Is not your hourglass tipped and your sand running out?"

"I don't know."

"Don't lie to me girl and I will treat you with respect. You must return the favor."

"Why is time short?" Scout asked once again.

Pandora took a step closer. Scout held tight to the Naga staff, tip pointed at the other woman's chest.

"You don't need that," Pandora said.

"You brought yours."

"Never show up empty-handed," Pandora said. "That is a truism through the centuries."

"Is it a gift for me, then?" Scout said. "Leonidas could use it and more."

"He would need the more," Pandora said. "Much more. And do you really want a gift from *me*?"

Scout gave her a few points for that repartee.

Pandora continued. "Let us be clear. You and I both know what will happen soon. Once the sun comes up, the Spartans will not see it set. But it is different for us."

"What do you want?" Lightning flickered. The thunder came not long afterward, indicating the storm was getting closer.

"It is not what *I* want, but what *you* need," Pandora said. She spun her Naga slamming the point into a body, holding up both empty hands. "We are sisters; we can work together. We are descended from what they call in this age Oracles or the Sibyls. We have always been here. Ever since the beginning."

"Atlantis."

"Yes. But men, they don't listen. One of our sisters, Herophile, prophesized the Trojan War, but Achilles and the Greeks still sailed. That was the beginning of this conflict between east and west so many years ago. But we, our line, live a timeless existence, above the squabbles of men. Can't you feel it?"

"I feel cold and there's a storm coming," Scout said.

"There is indeed a storm coming."

Scout was wondering why Pandora hadn't simply killed her.

"We live a timeless existence," Pandora repeated.

"Right. Except you just told me the clock is ticking and time is short."

Pandora didn't rise to the bait. "Xerxes is a follower of Ahuramazda. Do you know what that religion is?"

The data began to scroll in Scout's brain. "No."

"The followers believe that Ahuramazda created seven worlds, all branching from him." Pandora pointed at the other end of her Naga staff. "Seven is a number that comes up again and again. The oldest of the seven worlds is *Asha*, the Fire World. Fire is a sacred channel to eternal light. And to get to internal light, one must pass through infinite darkness."

"Okay," Scout said, tired of the mumbo-jumbo. "And that has what to do with what?"

"Do you know how those who follow Ahuramazda believe the world will end?"

"You talking?"

"Humor is excellent protection against reality."

"I'm in reality," Scout said.

"Really?"

Scout had to admit Pandora did have another point, since she was standing on the helmets of two dead men, in 480 B.C., dressed as an oracle's priestess, holding a Naga staff, inside of a time bubble before she was pulled back to her own time.

Pulled back if she were still alive. And for the first time, Scout wondered whether her body would be pulled back if she were dead? They'd gotten Ivar back but that was just before he had drowned.

The two Shadow agents she'd killed had simply crumbled inward to dust.

Then again, did it matter at that point past death what happened to the body?

Pandora wasn't done yet. "According to that religion, the world will end with purification by fire. A great river of flame will flow across the land and consume everything. Land, ocean, man and creature even unto heaven and hell. The entire world will be scorched and the human race annihilated except for the chosen ones. The angels of white, also known as the light travelers."

"Valkyries?"

"No."

"Then what does all that mean?"

The Sibyl suddenly snatched her Naga staff, pulled it out of the body, and threw it, just past Scout's left ear.

Scout dove to the right, twisting, landing on bodies. Seeing Pandora's Naga hit a Valkyrie in the chest, piercing the white armor. Pandora was past Scout, grabbing the seven-headed snake hilt, twisting it, the blade tearing a huge gash in the armor.

The white figure was floating a foot above the bodies, arms extended, foot long blades on the end of each finger. The face was smooth white except for two red bulges where the eyes should be.

Scout leapt to her feet and slashed.

The tip of her Naga sliced the right side of Valkyrie, just under the right arm to the hip. With a screech, the Valkyrie abruptly jerked back, like a puppet on a string, up into the darkness and was gone.

Scout turned, to discover that the blade edge of Pandora's Naga was on her neck.

"I could, right now, if I wanted to," Pandora. "I could've before if I'd wanted to. Have you been taught the four stages of awareness?"

"What?" Scout was confused, not so much by the blade but the question.

"I can tell you haven't been," Pandora said. "Whoever is guiding you has been a poor instructor. There is so much you do not know that you should. You deserve better because I can sense what is dormant in you. Great power. Pure.

"The stages: First. Awareness of self. Second. Awareness of others. Third. Awareness of the world. And last, awareness beyond the world.

We, the Sibyls, Seer, Oracles, whatever we are called in whatever era, live in the fourth stage, but you aren't there yet. Not even close."

Then Pandora surprised her, pulling the blade back. "We are kindred spirits. We need to work together to save the world."

"I don't think so," Scout said.

"I saved you from the Valkyrie just now. Is that not proof of my intentions?"

"No," Scout said, "because the Valkyrie was probably under your control."

Pandora laughed. "I would expect no less from one of my sisters. It was not, I assure you but I cannot convince you, correct? But ponder this, my sister. What if I've already accomplished what I needed to, here and now? Then there is no conflict between us. We both work for the greater good. I will help you with your task."

"Doubtful," Scout said.

"One half hour," Pandora said. "Be here in one half hour. It will still be well before dawn, when the men will begin the killing again. I will prove my intentions to you."

Pandora vanished into the darkness.

Newburgh, New York, 1783 A.D.

EAGLE WASN'T THERE AND THEN HE was there, but he'd sort of always been there. It was the best way to explain how he arrived, becoming part of his current time and place without fanfare or excitement among those around him. He was in the bubble of this day, not before, and hopefully he wouldn't be here afterward.

A thought he held on to as the whip cut into the young woman's back.

Tripped, he sprawled face down into straw covered dirt, hearing the whip strike home once more.

"Easy," a deep voice hissed. "Easy."

The hand belonged to an older black man, kneeling next to Eagle, shaking his head. Eagle looked back at the other four slaves, standing shoulder to shoulder, held back from helping by the invisible line of their status. No matter how much Eagle had prepared himself mentally for this role in this mission in the brief time he had, the reality of being thrust into this specific scenario had brought an instinctive reaction.

It is 1783 A.D. The world's population is roughly 900 million humans, of which only 3.6 million are part of the fledgling United States (less than one half of one percent); of the 3.6 million, approximately 600,000 are slaves (eighteen percent) and 60,00 free blacks (one point five percent); the Montgoflier brothers 'invent flight', demonstrating the first balloon in front King Louis XVI and Queen Marie Antoinette (the birds were not as impressed); an English clergyman concludes that some stars might have enough gravity to prevent light from escaping and he calls them Dark Stars, later to be known as Black Holes; the Two-Headed Boy of Bengal is born and would die four years later; Laki, a volcanic fissure in Iceland, begins a series of eruptions that continue for eight months and spewed forth gas which killed over half of Iceland's livestock, caused a famine which killed a quarter of Iceland's humans and caused crop failures and drought around the world, killing an estimated six million people.

Some things change; some don't.

"I do not take pleasure from this," George Washington said. "It is the law and we must respect the law. It is what makes us a nation. You know this is only a last resort. But she did not attempt to just run away. She tried to go to the British carrying some of my correspondence. That is treason and I have had white men executed for less. I am being merciful."

He gestured to the overseer. "That's enough." He stepped forward and looked at the other slaves. He gestured at the half-naked woman being unhooked by the oversee: "This is a waste and unnecessary."

Unnecessary, Eagle thought, taking a deep breath, trying to get his emotion under control. Washington might have executed white men for treason, but he didn't own them, so he had no financial investment; killing a slave was wasting money.

Eagle got to his feet, the man who'd tripped him also stood. Eagle stole a glance. The other slave's gazes were downcast, so he followed suit. A bit too late as Washington's boots appeared in front of him. He could sense the man's presence, his aura. One of those who commanded the room, or barn, they were in.

Eagle had to fight not to raise his eyes to look at the man who'd led this country to victory in the Revolution and would be its first President in six years. And was a slave-owner.

"Hercules?" Washington asked.

"Sir?" The man who'd tripped Eagle answered.

"Is everything under control?"

"Yes, sir. He just fell, sir. Not feeling well. Not a problem at all, sir. You know his head ain't ever been right since the fire."

"I want—" Washington began, but a voice called to him from outside

"General!"

Washington sighed and turned toward the barn door. "Yes?"

"Colonel Caldwell is waiting in headquarters, as requested, sir. And the officers are assembling at the New Building. General Gates is already there."

Eagle gave a quick glance, not quick enough as Hercules sharply elbowed him. He caught a glimpse of Washington leaving the barn, accompanied by another officer.

"Get back to work," the overseer ordered. "Hercules, take care of her."

The other four slaves immediately dispersed. Eagle had no idea what his work was or where it was, so he remained in place.

"What is wrong with you?" Hercules demanded of Eagle. He was already moving toward the young woman. "Easy, girl, easy."

Eagle followed him. "I'm sorry. Just lost my head for a second."

"Get some of that axle grease." Hercules pulled a clean piece of cloth out of his pocket.

Eagle was confused for a second, then saw a small bucket near one of the stalls. He brought it over. Hercules put his fingers in, pulled out a dab and gently began applying it to the open wounds.

"What about infection?" Eagle asked.

"You're really not right in the head," Hercules said. "That old beating coming back on you? The fire?" It was a question, but Eagle got the feeling they were suggestions for possible excuses.

The download confirmed that axle grease was a poor man's, a slave's, field expedient way of packing an open wound. It actually helped prevent infection.

Hercules was better dressed than Eagle. A black frock coat over a white shirt and black trousers, all relatively clean. His shoes were polished and, unlike Eagle's, intact. His name, surprisingly, was in the download: the head cook at Mount Vernon, also known as Uncle Harkless. Technically, he would become the first head chef for the President of the United States in 1790, when Washington moved the capitol to Philadelphia and established the 'President's House'. Eagle found it interesting that despite his apparent subservient demeanor, Hercules escaped Mount Vernon in 1797 and disappeared from the annals of history and thus from the download.

"Must be," Eagle said, running his hand over the scars scrolled on the right side of his skull.

"Now Nancy, you need be still," he said to the woman.

She wasn't paying attention to the ministrations on her back. A slight flinch was the only indication she felt the pain as Hercules packed the wounds. She was in her late teens, her skin black as coal, her face set in what appeared to be a permanent scowl.

"Get her blouse," Hercules ordered.

Eagle fetched it. Hercules helped her stand up. Eagle held the blouse and carefully slipped it on as she extended one arm and then the other.

She shook off any further help, buttoning it herself.

Hercules moved to a position in front of her and reached out, none so gently, gripping her chin. "Listen here, girl. The Master is right. White men *have* been hung for what you did. I've seen it. You know Master's a decent man. He took a chance bringing us up north with him. And you try to repay him by stealing and running?"

"No good man owns slaves, Uncle," Nancy said, shaking his hand off her chin. "And this new country he's fought to make? Not going to be any different. The British say any slave who comes to them will be free. And they ain't gonna be around much longer in the City."

"They say any slave who *fights* for them will be freed," Hercules said. "Big difference. How you going to fight in a man's war?"

"I was bringing them papers. They'd taken me in for that."

"Don't matter anyway." Hercules shook his head. "This war is over."

"Not over yet, or else why all the grumbling here?" Nancy gave a bitter laugh. "Why'd that man give me the papers to take to the British then, telling me they'd earn my freedom?"

"What man?" Hercules asked.

"Don' matter," Nancy said. "They say they're fighting for freedom, yet we're not going to see ours."

"It's called hypocrisy," Eagle said.

Both of them turned to him. Eagle belatedly put a hand to his head. "My head isn't right."

"That's for sure," Hercules said. "You get on back and rest," he said to Nancy. "I've got to go to the General." He looked at Eagle. "You take her place in the General's quarters today since you seem to want to be looking at everything and saying fancy words. Try some fancy words in there and you'd be getting a beating too."

Hercules walked out, leaving Eagle with Nancy.

"What's wrong with you," Nancy said, as soon as he was gone.

"My head," Eagle began, but she cut him off.

"You don't stand right," Nancy said. "Uncle Harkless saw it, but don' know what to think. He keeps what he sees real small and don' see nothing he don' want to that might cause him to use his God-given smarts."

"Your back," Eagle said, but was cut off once more.

Nancy pointed out the barn. "Get going. You keep acting like this, you'll get worse than me. As the man say, we got to know our place."

Ravenna, Capitol of the Remains of the Western Roman Empire, 493 A.D.

ROLAND WASN'T THERE AND THEN HE was there, but he'd sort of always been there. It was the best way to explain how he arrived, becoming part of his current time and place without fanfare or excitement among those around him. He was in the bubble of this day, not before, and hopefully he wouldn't be here afterward.

Since it was his second time trip, Roland was already used to it and didn't spare it a moment of wonder, awe, or confusion which helped save his life.

As he became aware he was *there*, he slipped in the mud and blood, which also helped save his life from the spear. Roland's combat reflexes took the Goth's head off.

They really had to get better with the timing on this time travel thing, Roland thought, as he spun about, ready for more enemies. A fifth person, a woman, in a long black robe, took a step back and vanished into a Gate.

That was different.

"Centurion!" Several soldiers came running around a bend in the path, swords drawn. Roland went on guard, but recognized they were equipped with the same uniform and armor he wore. While one checked the bodies, the others spread out, providing security.

It is 493 A.D. Clovis I marries the eighteen year-old Burgundian princess, Clotilde, who converts him to Catholicism; in the same year, her father is murdered by her brother, Gundobad; the Mor Hanayo Monastery is established in a former Roman fort on the Turkish/Syrian border; The Ui Neill Dynasty wanted to battle the Airgialla Kingdom for the body of St. Patrick but the legend is God flooded a river to keep them from fighting.

Here on a muddy road in the middle of forest, Roland had once more killed. He didn't keep a tally and he never looked back to try to count how many had departed the mortal coil at his hand. Roland knew to do so would mean there was something wrong with him as a human being; something more than what was actually wrong with him.

Some things change; some don't.

Riders came around the bend. Odoacer, First King of Italy, leaned forward in the saddle. "Did you kill all four, Centurion?" His voice was raspy, his face pale and exhausted. He had a thick white beard that matched his bushy eyebrows. But his eyes were sunk deep, shadows underneath.

"Yes, sir," Roland said. It looked like being king wasn't all it was cracked up to be.

"I need a man like you close to me. A killer. Especially this day."

Roland fit the bill of warrior. Six and a half feet tall, a giant in this day and age where the average height for a Roman was a foot shorter. He was well muscled, broad chested, and all he could be in Army terms. His most distinguishing feature, currently hidden under the centurion helmet was a scar running along the right side of his head the temple to behind his right ear. He'd had a tattoo done to partially cover it; barbed wire. While no one in this era would know what barbed wire was, he'd been assured when he was outfitted back at the Possibility Palace that tattoos were not uncommon now and any who saw it would assume it was a band of thorns.

Odoacer raised his right hand, while he pointed with his left at Roland. "You are now one of my twelve; a Protector." He gestured imperiously, which Kings actually get to do, at one of the riders around him. "Give him your horse."

Roland claimed the horse, swung up into the saddle and realized he didn't know how to ride a horse, and no matter how much knowledge they download into your brain, it couldn't—but then, he felt a surge of awareness flood his brain, and he had access to a slew of knowledge and advice about how to do exactly that from the best horse trainers, horse whisperers, jockeys, and anyone who had weighed in on the topic.

It was all a bit too much, especially for Roland.

Roland tried to sort through and focus on the advice concerning: *How not to get thrown on your ass.*

The horse skittered, backed up.

"Do you know how to ride, Protector?" Odoacer demanded.

The horse bucked and Roland flew backwards, landing on his ass in the muddy road.

The guy whose horse he'd been 'given' grabbed the reins, keeping it from stomping Roland's head, which he thought was pretty nice, considering what had just happened.

Odoacer muttered a curse, signaled to the others with him, and rode off. *So much for being on the inner circle.* Roland got to his feet as the guy remounted his horse and galloped after them.

Roland smiled at the four privates who'd been left behind. "Why ride when you can walk, eh?"

The four exchanged glances, but then looked at the four bodies they'd rolled to the side of the road and their smirks disappeared. They snapped to attention. Roland marched past them, leading the way to follow the King and his destiny with fate.

They'd barely gone a few hundred meters when a rider came back. The de-horsed, re-horsed guy. He leaned and held out his arm, reminding Roland of a high-speed recovery into a Zodiac during water ops where someone leaned over the gunwale with a padded loop of rope and—that was cut short as they gripped hands and the momentum swung Roland up behind him, the rear of the saddle slamming into his testicles, hearing the rider chuckle, knowing what had just happened. They galloped off, leaving the four privates slogging through the mud.

Roland grabbed onto the two 'horns' on the rear of the Roman saddle and held on grimly. It seemed to him that the rider was being particularly rough, although Roland had never been on a horse before, okay briefly, so he had no clue.

As they came out of the forest, Roland saw the walls of Ravenna in the distance, which led to a flurry of mostly useless data about cities and this era. What struck him of importance was that every city in this age that wanted to survive needed walls around it.

Roland noted all the hovels on the outside of the walls and understood that at a fundamental level. Some people got to be inside the walls, and others would always be outside. The difference was, of course, levels of wealth. He'd grown up 'outside the walls'.

Some things never changed

The trail merged with several others as they approached the city and then it became an actual road. A Roman road, a *via munita*, paved with blocks of stone.

Smoother than many roads Roland had driven on in his present. Especially where he'd grown up.

Of more immediate attention, flanking the road on either side, was a line of crucifixes spaced fifty feet apart. Most of the victims were dead, some long dead, given how picked apart their bodies were, but some were still alive based on their writhing, crying out in pain and begging.

Data flowed from the download: In the east, Constantine had outlawed crucifixion in 337 due to his newly found religious belief, aka Catholicism. Not because he thought it was cruel, but he believed it diminished what his new adopted Lord had been through. But this was the Western Roman Empire, even the dregs of it, and that law meant nothing here.

Roland looked up as they rode past. He'd seen many horrible things in his time under arms. Some worse than this. He was observing, taking it in, wanting to understand this era more than from the data in his head.

"Who did this?" he asked the rider.

"Theoderic," the rider said. "He's making a statement to our King, outside the walls of Odoacer's own capitol. Roman law means nothing to Theoderic. Doesn't mean much to Odoacer either, but he pretends, which could be his flaw. As you can see, Theoderic doesn't pretend."

"Who are these people?"

Roland could feel the rider shrug. "Criminals. The unlucky. I'm sure some were randomly chosen just to make the spacing even. Their crime was being in the wrong place at the wrong time. We know about that don't we?" The last was said as they passed through the sally port into Ravenna. The rider edged them to the left, into a side street.

Roland slid off the horse, his hand on the hilt of his sword. The rider halted and dismounted. He faced Roland, his own hand on sword. But neither drew.

The rider had short blonde hair, fair skin, blue eyes, and was shorter than Roland by almost a foot. He was barrel-chested, though, with solid, thickly muscled arms. His armor was dull, unadorned, functional. The dents in it were not for ornamentation.

Roland had no doubt the man's sword was functional as well.

He smiled at Roland, revealing numerous missing teeth. "I am Eric."

"Roland."

"A good name. Perhaps you are from the line of my people, far down the ages?"

Roland didn't reply.

"Odoacer made you one of the Twelve Protectors, but now, since he sent me back to pick you up, I assume we are thirteen. Is that an unlucky number in your time?"

Roland shrugged.

Eric laughed. "It is in this time. Of more immediate concern, it means Odoacer is feeling uncertain about the meeting tonight. To bring in another for protection. Tell me, traveler from a distant time. What will happen tonight at the banquet? Odoacer trusts Theoderic. I think him a fool for that, but perhaps he will prove me a fool. Will there be peace? Will the two rule together? That would make for a mighty army. One that could challenge the east. Restore the Western Empire. Perhaps they could rule as the Romans once did in their Republic and pretended to do afterwards, with two consuls, instead of one Emperor?"

Roland remained silent.

"A man of few words?" Eric drummed his fingers on the pommel of his sword. All around was the noise of commerce and trade. The rattle of cavalry riding by. Whores calling out for clients. Dogs barking. It smelled of sewage from the open ditches, but Roland barely noticed. Eric cocked his head slightly to the right. "You know what will happen, but you are not certain of your role in it?"

Roland cut to the chase. "I do not trust you."

"Nor I you. So what are we to do about that? Should we work together or just settle this now?"

"That would only prove who is the better fighter," Roland said. "Not who is right."

Eric laughed. "Isn't that the way everything is settled? It is never about right or wrong."

Roland considered that. "Sometimes it is."

"Ah. An idealist. Yet you appear a warrior."

Roland shrugged. "I've faced evil. Fighting evil is right."

Eric didn't respond to that. "Those four who attacked you. They were mercenaries. Their tribe is in the employ of Theodoric, but such men do blood work for whoever pays them, even if their tribe is under payment oath to another. Why were they after you specifically?"

"I have no idea," Roland answered honestly. "But if Odoacer and Theodoric are to join forces, and I'm Odoacer's man, why would Theodoric's men attack me?"

"He might not have ordered it," Eric said. "As I said. They work for money. Anyone's money."

"What do you think we should do?" Roland asked.

Eric squinted. "What I think matters nothing in this."

"This is your time," Roland said. "You're going to have to live with the results."

"And you? Won't you in your time?"

Roland shrugged. "Above my pay grade."

"Isn't everything for men like us?" Eric tugged on the bridle. "Ours is not to wonder the reasons and the whys. We just follow our orders and get things done. Let's drink some, see if we trust each any further, then go to Odoacer's fortress where the feast will be held." He led the horse toward a hitch outside a seedy looking dive. "And, if you trust me and want to succeed, you'll tell me what the result is to be this evening. Who lives and who dies." He slapped Roland on the shoulder as he invited him in. "Let us make sure it is neither of us, eh?"

The Missions Phase II

Rome, Roman Empire, 44 B.C.

"DID YOU TELL HIM?" Spurinna asked Calpurnia.

Caesar's third, and hopefully last, wife was in her atrium, knitting, which was actually called nailbinding in this era, Edith's nitpicking download informed Moms. A slave girl held the yarn as she worked.

Calpurnia glanced up. She was a slight woman, with hunched shoulders and sunken eyes. "I did not sleep well last night because of you."

"Is he here?" Moms cut through.

"And who are you?"

"My protégée," Spurinna said.

"I have not heard you had one," Calpurnia said. "And to answer your questions: yes and no. Yes, I spoke to him as you told me to. Perhaps not exactly as you would have wished. Would you like the words?"

Moms went back to her question. "So that's a no as to whether your husband is here?"

Calpurnia ignored her. "Let me try to recall, my dear Seer, although it was not long ago. Ah yes." She put the knitting down and spoke in a sing-song voice as she looked off into the distance. "Oh, mighty Caesar. As you know well, I have never stood much on formalities or even propriety. When you brought your slut from Egypt and placed her and her barbarians in our villa, I did not stand in protest although many urged me to. I also have never stood much on prophecies. But my mind was troubled during the night. Echoes of Spurinna's dire words. I am frightened, husband.

"There were horrid images in my dreams. An eagle falling. A dead lion. The dead climbing out of their graves. Battles above in the clouds between warriors. Blood falling on the Senate roof. The screams of dying men. A slut crying out. I am most frightened my Lord." Calpurnia looked at Spurinna. "Close enough?"

"Not quite what I told you to say," Spurinna said. "It might have been best not to mention Cleo—"

"That name is not permitted in this household," Calpurnia snapped. "This." She pointed down. "Is *my* home.

"Apologies," Spurinna said. "It might have been best not to mention the Egyptian slut because men are prone to anger at harsh words and in anger do not think straight."

Calpurnia scoffed. "There are things besides anger that keep men from thinking straight."

Moms jumped in. "But you told him not to leave?"

"No is the answer to your question, protégé. He is not in the house. Why did you ever think he would pay attention to me?" Calpurnia asked Spurinna. "As you instructed, I told Caesar I had already sent word to Antony that he was ill and would not be attending the Senate. He laughed. He walked out and his last words to me were: 'Caesar goes forth.' As if there were someone else walking out the door. It is fortunate his mighty head was able to pass through the doorway."

"So he is gone," Spurinna said. "Despite my warning and your entreaty."

"He does not bear the words of women well," Calpurnia said, going back to her knitting. "Except for that Egyptian slut."

Petrograd, Russia, 1917.

DOC WANDERED AIMLESSLY, quickly learning that the only part of the palace that still had heat was the family wing. He'd yet to meet another person. No guards, no servants. He wondered who was stoking the boilers to keep this area warm. He knew the Tsar was in here somewhere, having been brought back on the 9th of March after drafting his abdication on the 2nd in his Imperial train car, idled at a siding in Pskov. A document that had gone through revision after revision by the Bolsheviks, who were unwilling to allow a transfer of the monarchy, but wanted it finished. Today was the day it would officially be terminated.

Revolutionary soldiers surrounded the palace, but they were keeping their distance, under orders not to provoke an incident until it was decided what would be done with the royals.

He had some time to reflect now that he was done with his mission. The time travel had been just as Roland had described, painless and instant and utterly confounding to Doc, who wanted a scientific explanation for everything.

On top of that, Roland being right was almost as surprising as being here, inside Alexander Palace in what Doc had to assume was 1917.

Not understanding the science was going to drive him crazy. Doc knew the danger, but because he was an intelligent man, he had to stop his mind from careening down the blind alleyways of ignorance searching for enlightenment.

He did his best, remembered Nada reeling him in on so many missions, slamming him back into the real world and the real problem. Usually just before they would have gotten killed if they'd followed Doc's scientific inquisitiveness rather than Nada's survival instincts.

The palace was quiet. Far too quiet for a palace. He'd watched Downton Abbey and knew even a great house was full of noise, never mind an Imperial Palace. But not a sound. There were no guards at any of the many doors he could see.

Glancing out a window Doc could see the massive boulevard leading up to the palace. It was empty in the mid-day light. No inflamed hordes of the peasant working class coming to finally take down the bourgeoisie. Strange to think he was in the midst of the most significant revolution of the modern era and it was so quiet and still. He could see some guards in the distance, gathered round a fire, more intent on staying warm than guarding.

The download flooded his brain with information, so much that Doc couldn't move, mesmerized an almost orgasm of data. While the Palace in modern days was considered part of St. Petersburg, technically it was outside the city, at Tsarskoye Selo, 15 miles south of the city that helped explain the lack of crowds outside.

But St. Petersburg had been renamed Petrograd in 1914 at the start of Russia's involvement in World War I to get rid of the German dangler: *Burg*. Doc imagined Peter the Great, who'd founded the city in 1703 after capturing the area from the Swedes, wouldn't have been too happy about that. Peter the Great had wanted a year-round port and it fit the bill so he took it from the Swedes. He eventually moved his capital here from Moscow and, searching for a name, decided on the simplest solution: name it after himself.

Petrograd, as a name, wouldn't last long, with its ties to the Tsarist past, and would be renamed Leningrad in 1924, just five days after the namesake passed away. But then Lenin's communist legacy eventually passed away and in 1991, it went back to St. Petersburg.

The cycle of history, Doc thought. He looked back at the wing where the Tsarina had ensconced herself and her children. Like many people in huge mansions and palaces, the Tsarina spent most of her time in one small room, the antechamber off her bedroom. A tiny enclave in this football stadium of marble and gold and paintings and sculptures and tapestries and tall, closed doors. Doors that should have two Imperial Cossack guards with lances flanking them.

But didn't.

Those days were gone and the revolutionaries controlled the area, making the grand palace a grand prison. He took a turn, following the floor plan from the download, not quite certain why he was drawn to these rooms; perhaps it was the unnatural attention that Anastasia had directed at him?

He paused at a door, marked with a small lilac. Doc opened it, peering in. Afternoon light filtered through a dirty window, revealing a bedroom. The beds were un-made, clothes scattered about.

The download informed him that the Duchesses shared rooms. The eldest, Olga and Tatiana, in one, while Anastasia shared hers with Maria.

Compared to their mother's boudoir, the girls lived austerely. The beds could hardly be called that, more a cot with no pillows. A single desk with a chair on either side.

Doc shut the door. He opened the next one. Another bedroom, two cots, but everything in its place. Blankets folded. A book was open on a desk. Intrigued, bored, against his better judgment, he slipped in the room.

The book was a diary.

Like the download he couldn't turn off, Doc was drawn to it. He leaned over. A pencil between pages marked a spot further in the diary, but Doc read the open page:

I know that I'm a princess, but I don't want a prince. How funny that I'm the only girl who doesn't want a prince, but rather desire an ordinary boy who loves me and not the shoe which I leave behind. I want no pumpkins which turn into carriages and certainly no wicked stepsisters as my sisters are enough for any lifetime. I want a true friend in a boy who will always care for me like papa cares for mama and combs my hair and laughs at my little stories and tell me over and over that I'm the prettiest when I know I'm not.

I don't want a prince at all and I'm so lucky because I'm the youngest and will be able to have a real marriage for love and not for country or position or for treaty. I know those are needed, but mama said no to the first who was presented to her by her grandmother. To defy the great-grandma Victoria! Even her own son would not do so. But mama did and great-grandma granted her wish to be with papa.

And if she had not? I would not be here. I would not be writing this. So strange.

But once mama met papa, he was all she had room for in her heart.

Still, papa was a prince. If only he'd been a farmer. I'd still be here, mama would still have a full heart, but all these troubles would not lie on our heads.

If only.

If only.

If only HE had not come into mama's life because of little brother. HE is not real. HE is not of us. I know it but I cannot tell anyone. They would think me crazy, even though they should see that HE is the crazy one. All the country can see it, but not mama. Even Papa knows it, but he gives way.

Doc stared at the word: *HE*

He had no doubt who Anastasia was referring to: Rasputin.

He re-read: *HE is not of us.*

What did that mean? What had happened here? But Rasputin was dead and his legacy already a part of the future history. If Rasputin was a time traveler—and he wasn't Time Patrol, even Dane wouldn't forget to mention that little nugget—then?

The Shadow. It had already sown its seed of change well before Doc's arrival. He'd been just in time.

Doc flipped through the pages, skimming the whimsy of a teenage girl, searching for more reference '*HE*'.

He found another dated December 1916.

HE sent a letter to mama, which caused her great consternation. She threw it to the fire, but I retrieved it before it was burned. I copy HIS words, so that someone who reads this after I am gone may know:

Doc swallowed, sure there was no way Anastasia meant a time traveler, but rather someone reading her words later on. But still—

He read the transcription of Rasputin's letter:

I write this letter, the last letter, which will be left after me in Saint Petersburg. I have a premonition that I will die before 1 January. I speak to the Russian People, to Papa, to Mama and Children, to all of the Russian Land, what they should know and understand. If I will be killed by ordinary people, especially by my brothers—the Russian peasants—then you, the Russian Tsar, should not worry about Your Children. They will lead in Russia another hundred years.

But if I am murdered by the boyars and noblemen, if they spill my blood, and it stays upon their hands, then twenty-five years will pass before they will be able to wash my blood from their hands. They will have to flee from Russia or die. Brother will kill brother, everyone will kill each other and hate each other, and at the end of twenty-five years, not one nobleman will be left in Russia. Tsar of the Russian Land, if You hear the ringing of the funeral bell at the death of Grigory Rasputin, then know this; if in my death are guilty someone of Your relatives, then I tell you, that none of Your Family, none of Your children and Relatives will live more than two years. And if they live, they will pray to God for death, for they will see the disgrace and shame of the Russian Land, the arrival of the antichrist, pestilence, poverty, desecrated temples of God, holy places spit upon, where everyone will become a corpse. Three times twenty-five years will the black bandits, servants of the antichrist, destroy the people of Russia and the faith of the Orthodox. And the Russian Land will perish. And I perish, I have perished already, and I am no longer among the living. Pray, pray, be strong, think of Your Blessed Family.

The download was already casting doubt on the validity of the words Anastasia claimed were written by Rasputin. There had always been rumors of such a prophecy, but scholars had disputed it, claiming that the language in it was not such that would be used a Russian at that time.

Unless Rasputin wasn't of this time, Doc thought. There was no reason for Anastasia to be making this up. She was here. Now. Historians weren't.

Anastasia's brief comments following the transcription indicated her thoughts ran in the same direction:

I fear HE is right. I have always known HE is not of us. Not of now. HE knows things he should not. HE does things no one should be able to do. I fear for all of us.

I would pray to God as Mama, and especially Papa, do. But God would never have allowed HIM to come here. I have prayed for Papa but it does not stop what is happening. I wonder, and I would never say this: Where is God? Why has He abandoned us?

Doc checked the rest of the diary, but there wasn't another reference to *HE*. Not even a mention on the 30th of December 1916, when Rasputin was killed.

Doc went to the most recent entry and the first sentence chilled him, even though the room was heated.

When she died, she was only a teenager.

Doc forced himself to continue reading.

There was a boy somewhere who loved her, without ever having met her. But he knew her very well. He would never be able to tell her that he loved her, because now she was dead. But he thought, and she thought, that in another life, whenever that will be, that they might meet and fill each other's heart.

Goodbye. Do not forget us.

Nothing more.

Doc glanced over his shoulder at the door. He felt as if Anastasia were watching him, even though the door was closed and he was alone.

Palos de la Frontera, Spain, 1493 A.D.

"THERE'S ANOTHER BAR HERE, RIGHT?" Mac asked.

There was movement on the deck of the ship, but no one had disembarked. A small boat with two men and a woman holding up a baby had rowed out not long ago. She'd called out, holding up the baby. A man had come to the side and there had been a conversation, too distant to make out, then the rowboat had come back, the woman looking none-too-pleased.

Geert was surprised at the question. "It is a harbor town for sailors. Of course, there is a bar. But our vows preclude—"

"Your vows," Doc said.

Geert was quiet for a moment, then pointed. "Come. We will choose one where the Swiss are not."

Mac walked alongside Geert to town, which was so small it wouldn't have qualified for a single stop sign if there were cars. A dark opening beckoned in one of the buildings facing the waterfront and Geert ducked in. Mac glanced over his shoulder and noted that one of the Cente Suisse was following.

The tavern was crowded, sailors and fishermen discussing the appearance of just one of Columbus' ships. They'd been gone since the 3rd of August the previous year. There was much speculation, and concern, over the missing *Santa Maria* and *Pinta* and their crews.

Geert made his way to a dark corner and Mac followed. Then they jostled each other, both wanting to sit with their back against the wall, until they settled on bracketing the corner, each with a wall behind them. A young boy came by and Geert ordered something.

"The town had to help pay," Geert said, indicating the men.

"Pay for what?"

"For Columbus' expedition. Ferdinand levied a tax on the town to help finance it. They all have a stake. Not that they will see any reward. It is the nature of Monarchs to demand money, rarely to give it. The town paid with the *Nina* and the *Pinta* and a large part of their crews. Captained by two brothers from here, the Pinzon's. It is an interesting story and I have had nothing else to do this past week than listen to stories."

Mac saw the Swiss Guard enter, check the interior, and after ascertaining Mac and Geert's location, taking a seat where he could watch them. Nothing subtle about it at all.

"Columbus got Isabella and Ferdinand to assist in financing," Geert said, "and that was in no small part due to Father de Cisneros from the Friary. He is Isabella's confessor. Who knows what secrets he has hidden in heart that she has whispered to him, eh?"

The boy brought two mugs and Geert immediately drank half of his. Mac saw no reason not to follow suit.

"And, yes," Geert said, "I see the Papal pig over there. One has shadowed me every time I left my room at the Inn. They are most suspicious of any strangers in town. Where was I?

"Ah. The ships. The King and Queen ordered the town to provide two vessels. The town refused. Father de Ciscneros cajoled them and they finally agreed but only on the conditions it was two of their own ships, with their own crew, with their own trusted Captains. Thus the Pinzon brothers and the *Nina* and *Pinta*." Geert leaned close to Mac, his breath foul. "Some say that Martin Pinzon, the older brother and captain of the *Pinta*, had already found landfall to the west four years ago, but if so, there is no official acknowledgment of it."

The download confirmed the rumor, but not the fact.

"Now all are worried where their sons and husbands and fathers are."

Mac knew their fates. After 'discovering' San Salvador on the 12th of October the previous year, the small fleet moved on and made landfall in Cuba on the 28th. At which point, Martin Pinzon parted ways with Columbus, taking the *Pinta* in search of a place he'd learned of from the natives that was supposed to be full of gold.

Then Columbus' flagship, the *Santa Maria* foundered. Columbus was rescued by the *Nina*, which he made his new flagship. Unfortunately, there wasn't enough room on the smaller ship for both crews, so Columbus left forty men ashore, with orders to use the wreckage of the *Santa Maria* to build a fort.

Columbus sailed further along the coast and, amazingly, linked up with the *Pinta* along the coast of Cuba. A fierce argument ensued between Columbus and Pinzon, not only over Pinzon's disappearance, but the stranding of the forty men, many of them from Palos de la Frontera.

Over Pinzon's objections, the fleet, now down to two ships, headed back to Spain, leaving the men in Cuba. The ships were separated in a storm on Valentines Day. As far as Columbus and everyone else knew at the moment, Pinzon and the *Pinta* had been lost.

Geert had been silent for a little bit, leaving Mac to his thoughts, but he picked something up from Mac's expression. "They are all lost?"

"No," Mac said. Which was true and not true. The forty men Columbus had left behind? None survived to the next year. But the *Pinta*? Was he breaking Rule One by telling Geert what would happen any minute now? "Not all of them." Of course, Mac, thought, what if the *Pinta* didn't show up? Then things had already changed and—

Mac picked up the mug and drained it. "Another," he said to Geert.

Geert made a signal and the boy hustled back with full mugs.

"So," Geert said. "Not all are lost. The others will show up?"

"Some of them," Mac said.

"Keeping secrets," Geert said. "Very smart. All is intrigue. King John, King Ferdinand, Queen Isabella, the Pope trying to dip his hand in. And speaking of—"

Mac had one hand on the hilt of his dagger as there wasn't room for the rapier. The Swiss Guard took the seat at the other corner of the table, his back to the room, his focus on Mac and Geert. He was a big man, over six feet. He had two scars on his face, evidence of past violence.

"You are Franciscans? From the Friary?" His accent was one Mac couldn't place, his Latin barely understandable.

"No," Geert said. "You work for the Pope and don't know what a Franciscan looks like?"

The Guard shrugged. "You priests are all the same to me." He nodded at Geert. "You have been here a while. You," he indicated Mac, "are new. Why are you here?"

"Why should I tell you?" Mac asked in response.

The Guard looked bored. "My sergeant sent me to ask. I go back to him without an answer? He will not be happy. Then I will not be happy. I would like to be happy."

"Wouldn't we all?" Mac said. He was dealing with a Roland: dumb, but dangerous. "Maybe you tell us why *you're* here and we figure things out? Why we're all here?"

The Guard shrugged. "We're here to get the report of the man, Columbus. Bring it to Rome."

Mac hadn't expected an immediate, direct response.

"Is Columbus on the ship?" Mac asked.

"He was on it in Lisbon," the Guard said. "He sailed from there on it. We have not seen anyone get off the ship. So he is on it."

Mac was back-pedaling in the face of Roland simplicity. He tried to think of an explanation why he was here that wouldn't reveal his true mission, explode this simpleton's brain, and keep from getting stabbed.

Geert beat him to it. "We are here to pray for the safe return of all the sailors from this town." He reached into a pocket on his robe and pulled out a small bag of coins, which he jiggled. "They have paid us for our services."

The Guard laughed. "Priests." He spit. "Pimps and whores. But the town has their own priests from the Priory. You are strangers. Why would they bring in strangers to pray?"

Mac and Geert exchanged glances. A good question to which they had no answer.

The Guard leaned forward. "My sergeant told me, to tell you, to leave. He is under orders to protect Columbus and protect the report. Strangers make my sergeant nervous. He doesn't like being nervous. He sees danger everywhere and you two, whatever you are, who should not be here, make him nervous." The Guard stood. "If we see you again, we will kill you. We have the Pope's blessing for that."

There was a ripple of excitement as a man appeared at the entrance. The news flew across the room: The *Pinta* had been sighted.

"Our prayers have been answered," Geert exclaimed.

The Guard thumped a heavy fist onto the table. "Now answer my sergeant's prayer and leave the town."

Thermopylae, Greece, 480 B.C.

"WHERE WERE YOU JUST NOW?" Leonidas reached down from the top of the wall and gripped Scout's hand, pulling her up and over.

"I spoke to Pandora," Scout said.

"And you're still alive," Leonidas said, "so I take it that it didn't go badly. Did it go well?"

"I don't know. I must speak to her again shortly."

"How did you get past my sentries? They would not fail in their duty."

"They did not," Scout said. "I am a priestess of the Delphic Oracle. We can do much that men cannot see." Scout felt like a fool saying that, but she had to stay in character. And one shouldn't feel like a fool when standing on a rampart of stone and dead warriors.

They climbed off the wall. Leonidas put an arm around her shoulder, an unusual gesture for the King.

"You are shivering," he said. "Come to the fire."

They went to their spot in the camp. Scout held her hands out, warming them. Lightning flickered, followed by thunder, but the storm had stalled off the coast, neither approaching nor passing.

"It is not the cold that makes you shake," Leonidas said, moving to the other side of the small fire, looking at her in the flickering light.

"It is the cold," Scout said, without any conviction.

Leonidas smiled sadly. "It is not bad to admit fear. Many think Spartans have no fear. As if we weren't humans but rather some species born out of rock. I told you of *phobologia*, our fear training. Where we master our muscles and reactions. That doesn't mean we don't fear. Rather we have been trained to act in spite of it. And," Leonidas continued, "there are worse things than fear."

Scout looked up from the fire. "Such as?"

"You saw," Leonidas said. "When we departed Sparta. Our wives did not wish us well or even that we return."

The data was there. "*'On your shield or with it'.*"

Leonidas nodded. "Do you know why they say with shield and not with our *xiphos* or spear?"

Of course she did. "No."

"A Spartan who drops his sword or spear only disarms himself. A Spartan who drops his shield exposes the man in the shield wall to his left. Leaves him open to the enemy. That is the greatest disgrace. It is punishable by immediate death." Leonidas stared at her, eyes glinting in the firelight. "Cowardice. Failing one's comrades in battle. That is unforgiveable." He paused. "As is treason. Betraying one's comrades and betraying Sparta."

Scout understood the implication. "I have to learn what Pandora has planned."

Leonidas shook his head. "Gods and oracles. As if we were all just pieces in their game. I wish I understood what the game is? What the purpose of all this is?"

"Defending Sparta," Scout said. "And in doing so, saving Greece."

"Noble concepts," Leonidas said. He sighed, so deeply, Scout sensed it was down to his soul. "I die soon. The way a Spartan should die. In battle. But . . ."

His voice trailed off.

"Why do you doubt?" Scout asked.

"That is a good question," Leonidas said. "I've never doubted before. If I had ever showed doubt or weakness, I would not be King." He shifted his gaze, looking around the camp. "Every man here, every Spartan, is judged immediately after birth by a committee of elders. Those who are infirm, sickly, who do not appear to be able to develop into a warrior, are taken to a hill and left to die."

"And the baby girls?"

"The same. They are evaluated in a similar way, except in terms of being able to bear warriors. When the boys see their seventh year after birth, they are taken from the family to live in the *agoge*. Where we live until we see our thirtieth year. The *agoge* remains a part of us until we die.

"In our late teens, we are sent out into the wild, naked, with no weapons. No supplies. For two weeks." A faint smile. "The lucky ones go in summer. The unlucky, winter. But each season has dangers. We must not only survive, we must kill a *helot* to prove we can kill. After all, what good is a warrior who can't kill a person?

"Then at our twentieth year, we become a citizen. We can marry, but must still live in the *agoge* and train. After all that, after all my victories as King, I should not doubt. Especially now, as I face my greatest battle."

"Why do you?"

"Because of you," Leonidas said.

Scout felt a hand squeezing her heart.

"I don't think you are a priestess of the Delphic Oracle either."

Scout remained still.

Leonidas continued. "I do not believe you are the Cyra of Delphi I traveled with these past weeks. You look like her, but you are not her. Something has changed. You have changed. During the night. Your questions about what you should already know, what you witnessed, indicate that. But more so, it's a feeling. The one a good soldier gets before walking into an ambush. The awareness of something amiss."

He waited, but Scout gave no reply.

"You do not deny it," Leonidas said.

"Do you think I am an ambush?" Scout asked.

Leonidas was still as a statue. Scout fought to remain as still.

The Spartan King finally spoke, answering her questions with his own. "Can you tell me who you are?"

"I can not."

"Can you tell me why you are here?"

Scout sighed and he took that as a no.

Leonidas drew a callused hand through his beard. He looked to the east. "Dawn is still a few hours away. Your time to meet Pandora has come." He indicated the wall. "I will see you over the wall. But when you return, if you return, I need truth. A man about to die deserves that."

Newburgh, New York, 1783 A.D.

EAGLE STOOD OUTSIDE THE CLOSED door leading to Washington's office, having little clue what he was to do. Nancy's instructions had indicated he was to be some sort of waiter, but he wasn't sure of the protocol. Just walk in? Knock?

Hercules came bustling by, carrying a tray with bread on it. Eagle could hear muffled voices from the room, but nothing distinct.

Hercules came back out and poked Eagle in the ribs. "What are you standing out here for? I know you're a field man and not used to inside, but you got common sense. Get in there. Fill the wine. The beer. The water. Otherwise stand in the corner. And don't say nothin'. And don' act like you hear nothin'. Cause you don't hear nothin'. You don't see nothin'. Understand?"

Eagle nodded and went in, discreetly checked the wine glass in front of Washington, full, the beer mug in front of the other man, also still full, water glasses, still full, and went to the darkest corner. Washington's office was inside a one-story log building. Much like dozens of other log plank buildings haphazardly scattered about the cantonment. There were also numerous tents of varying sizes.

The download informed him that there were over five thousand troops here, with about five hundred family members. This was what was left of the majority of the Continental Army, with men drifting away every day to go home, now that the fighting was over and there had been no pay for eight months. In fact, many of the officers were using personal funds to pay for food and supplies for their soldiers. Not only weren't the soldiers being paid, the officers knew that the promise Congress had made in May 1778, right after the awful winter at Valley Forge, of a pension of half their pay once they were discharged, was now an empty one.

The country had a fundamental problem: Under the Articles of Confederation, Congress had no power to tax. It had to ask the states for funds; which was rarely forthcoming. The previous year a delegation of officers had been deputized to appeal to Congress about the pay issue. Their appeal was rejected. The issue had simmered all winter, with officers and troops confined to the Newburgh Cantonment and mostly indoors, with little else to discuss while the winter raged outside.

"Let me talk to the officers," the other man in the room said. He wore a blue uniform, the left sleeve empty and pinned to his lapel. His one hand rested on a black, leather-bound book.

Washington was seated behind a wood table, leaning back, legs stretched out, staring out a window toward an open field where some troops were drilling without much enthusiasm. Eagle figured the speaker was Colonel Caldwell and—

Eagle stiffened as the facts from the download belied what he was seeing: James Caldwell was killed on 24 November, 1781. Shot by an American sentry after he refused to have a package he was carrying inspected. The sentry was hanged for murder just two months later. The suspicion was heavy that he had been bribed to kill Caldwell. By whom or for what reason, the download had a gap.

Prior to his death, the British had dubbed Caldwell the High Priest of the Rebellion. His church was burned down and he'd taken up arms, flanking his Bible with pistols on the podium whenever he preached. Up until he was killed.

But here he was.

Washington glanced over at Caldwell. "Put the fear of God in them, James?"

"It works when all else fails."

"Money works," Washington said. "If Congress would follow through on the promises it made my officers, we wouldn't have this issue."

"If Congress had followed through on half its promises," Caldwell said, "our country would be in much better shape, General. I fear the states will spin off once a treaty is signed with Britain. We'll have thirteen weak, bickering siblings instead of a nation. And what of the west? There are agitators already whispering about starting their own little kingdoms. That Sevier fellow in North Carolina over the mountains is acting like he wants his own country." He shook his head. "You said you would not go to the meeting, because you didn't want to sanction it with your presence. Who is to speak then?"

"I was thinking General Gates. His adjutant wrote the damn letter of discontent. And Gates is already at the New Building."

"You mean the Temple?"

Washington chuckled. "You spend more time in there than anyone, I will admit that."

Caldwell wasn't put off so easily. "Gates? Sir, he actively went against you in '78. Tried to get you replaced. You place too much trust in those who have proven themselves unfit. Camden was a disaster. He should have been court-martialed."

Washington was back to watching the troops. He waved a hand without much vigor. "We've had enough of the past, James."

Caldwell leaned forward. "Sir. Hamilton is playing this. Surely you know that? Leveraging the Army against Congress to advance his agenda. I fear he will destroy all in order to achieve his own goals."

"Hamilton is a man of contradictions," Washington said. "He is very smart. Smarter than both of us. I don't waste time trying to unravel his machinations. I just watch for them." He reached out, fingers grasping, found the water glass and took a deep drink, putting it back down, still focused out of the building. "Hamilton and his cronies are indeed leveraging some of the officers. They play a bigger game than funding the army. They want a stronger Federal government. Not, as you said, thirteen bickering siblings. Hamilton also wants a Federal bank. I'm sure he sees himself at the head of it.

"But you know," Washington mused, "he might just be right about that issue. Time will tell. We need peace first. True peace before we can tackle so many of the issues confronting us. And I fear—" he glanced in Eagle's direction for the first time, and then back at the soldiers—"that there are some that will have to be put off for a future generation. Country first."

Eagle didn't need the download to confirm that line of thought amongst most of the Founding Fathers. They were, mostly, very smart men, some brilliant. Most knew intellectually that slavery was a doomed institution. Many even objected to it on moral grounds. But it was a reality and to fight that battle before the country was on solid footing threatened to divide the northern colonies from the southern before they were even joined.

The issue had been put off and the grandchildren and great-grandchildren of those men would pay the price in blood during the Civil War. Eagle wanted to speak up, to warn of that storm over the horizon, of the hundreds of thousands who would die, white men. Of the millions of blacks who would live their lives as slaves before that great war would decide the issue.

Caldwell interrupted Eagle's dark musings. "Hamilton is a dangerous man, sir. He's a bastard and—"

"Let us not hold his birth against him," Washington said, a slight edge to his voice. "A person's birth is not their choice."

Exactly! Eagle wanted to scream.

"Hamilton served me well at critical times in the war," Washington said. "I could send him to relay a verbal order and be assured he would deliver it correctly. That is a rare talent and essential in an aide-de-camp."

"Jefferson and Adams despise him, sir," Caldwell said.

Eagle had to wonder, through his anger and frustration, what agenda Caldwell was pushing. Hamilton had been, would be, instrumental in the formation of the United States. Not in the framing of the Constitution, but in the area of financing. And no country could survive without financing.

"I know they do," Washington said. "But you and I understand something that Jefferson and Adams do not. We have faced the enemy. So has Hamilton. Such men hold a special place in my heart. As you do, my friend.

"Nevertheless, we must beware." Washington waved a hand toward a pile of correspondence, without looking at it. "There's a letter in there from him. He tried to enlist me in the effort against Congress. To take charge of the officers' efforts. That is why I cannot be at that meeting. It will reflect poorly on me and send the wrong message to Hamilton and to Congress."

"He asked that directly, sir?" Caldwell was surprised. "In writing?"

"Yes. I replied to him immediately. Informed him I would not introduce the army into this matter of a central government. Down that path lies a dangerous forest. The army must be separate from politics."

"The war is not over, sir," Caldwell argued. "All assume peace is a given, but what if the British change their minds? We are counting on the same fools who cannot pay us to negotiate the peace in Paris. We should not be waiting. We should force British government to negotiate in faith. Take New York City and—"

Washington's low murmur cut through Caldwell's exhortations. "They have no spirit."

"Sir?"

"The soldiers," Washington said, nodding toward the parade field. "In some ways, this winter was worse than Valley Forge. There was little spirit. No common foe, other than Congress."

Eagle came forward with a jug and began filling the glass. Washington turned his chair, wood scraping on wood. Eagle retreated back to the corner.

If he were a demon, Eagle thought, then Caldwell was a ghost. A sign of history already changed before this bubble in time.

Washington looked at Caldwell. "I know you hate the British, James. You have every reason to. Far more than most."

The information was there: Caldwell's wife had been killed by the British during the Battle of Connecticut Farms the previous year, the last major attempt by the British to gain victory. A Hessian General had led an attack out of New York City toward Washington's old encampment in Morristown, but had failed. The event of her death was also hazy in the download, as the records indicated she'd either been shot accidently; or had been targeted by the British who'd already put a price on her husband's head.

"More the reason to allow me to speak to the officers," Caldwell said. "I can redirect their anger from Congress to the British."

"What good would that do?" Washington asked. "Our fighting is over. Men would die needlessly attacking New York City. It would violate the truce. If the British come back in force, they might well win back what they believe they have lost. The French have gone home. They have their own problems because of the war. They lent us quite a bit of money. Something else the Congress is unable to pay. Also," Washington gave a low laugh, "I imagine the British government listens to their soldiers about as well as ours does. Which is to say, not much at all."

"Then let me appeal to the officers' faith, sir."

Washington seemed to be considering it. "Remember, though, that you have enemies inside the ranks. We know that." He indicated the empty sleeve.

Eagle was invisible, a nothingness. A void whose only use was to fill glasses. His status made him inconsequential, not even human.

"General," Caldwell repeated. "We need to draw out the ringleaders."

"We do need to stop the discontent," Washington said.

"You cannot trust Gates, sir," Caldwell insisted. "We have to find out who else is in his inner circle of malcontents."

Washington nodded. "You have a point. My loyalty blinds me at times." He drummed his fingers on the desk in contemplation.

Caldwell shifted in his chair, looked at Eagle with a frown on his forehead, as if he could sense the raging turmoil inside Eagle.

"Perhaps," Washington began, "it *might* be for the best if you addressed the officers. Appeal to their faith yes, but we must give them more than that. We must appeal to their hope for the future. Like you, many of these men lost everything in the war. Their homes gone. Their livelihood gone. They must believe they have not lost what they were promised in order to rebuild their lives."

"How will I do that, sir?" Caldwell asked. "We can make no promises beyond those that were already made."

"Tell them I sympathize with their grievances. Most know that, but they should be reminded. And words are not enough on my part. They must know that I am taking action. I will go to Philadelphia. I will make a personal appeal to Congress."

Washington never did that, Eagle thought. Of more pressing concern: *Why was Caldwell still alive? Why was he so opposed to Hamilton? Why did he want to address the officers?*

Washington pulled a pocket watch out of his uniform vest. "The meeting will convene in under an hour. I will prepare to leave. Even though it is nearly dark, I will ride out, past the New Building, and they will all be able to see me depart, knowing that what you tell them is not only true, but being acted upon immediately. I will stop at the first inn on the way to Philadelphia and continue on in the morning." Washington looked to the door. "Hercules!" he shouted.

The door swung open. "Sir?" Hercules glanced over at Eagle, then back at Washington.

"Prepare my valise. We depart for Philadelphia within the half hour."

"Yes, sir."

Eagle knew this was not how it needed to play out. Caldwell was a wild card, perhaps an agent of the Shadow? Perhaps merely saved by the Shadow, the musket ball that should have killed him, instead just taking an arm? What would happen if Washington were out of the Cantonment and Caldwell had free rein to say whatever he wished to a cauldron of unhappy officers? The wheels of history were sliding off the tracks.

Washington stood. "Keep things in check until I return, James."

Caldwell got up. "Yes, sir."

Washington strode around the desk and out of the room. Caldwell stood up and gave a slight bow as the General passed him. Eagle was trying to determine his best course of action; but Caldwell didn't leave. He stopped at the door, then swung it shut and turned back to the room.

Eagle was gathering the various glasses, while trying to figure out how to get to Washington and change the course of action. He was surprised when Caldwell pushed by him to Washington's desk and began rifling through the stack of correspondence.

"Sir!"

Caldwell was surprised. He glared at Eagle. "What is it?"

"That's the Generals' private—"

"Shut up," Caldwell said. With only one hand, he had to shove the papers along the top of the desk, scanning the parchments.

Given that Caldwell shouldn't even be here, Eagle wasn't about to walk away. He could hear Nada's advice when in an uncertain situation: look for the wild card. The one that doesn't belong.

Eagle looked down as Caldwell paused at a certain document. A letter. Signed by Alexander Hamilton.

Eagle reached out. "Sir-"

Caldwell drew a flintlock pistol from inside his frock coat, pulling back the hammer and aiming it at Eagle. "How dare you talk to me like that."

Caldwell stepped back from the desk, keeping the pistol trained on Eagle who was also backing up, around the desk, getting some space between them.

"Open the door," Caldwell ordered. "You say nothing, nigra, you get to live."

The muzzle of the flintlock was huge, fitting a round bigger than .50 caliber: a huge round ball of lead. Mass times velocity. At this range, Caldwell couldn't miss. Eagle moved sideways, reaching out, grasping the latch and swinging the door open.

"Hercules. Get in here!" Caldwell yelled.

The chef appeared in less than 10 seconds, taking in tableau. "Sir. No need for that. Samuel, here, he got hurt in the head. He's never been right since."

"He questioned me," Caldwell said.

"He was going through—" Eagle began, but then he saw Caldwell's finger twitch.

108

It happened in slow motion, as events like that happened when a surge of adrenaline exploded into a person's system. The finger twitching, pulling back. The click of the release. The hammer rotating forward toward the priming pan.

Eagle was moving, throwing himself to the side, toward Hercules.

Out of the corner of his eye he saw the flash as the flint on the hammer hit the steel of the frizzen, then the spark struck the powder in the pan.

The roar of the pistol reverberated in the office.

The heavy lead ball hit Eagle, slamming him against the log wall.

Ravenna, Capitol of the Remains of the Western Roman Empire, 493 A.D.

ROLAND HAD THE LARGE MUG TILTED, the foul concoction inside passing for ale or beer or whatever, but he was peering around the edge at Eric. Who had his own mug to his lips, watching Roland.

Eric gulped, and continued gulping. So Roland did the same. About halfway through, Roland realized this was a classic laying the schlong on the table, mine is bigger than yours, manly man sort of thing. At least that was how Neeley would describe it and dismiss it.

But manly man things were important between men. So Roland matched Eric swallow for swallow.

They went on until both mugs were empty. Eric slammed his down on the table, and Roland followed a second later.

"Ah!" Eric exclaimed, wiping a dirty sleeve across his mouth.

Roland didn't both cleaning up. The download was trying to let him know that drinking anything fermented was actually healthier in this age than drinking the water because—Roland cut that irritating information off.

The tavern resembled bars Roland had been in before: a hole in the wall, dark, dingy, filled with the type of people who'd be drinking in the middle of the day, and made their livings in ways that allowed them to drink in the middle of the day and not be killing themselves trying to plow rocks into crops.

They preferred to kill others.

At least no one would be pulling a Mac-10 and spraying the room; like a bar Roland had been in once before in some crap-hole part of the world. But there were enough swords, spears, axes, and hidden daggers to make it dangerous enough.

"They attacked you first, I assume," Eric said.

"Who?"

"The Goths," Eric said patiently. "Who you killed."

Roland had no idea. "Yes."

"They must have been waiting," Eric said. "An ambush."

"How would they know where to wait?" Roland asked. "And when?"

Eric shrugged. "As you said. That's above my pay. From what I understand, the Shadow is resourceful."

Roland considered it. Dane had mentioned that the Shadow made this bubble in time. So that meant any agent of the Shadow would have a good idea of when. And where? Perhaps they hadn't been waiting for him, but for Odoacer? And Roland had just been in the way? But then it would have been just the four against the Twelve Protectors, and the four Infantrymen. Not a smart ambush.

"How did *you* know who I was?" Roland asked the obvious.

Eric shrugged. "Just felt it. Moment I saw you. Just knew it. You're not of this time."

"Doesn't that mean everyone else can feel it too?"

"Everyone else can't conceive of it," Eric said. "When you can't conceive of something, you're blind to it. And, you have to remember, I was recruited to be a member of the Time Patrol."

Roland tried to process that but couldn't. "How come I don't feel that way about you?"

"Because this is *my* time. I belong here. I'm like everyone else around you." Eric pointed a finger, the nail black and half smashed off, at his own head. "I just know some things others don't."

"How did you get recruited?" Roland asked.

Eric smiled. "You have your time and your secrets. I have mine."

Roland didn't buy that answer and Eric must have sensed it.

"Listen, my friend. I know you cannot tell me of the future. You are from a different part of the Time Patrol. One that moves back and forth in time. Me? I'm stuck here. In this time. I was born here. Will die here. I'll never travel like that. I have no idea how you do it. I don't even really know *why* you do it, other than I was told it is for the safety of all of us through the ages. I know nothing of the time in which you live. How different it is. Whether the ale is better than this swill." He indicated the mug. "And you don't know much about me and my part of it. And that's all for the best. We could only tell what we know if we're captured."

That made sense to Roland. The standard of covert ops. *The need to know*. Roland already knew the joke would Mac crack reference that.

"What now?" Roland asked.

"Whatever is to happen at the banquet shortly," Eric said, "we have to assume that the Shadow wants the opposite to happen."

Nada had also had a Yada about assuming, Roland remembered. One that wasn't very original to him.

Eric shifted in irritation or perhaps from fleas and lice. "If you would tell me what is to occur, we can make plans."

"One of them kills the other," Roland said.

"Which one?"

"Which one kills? Or which one gets killed?"

Eric stared at him, his good humor fading momentarily. "Are you that dense?"

Roland now understood the cheap thrill Mac got from jerking someone's chain. "One of the kings kills the other."

"Everyone in your time as funny as you?" Eric gestured. A few seconds later a woman who appeared to be in her sixties appeared with a large pot. She poured, none too carefully, filling both mugs. Giving the era, Roland figured she was probably in her late twenties. Her clothes were an amalgamation of rags sewn together. The skin on her hands cracked and dry. Her shoulders slumped, indicating her life was already defeated and she was only living because humans almost always fought to live, no matter the circumstances.

Eric picked up his mug and began to down it, but Roland didn't follow suit. He was watching three men entering the tavern. They were much too curious about checking out who was inside than looking for a place to sit.

Halfway through, Eric realized Roland wasn't drinking. That didn't stop him from finishing the mug and slapping it back down on the table. "Too much for you? Head spinning? Used to finer drink? I imagine it is indeed much better in your time."

"There are three men near the door," Roland said.

Eric wasn't an amateur. He didn't turn to look. "Armored?"

"Just leather jerkin. No insignia. They do have swords."

"Everyone has swords in here."

The bar 'maid' went to the newcomers and blocked their view of Roland and Eric. One of the men shoved her out of the way.

Roland sighed. "They're not here to drink."

"There's a back door," Eric said, glancing over Roland's right shoulder. "Your choice."

"If they're here for us then it's better to deal with it when we can see them rather than an ambush."

Erich laughed. "'Us'? So we're a team now? You trust me?"

Before Roland could answer, the three were approaching, amateurs, bunched too closely. Eric picked the pending attack up from Roland's eye movement. He threw his chair back, coming to his feet as he drew his sword. Roland slid the *spatha* out of its scabbard and shoved the trestle table out of the way.

By the time he did that, Eric had already spitted one of the three through the heart with the point of his sword. But the man went down awkwardly, turning, twisting the sword in Eric's hand. He didn't let go soon enough and was pulled off balance. Roland was a second late trying to block the center man's slash at Eric. The edge of the blade hit Eric's armor on the shoulder, skidded and sliced into the neck.

The swordsman didn't have a chance to savor his success. Roland swung his sword so hard it took off his head and had enough momentum to sink into the shoulder of the surviving attacker. Roland jerked the sword out and stepped back, reassessing the situation.

The first two attackers were dead. Eric was sitting with his back against a bench, hand trying to stem to the flow of blood from the cut on his neck. The last attacker was on the dirt floor, moaning in pain, holding his shoulder. Roland knelt next to Eric and checked the wound.

Eric nodded ever so slightly toward the man he'd killed. "He died funny."

Roland knew exactly what Eric meant. "He did." The man should have gone down the exact opposite of the way he had. Dead meant dead, and a dead person usually dropped straight down like a stone, but that man had died, and fallen, as Eric said, funny.

It happened at times. The vagaries of the variables in combat.

Roland grabbed a dirty rag off a nearby table and pressed it against the wound. Eric looked at his hand, at the blood.

"Too deep," Eric said. "Black blood."

Roland wished he had a medkit with a Quickclot; he wished Doc were here; he wished he didn't have to see another warrior he'd fought beside die, even if they'd only just met.

"You are not very good," Eric said.

"I moved as fast as I—"

"No," Eric said. "Not that. You're a good fighter."

"What am I not good at?" Roland asked, trying to keep Eric engaged.

"Your face. As soon as you saw the wound, before I even saw the black blood, I knew I was a dead man. You didn't hide it in your face."

"My—" he almost said girlfriend, which seemed inappropriate somehow, here, and now—" my friend says that of me. She says she can read me quite easily."

Eric smiled, revealing blood on his teeth. "If she is still your friend, as you call her, then she must like that about you. A wench to hold on to."

The rag was soaked through with dark blood. In his peripheral vision, and by the growing lack of sound, Roland could tell the tavern was almost empty.

"She is a good woman," Roland said. He'd never been good at small talk, but from the first time he'd held a dying man, he'd known one had to keep speaking. A warrior could not go into the darkness with silence from the living next to them.

"I am not your enemy," Eric said. "I am what you thought I was. Your contact. Now you must do what must be done on your own. I know you can do that. Whatever it is."

"I will," Roland promised. "But there is a Shadow agent here."

"How do you know?" Specks of red froth were on Eric's lips.

Roland nodded toward the two dead and one wounded. "Someone sent them. Someone sent the four who attacked me earlier. There was a fifth person there. But she simply disappeared. Must have been a Gate there. She was different than the others."

"Ah." Eric's eyelids were fluttering. "Tell me, fellow warrior. Which king dies tonight?"

"Odoacer."

"I suspected so." Eric managed a slight smile. "If you'd told me, I could have wagered on it and earned some decent coin. I also suspect the ale is better in your time."

And then he died.

Roland lowered Eric to the floor, placed his hand on the man's forehead for a brief moment. "Safe travels."

Roland stood, walked over to the wounded man, grabbed him by the neck and dragged him out the back door of the tavern into a narrow alley reeking of sewage and rotting garbage.

The man was still moaning and whimpering like a hurt dog. Roland patted him down, finding a small pouch of coin.

"How much were we worth?" He glanced in, but had no clue what the roughly minted coins equaled. He imagined it was in his download, and even as he thought it, the data began to flow, but he easily cut that off. He put the pouch into his belt.

"Who sent you?"

The man shook his head, but without much vigor.

Roland pushed his blood-covered hand into the man's shoulder wound as he shoved the bloody rag into the mouth to muffle the scream. "Who sent you? Do not make a noise other than to answer my question. Do you understand?"

The man nodded.

Roland pulled the rag out.

"I don't know."

Roland moved toward the wound, but the man was crying. "No! He had coin. Paid us well."

"Dark hair? Smoothly cut beard? Sideburns to here?" Roland pointed at his own face. "Dressed in a brown tunic and black trousers?"

The man nodded vigorously. "Yes. Do you know him?"

"No."

"Was a woman with him?"

"Yes."

Roland could hear someone shouting orders from inside the tavern. The clatter of armor and weapons. The rear door opened, a soldier stuck his head out, saw Roland, and popped his head back in.

"Killing for money." Roland shook his head as he slid his dagger underneath man's rib cage, into his heart, twisted. He was dead before Roland pulled the blade out.

Roland stood up as three soldiers burst out of the door, weapons at the ready. A fourth, the red crest on his helmet similar to Roland's followed them, his weapon undrawn. He glanced from the body to Roland who was wiping the blade clean.

"Did he kill the Protector inside?" the man asked.

Roland nodded.

"King Odoacer sent us for the two of you. Be at *Ad Laurentum* Palace. An hour before sunset. He meets Theoderic.

The Missions Phase III

Rome, Roman Empire, 44 B.C.

DEPARTING CAESAR'S HOME VIA THE REAR entrance, Spurinna was met by a half dozen men and women, all slaves, who approached one by one and whispered in her ear before scurrying away.

"No one has seen Caesar," Spurinna summarized to Moms when the last one was gone. "It is possible he has gone to Cleopatra. He does on occasion."

"How far is it to the villa?"

"Not far from here," Spurinna said. "I know the quick way. It is just outside the walls. Caesar has her as close as he can. A foreign leader is not allowed inside the walls of Rome without the Senate's approval and Cleopatra—" she left the rest unsaid. "Come." Spurinna strode off at a surprising pace, the urgency of the task pushing the pain back.

"Does he disappear often?" Moms asked.

"On occasion."

"For any reason besides seeing Cleopatra?"

Spurinna glanced at Moms as they negotiated back alleys of Rome. "There are secrets that are not secrets. There are secrets that can be uncovered with some digging. And then there are fatal secrets. The ones if a person, regardless of station, is found in possession of, death is immediate. Caesar's disappearances are one of those."

"And, of course, you are in possession of that secret."

They reached a narrow gate in the wall surrounding Rome.

"I am. And if I tell you, then you will have that burden."

"I am not here long," Moms said.

"I suspected you won't be. When Caesar disappears, he goes to see a healer."

A rush from the download gave Moms the information. Modern scholars still couldn't agree on what had been wrong with Caesar, but all agreed he'd been an ill man later in life. Most accepted the diagnosis of Caesar's contemporaries who wrote that he had epilepsy.

"People know of Caesar's seizures," Moms said.

"They do. Epilepsy. And that works to Caesar's advantage." They were approaching a spacious villa on a small hill.

"I don't understand," Moms said.

"Epilepsy is viewed as being visited by spirits. A holy affliction." Spurinna nodded toward a path that went to the left of the house. "This way. Always the slave's entrance for me. Never the front." She paused before the entrance. "It is not epilepsy. The best healer's know the sure signs and he has seen the best healer's and they also bear this fatal secret."

"What is it?" Moms asked, but the download already provided an answer.

"Caesar's father died without any warning signs while putting on his sandals," Spurinna said. "It is in Caesar's bloodline that he has the sickness of the head-heart."

"Strokes," Moms said. "A series of mini-strokes."

"If that is what you call it," Spurinna said. An old slave-woman appeared and gestured for them to follow. "If the word was in the street that Caesar could die at any moment, that would change things. Lead to uncertainty. Upheaval."

"More than you already have with an assassination plot in place?" Moms asked, but didn't expect an answer.

That Egyptian slut was sitting in a high-backed chair set on a wood dais built six inches above the marble floor, a Nubian guard on either side. The guards were splendid looking warriors, each over six feet, well-muscled. But Moms knew the moment she saw them that they were not mere ornamentation. They held spears in one hand, the other hand gripping the top of tall shields resting on the floor and angled forward. Each had a sword on one hip, a dagger on the other. The way the two glanced at Spurinna, dismissed her as a threat, then checked Moms, and kept their gaze on her, indicated they were experienced warriors.

Cleopatra had a small table on the right arm of the chair. Next to it was a holder, much like a quiver, containing scrolls instead of arrows. There was a similar one on the other side. Both had numerous documents poking up.

Cleopatra was aware of their entry, but held a hand up, indicating they wait, as she scanned a document. She snapped her fingers and a nearby slave scurried forward with a quill, tip freshly dipped in ink. Cleopatra scrawled, then handed the parchment and quill back to the slave. Who blew on the fresh ink, drying it, then rolled it shut. Produced a seal and hot wax from another table and affixed a seal, once more blowing it cool.

She handed it back to Cleopatra who inspected the seal, then slid it in the quiver on the left side of the throne. Cleopatra reached down for another document from the right when Spurinna cleared her throat loudly. "Your Majesty—"

Cleopatra shifted her gaze to the old woman. "Is this about Caesar once more? Is it not the Ides already?"

"Your Majesty," Spurinna began again, but Cleopatra pointed a single finger at Moms, the simple movement enough to silence the Seer.

Cleopatra was what would be considered in Moms' era, Rubenesque, but in this era was considered perfectly proportioned. Her hands were unique. Long, with very slender fingers. They commanded, whether in signing or signaling. "I have not seen you before."

It wasn't a question so Moms said nothing.

Cleopatra pulled the hand back and the finger tapped on her lower lip. "Do you bring me word of Caesar?"

"No, Majesty," Spurinna said. "I was wondering if you had a chance to speak with him after our last conversation and—"

"To warn him, you mean."

"Yes, your Majesty."

"One does not warn Caesar. That is why he is Caesar. He is Dictator in Perpetuity; isn't that what your Senate proclaimed him? In fact, the Senate also proclaimed that, in case of death, he would be a God of Rome." A slight smile curled Cleopatra's painted lips.

The room surrounding her chair, more a throne, was the opposite of Calpurnia's atrium. The walls were hung with tapestries depicting Egyptian scenes: battles, buildings, Pharaohs, Gods. Incense floated up from several pots, tinting the air with something pleasant. Other than Spurinna there was not a Roman in sight.

Cleopatra had made the summer villa her court, an enclave of Egyptian royalty next to the Roman capitol.

"That is true, your Majesty," Spurinna said. "I was just—"

"Seeing if I did your bidding?" Cleopatra leaned forward on the chair. "Does a Queen do the bidding of others?" She didn't wait for an answer, as she glanced left and right, at her two guards, assessing. "You." She pointed at Moms. "You bother my men. Why is that Kashta?"

The Nubian on the right answered. "She is not a priestess, Majesty. She is a killer."

"An Amazon perhaps?" Cleopatra said. "We have legends of those in my country. Why then, Seer Spurinna, do you bring a warrior into my court, cloaked as a priestess? Do you have designs on my life?"

"Of course not, your Majesty. We are merely—"

"Checking on Caesar. What he knows. What he doesn't know. Why not ask him?"

"We can not find him, your Majesty," Spurinna said.

"Does it speak?" Cleopatra had extended an elegant finger toward Moms.

"I speak, your Majesty. I have nothing to say."

That same half-smile, almost seductive. "A rarity in a woman."

Moms could see why people still spoke of this Queen millennia after her death. Edith Frobish dismissed her too easily. Cleopatra's power was her own. Exercised through men only when it fit her desires. Even to the end, fourteen years from now, if history held true, surrounded in her palace by Augustus and his forces in Alexandria, she fooled Antony by having word sent to him that she'd killed herself. Leading to him falling on his sword. A ploy so she could present the body to Augustus and try her wiles on him in order to escape his net.

It hadn't worked. Wouldn't work, Moms knew.

"You smile," Cleopatra said, catching Moms off-guard. "A pleasant thought, perhaps?"

"Not particularly, your Majesty."

Cleopatra stared at her for several seconds. "You disturb me."

Kashta took half a step forward, lifting the shield off the floor, but Cleopatra's slight hand gesture stopped him.

"You are more than a warrior," Cleopatra said. She stood up and walked forward, the two Nubians flanking her, spears and shields at the ready. She stopped in front of Moms. An odor masked the incense. Moms nostrils flared, taking it in. It stirred her, but before she could try to decipher what it was, Cleopatra put her hands on either side of Moms' head, incredibly long fingers cradling it.

The tableau was frozen for several moments.

"We share something," Cleopatra whispered, her voice seductive.

Moms met Cleopatra's gaze.

"Tell me," Cleopatra said. "What is my future?"

"I am not a Seer," Moms said.

Cleopatra pulled her hands back. "You want an answer from me about Caesar. You must tell *me* something I don't know."

Moms considered that. "I see three obelisks, Queen. Monuments to you. They will survive through the ages. Each will end up in the center of the three most glorious cities in the world. They will be called Cleopatra's Needles."

The download was an irritating buzz, Edith's influence trying to poke through to point out that none of the three obelisks had anything to actually do with Cleopatra. In fact, at this moment, all three existed, were already over a millennia old, and still in Egypt.

Now wasn't the time to mention that, Moms decided.

Cleopatra abruptly turned and went back to her throne. "That is not my future. That is the future of three pieces of rock. Still, it is a form of immortality. Don't we all desire that? To survive in one form or another past life itself?"

She pointed at Spurinna. "I did not speak to Caesar as you requested. One does not speak like that to Caesar. And," a coy smile, "Caesar has his own reasons for what he does. It is still the Ides. Perhaps you can find him before your prophecy comes true? If it comes true."

Cleopatra flicked her hand. "Go." She reached down and retrieved a scroll from the right quiver.

As Moms and Spurinna reached the threshold, Cleopatra's voice carried after them. "I am not the one you should have come to. It is Marc Antony who holds sway this day. Caesar's fate is in his hands."

Petrograd, Russia, 1917.

THE HEAT FROM THE FURNACE blasted Doc. He used a shovel to flip open the door. Doc reached inside his coat and pulled out Anastasia's diary.

As he moved to toss it in the blaze, Doc felt cold steel across his throat.

"I am here in peace," he said, trying to turn his head, but a hand gripped his hair, knocking his hat off.

"There is no peace in Russia any more," the man holding the saber said.

"I have—" Doc began, but the man cut him off.

"Why do you have the Little One's book?" Before Doc could answer, a second question: "Why were you in the Tsarina's bedchamber? The Duchess's rooms?"

"I have the Tsarina's blessing," Doc said.

"Step back." The man punctuated his order with pressure from the blade. They moved several steps away from the furnace.

"Drop the book."

Doc let it drop to the floor.

"I saw you leave the Tsarina's bedchamber. How does she fare?"

"It would be easier to tell you without the sword at my throat," Doc said.

The blade was withdrawn, his head was released and Doc finally got to see a Cossack. He was dressed in black and had the special insignia of the Tsarina's personal guard emblazoned on his chest. He had a cavalry saber in his hand, pointed in Doc's direction. He was covered in coal dust, which explained both the blaze in the furnace and the warmth in the Tsarina's private wing of the palace.

"Where are the rest of the guards?" Doc picked up his hat.

The Cossack spit in disgust. "Like rats. They've run. Abandoned their duty. We are now prisoners. But the Bolsheviks do not know I am here. Working the cellar. Keeping the family warm. I walk the servants' secret passages. What was your business with the Tsarina?" He still had the saber half at the ready. Apparently he didn't consider Doc much of a threat, which echoed Doc's own thoughts about himself.

"May I?" Doc asked, indicating a pocket.

"Yes."

Doc pulled out the icon and showed it.

The Cossack flicked the point of the saber up, the tip on Doc's jugular. "Where did you get that? How did you know that whore-mongerer? That charlatan?"

Good question, Doc thought. Good old Edith never missed a beat, except this answer wasn't going to fly with a Cossack: she'd discovered it in a secret FBS vault in Lubyanka. The infamous headquarters for the KGB for so many decades during the Cold War.

"From his body," Doc managed.

The Cossack did not pull the tip of the blade back. "I have heard his body was burned. The ashes spread so that no part of him would ever be found again."

"I have shown this to the Tsarina," Doc said. "She verifies it is what she gave Rasputin. I am in her favor, so remove your weapon from my throat."

"Rasputin was in her favor and they killed him."

"I am not Rasputin," Doc said.

"But you bear his icon and you have been in the Empress's bedchamber."

"The Duchesses were there. The Prince."

"I know." The Cossack lowered the saber once more. He seemed more tired than guarded. "If she had been alone, you'd already be dead. I have secretly watched as much as I can. I saw you come out. I heard their voices, so I know they were there. I cannot watch all. And now—" his voice drifted into silence. He leaned over and picked up Anastasia's' diary. "Did the Tsarina give you permission to go into the Duchesses' room? Take her book?"

"Yes," Doc lied.

"Why?"

"I do not question the commands of her most Excellency," Doc said. "Do you?"

The Cossack frowned. "I follow orders, but now it seems no one else does. I do not understand why she would want the Little One's book burned."

Because no one ever found it, Doc thought. The download had confirmed that of the four girls, only Anastasia's diary had never been uncovered. Which had contributed to the myth that she had escaped her family's fate and was alive. But most importantly, it had to be destroyed because of what it said of Rasputin. "She wants the Little One's secrets to remain her own secrets."

That seemed to make sense to the Cossack. "The Tsarina and Tsar have been burning many papers." He snorted. "They should give them to me. We don't have that much more coal. I could burn the books and papers faster. And with better use." He handed the diary to Doc.

"If I discover you have lied to me," the Cossack said, "I will kill you."

He said it the way Roland, or Neeley or any of the killers Doc served with, would. Matter-of-fact. Just the reality. Nothing personal. The worst kind of way to hear that specific threat because it made it a guarantee.

"Do you have a name?" Doc asked.

"Krylo. And you are?"

"Doc."

"Are you English? You speak with a strange accent."

"American."

"I have never met an American," Krylo said.

"May I finish my task?" Doc asked.

Krylo nodded.

Doc tossed the diary into the flames. He watched the fire consume Anastasia's dreams and her prescience.

"The Tsarina and her children will be fine," Doc lied. "All will turn out well."

Krylo wiped the coal dust off the steel and sheathed his saber. "That is what the others also say."

"The 'others'?"

"The Count and his guards. He says they are here to save her and the children. They have come on orders from her cousin, King George, to take the Tsarina and Duchesses and the little Tsar to her family in England. They arrived an hour ago."

There was no count in the download. No rescue by King George.

It ain't over until it's over, Doc thought. And knew that when he was using Yogi Bera quotes, he was pretty far down in the barrel.

"Take me to this Count."

Palos de la Frontera, Spain, 1493 A.D.

"THAT IS COLUMBUS," Geert said, pointing at the small boat being rowed toward the quay.

Mac and Geert were peering around the corner of a building, near the southern edge of town.

Mac wasn't impressed. The famed explorer was hunched over, a heavy cloak over his shoulders. He had something wrapped in a scarlet cloak in his arms. It was obvious the sudden appearance of the *Pinta*, on schedule according to history, surprising to everyone else here, had finally spurred action.

The sun was setting on the grey day, lanterns being held by some of the crowd along the shoreline, excited about the arrival of the second vessel. The six Cente Suisse were on the quay, waiting. The *Pinta* was only a quarter-mile away and closing in.

"Where has the *Pinta* been?" Geert asked. He was beginning to get twitchy, the Guard's threat resonating his fear. Mac suspected Geert actually *was* a monk, with little military experience despite his bravado earlier about life or death.

Mac wished his headache would go away. A figure pushed his way through the edge of the crowd and it parted, allowing free access. Dressed in a brown robes, the white haired Franciscan even managed to get the Swiss Guard to step aside. He held up a crucifix in his left hand as Columbus' small boat bounced up against the rocks of the quay. The priest's right hand moved in the sign of the cross, blessing the explorer. He had a leather purse at his side, the strap over his shoulder.

Columbus stood, a bit unsteadily, one of the rowers reached out and grabbed his leg to keep him from falling over. Columbus gave a slight bow in the direction of the Franciscan and climbed out of the boat.

A loud splash diverted everyone. The *Pinta* had just dropped anchor.

Such was history, Mac thought. If the *Pinta* had arrived first, perhaps Martin Pinzon would be celebrated at the discoverer of the 'New World'. It was rather amazing that separated by the storm for weeks, both ships had managed to arrive at the same place, on the same day, just hours apart.

The Swiss surrounded Columbus as the crowd surged forward, asking, begging, demanding information about loved ones.

Columbus could care less. Protected by the Swiss, they bulled their way to the main avenue leading to the Friary.

No one followed, their focus on the ships. Boats were being launched from shore, heading to both, rowed by locals.

"Go after him?" Geert asked.

Mac had no clue. The last mission had been easy: either Raleigh's head got chopped off or not. This one? What was the variable? Columbus' report? But the word of the discovery was already out; the two weeks stay in Lisbon had done that. Columbus wasn't that important any more, now that the *Pinta* was here. Pinzon knew how to navigate to the—the download popped up some information about Pinzon causing Mac to re-evaluate.

Mac had started out in the Army as EOD: Explosive Ordnance Disposal. A job in high demand. He'd gone from EOD into Special Forces as an engineer, more commonly referred to as a demo man. He'd been the best but that hadn't been the only thing that had attracted the attention of the Nightstalkers. Yes, he could take apart IED and booby-traps and he could build even better ones, but the key to both emplacing them, or finding them, was understanding the target. It was why he was the best: he wasn't as smart as Eagle, but he was analytical.

Geert was antsy. "Once Columbus is in the Friary, it will be very hard to see him."

"He's already back," Mac said. "He's written his report. We can assume he's already told King John everything he discovered in the New World. Here, now, the Swiss will take the report to Rome where it will be published. That's a done deal. The New World has been discovered."

"Then why are we here?" Geert wanted to know.

Mac was staring at the priest on the quay. "Who is that?"

"Friar de Cisneros," Geert said.

"Why didn't he go back to the Friary with Columbus?"

Geert shrugged. "To bless the rest of the sailors as they come ashore, I suppose."

De Cisneros was looking at the *Pinta*. There was something in the way he stood, his demeanor, which stirred Mac's personal demons.

A piece of the download concerning the significance of this return from the New World finally clicked into place.

"What is it?" Geert asked, sensing the change.

"When you look at Friar de Cisneros," Mac asked, "what do you see?"

Geert was puzzled. "A Franciscan. What do you see?"

"Guilt."

Thermopylae, Greece, 480 B.C.

"IT IS CONSIDERED WISE TO BE leery of strangers bearing gifts," Scout said. "I'd say you top that list of strangers."

Pandora had a wooden box in one hand. The box was square. Roughly fifteen inches to a side. In the other hand she had the Naga. The storm raged offshore, occasionally lighting the field of death, but it was stalled.

"Ah, some say it of me," Pandora said, "but the Trojans truly learned it almost a thousand years ago."

"That was just a wood horse," Scout said. "You unleashed horrible plagues on mankind."

"You're wrong," Pandora said, as she put the box down on the armor covering the chest of an Immortal. "There is a very important distinction to be made. *I* did not open the *pithos*. It was a man who opened it, even though he had been adequately warned. That is where the blame should lie."

"Splitting hairs," Scout said.

"Hah. You want to split hairs, as you say? Then who invented the plagues that were unleashed? Not I. Shouldn't the blame fall there? To the originator of all?"

"God?"

Pandora shrugged. "In this age, they believe in more than one God. Which makes more sense than a single one. Gives people someone to blame regarding various things. Someone to pray to for various things. More complex, yet simpler in a way. Rather than jamming everything into one. That gets confusing, don't you think?"

"You're supposed to be molded by the Gods themselves," Scout said.

"As was Adam. But then Eve came from him; just a rib. In the faith in that book, women aren't even given the honor of being direct from God, but rather are just an offshoot of man."

"Enough theology," Scout said. "You're going to show me what's in the box, otherwise you wouldn't have brought it. So show."

"I told you I would bring a token of good faith," Pandora said. "But not yet. Patience. I told you I would also teach you. You could not see me the last time we met. But I could see you. Do you wonder at that?"

"You own a pair of night vision goggles," Scout said.

"I don't know what that is," Pandora said. "I see with the Sight. You can too. You just haven't been taught how. It comes and goes for you. Much like the lightning. But if you master it, you can see all the time. Feel the disturbances around you."

"Like you?" Scout said.

Scout was startled as Pandora's voice whispered from behind, close to her ear. "The time for humor is long past, my dear."

Scout started to turn, but a hand was on her shoulder.

"You didn't see me move, because there was no lightning," Pandora said. "You didn't hear me move, even though there was no thunder. But I moved. The sight is not the eyes. Hearing true is not the ears." The hand slid up to Scout's neck, shockingly cold, as if no blood ran in Pandora's veins.

Scout tensed, remembering Luke's embrace and how he tried to choke the life out of her. But the cold hand continued up her skin until it rested on the back of her head. She felt Pandora's fingers squeezing.

"Here." Pandora's voice was seductive. Not a mother at all; more intimate than a lover. "Here is where you see. Where you hear. From the inside out. Not from the outside in. You reach out with the Sight. To all around you. You are part of it. Part of the world around you."

Scout tried to hold on to Nada, to one of his Yada's, but this was far beyond what he'd ever faced, even in death.

Pandora's voice continued, enticing, the words no longer coherent, but going into Scout, into the place where Pandora's hand cradled her head. A small, tiny part of her that was still Scout realized that Pandora was no longer speaking aloud. That the words, more than words, were flowing into her from the hand, from the essence of Pandora.

Scout's knees grew weak and buckled. Only her grip on the Naga staff kept her from collapsing.

Pandora abruptly withdrew her hand and Scout gasped at the disconnect. She felt a hole inside herself, one she hadn't even known was there.

Pandora was once more in front of her, standing behind the box. "Enough for now. Are you beginning to understand?"

Scout took several deep breaths. "I don't—" she paused. "Someone is coming."

"Good," Pandora hissed. "Very good. You see him before he can see you. Very good. Who is it?"

Scout closed her eyes, confused. "A sword? A dagger?"

"Good. He is called Xerxes Dagger," Pandora said to Scout. "A dangerous man. An assassin."

Lightning flashed, illuminating a slender man, weaving over the bodies, feet lightly touching down, approaching at a run. He halted ten feet short of the two of them.

"Curious," he said. Not an inch of skin was revealed, his body, his head, wrapped in black cloth. He wore no armor. Just a sword on a belt on the right side and a long knife on his left. His eyes peered through a narrow slit in the cloth. "The King wonders where you have gone," he said to Pandora, but he was looking at Scout.

"I gather information," Pandora said.

"And in the box?" Xerxes Dagger asked. He was known by no name and no other title in the court. When Xerxes gave him an order, it was considered completed as soon as it was uttered. And the orders always involved killing someone.

"A present for my friend," Pandora said.

"And your friend? Who is she?"

Scout didn't like the way he was looking at her. She realized she wasn't a person to Xerxes Dagger. There were no other people to someone like him. Everyone and everything was just part of a game in his mind, existing only for his amusement. His reality was himself.

Pandora ignored him. "Are you my friend?" she asked Scout.

Scout fingered the haft of her Naga. She wished Nada were here. Or Roland. Or Moms.

"Yes," Scout said.

Xerxes Dagger asked once more: "And in the box?"

"You know what's in the box," Pandora said. "Else you would not be here."

Xerxes Dagger shifted his gaze from Scout to Pandora. "You have been troublesome ever since you arrived in Court. You've made a few good guesses. But your map of the pass was wrong. And I wonder about what you did in that town we sacked in Macedonia. The King fears intrigue. He has men searching for the baby you saved."

Scout turned from him to Pandora. "What baby?"

"Hush," Pandora said. "They will never find him," she said to Xerxes Dagger.

"When this battle is over and the King releases my leash, I will find the baby. Your efforts will have been in vain. No one escapes me."

Pandora sighed. Despite the dark, Scout could clearly see her now. She was older than she'd looked in the lightning glimpses. Their eyes locked. A hint of a smile on Pandora's cold face.

Scout spun to the right, bringing the Naga up and level, blade swinging toward the Dagger.

Except he wasn't there. Moving faster than her blade, he ducked low, drew his dagger and lunged, the blade pointed straight at her heart. Scout fought to counter-act her own momentum, knowing she was going to be too slow, that she was going to die, just as she'd killed those two—

Pandora's Naga sliced down through the Dagger's arm.

The blade, and severed hand, dropped, but the Dagger wasn't stopped so easily. He twisted, falling to his side, rolling, pulling his sword out with his surviving hand.

And then both Naga's pinned him to the ground. Blood frothed on his lips as he struggled.

"Hold him," Pandora said, withdrawing her Naga.

Scout leaned on the haft of her Naga, the blade through the Dagger, through the corpse underneath him and into the ground. He reached up with both arms, forgetting he was missing a hand. His one hand grabbed the shaft of Scout's Naga and he pulled himself up several inches. If he'd have had the other hand, Scout believed he would have come all the way up and strangled her.

Pandora knelt next to him, a finger on his chest, halting his upward progress. "You are not human. You are an animal. Your kind is the scourge of worlds."

Xerxes Dagger tried to spit blood at her, working his jaws, his mouth, but he died before he could finish the task. His body slid back to the ground.

Pandora stood.

Scout did the same. "You used me to distract him."

"Yes. We have skills, you and I, but he had skills too. Animals like him? One on one? Direct combat? I'm not sure I could have taken him. The Sight doesn't work on his kind."

"And what kind is he?" Scout asked.

"There are those," Pandora said, "who have a different kind of sight. Who are not of any world or time."

Scout looked down at the body. "Is he from the Shadow? I've fought those before."

"Those were amateurs," Pandora said.

Scout's head snapped up. "How do you know that?"

Pandora held up the hand in which she'd cradled Scout's head. "I saw things in you. I saw you kill in that other time. But you almost failed. You let them get close."

"Not big on compliments are you?" Scout asked. "Reminds me of my mother."

"Ah, poor dear." Pandora shook her head. "You know nothing of your real mother."

Great, Scout thought. This was getting worse than *Luke, I am your father*.

"That's good news," Scout said. "Always hoped I was adopted. Since you want to teach me, tell me of the Shadow."

"You're not ready."

"You don't know what the Shadow is." And Scout sensed the flash of anger from Pandora before she could suppress it.

But Pandora was already moving on. She leaned over and opened the lid of her box. Then reached in and lifted a head by the hair. A savage red line indicated where it had been severed from the body. A stump of white protruded from the bottom; the spine.

It was not as shocking as it might be in another scenario, given they were standing on a field of dead.

"Anyone I should know?" Scout asked.

"Good question," Pandora said. "I don't know what you know. Do you know who is to betray the Spartans later this morning? Lead the Persians around them on a goat trail in the mountains?"

Scout knew, but if she revealed she knew, then . . .

"I assume it's the head you're holding," Scout said. "How did *you* know?"

Pandora dropped the head into the box and kicked shut the lid. "He went to Xerxes last evening. Ephialtes. A local. Wanted a reward. Told mighty Xerxes that he knew a path. A narrow path. Through the mountains and then back to the coast. Behind the Spartans."

That was the name in the download. Ephialtes, a goat herder, who went to the Persians with word of the trail. Like Quisling, Benedict Arnold, and others, his name would become synonymous with traitor in Greece for future generations.

Apparently not any more.

Scout felt a tremor and for a moment thought earthquake, but realized it was inside her. A ripple. Had she already failed? History had already changed in this detail, inside this bubble, via this severed head in the box.

"The Persians will win regardless," Pandora said, as if sensing her thoughts. "Even without—" she tapped the box with the tip of her bloody Naga. "It's simply a matter of time."

"But time is short," Scout said.

Pandora smiled as lightning flickered. "Perhaps it's already too late for you? I can tell you are upset by this." Once more she indicated the box. "Which means you thought Ephialtes *would* lead the Persians to envelope the Spartans. That it's the way history records events in *your* timeline."

"What do you mean?" Scout asked. "You're not of this timeline?"

"I told you," Pandora said. "I am timeless. You could be too."

I'm outta here soon, Scout hoped. She had to hold on to that.

"The Persians will win regardless," Pandora repeated. "The battle. But the war? No. They will lose. Leonidas and his men have held long enough. For both the Greeks and for you. And for me."

"How is that?" Scout asked.

"I told you," Pandora said. "I've already accomplished my mission here and now."

"The baby."

"Yes."

"Who is it?"

"That's not important," Pandora said. "It's who comes forth from the baby's lineage in one-hundred-and-twenty-four years according to the Prophecy."

Scout had never particularly cared for math, and given they were B.C., not A.D., Scout took a moment to figure it:. "356 B.C.," Scout said. "Alexander the Great was born that year."

"And who is that?" Pandora asked. "It sounds as if the Prophecy in this regard was quite on target. The Great? What will he do that is so great? Will he stop men like that?" She indicated the Dagger's body. "Will he stop war? Will he put mankind on a better path?"

Not exactly, Scout thought, shutting down the spigot on Alexander's various conquests. All of which ended up accomplishing what exactly in the long run, except etching his place in the history books? His empire did not last past his death.

"And what of your mission here and now?" Pandora pressed. "What will it accomplish?"

"I don't know," Scout answered honestly.

Pandora pointed at her box. "Perhaps I've done it for you?" She looked to the left. "Dawn beckons. Despite this," once more she indicated the box, "your Spartans die today. But then the Persians lose anyway. How futile. Take your King back to his home. Let him, at least, live."

Pandora faded back into the darkness, leaving Scout alone in the field of the dead. She went back, climbing the wall, not bothering to sneak in. As she clambered down, Leonidas was waiting for her, his sword drawn.

Scout didn't react as Leonidas pressed the edge of his sword against her neck.

"Speak the truth."

"I don't know the truth," Scout said.

The blade pressed deeper into her skin. "What happened?"

"I met Pandora," Scout said. She decided to skip to the headline, or at least what Leonidas would consider the headline. "We killed Xerxes' Dagger. He came after us. He wanted to kill us."

"He and I have that in common," Leonidas said, but the pressure from the blade lessened. "Xerxes Dagger? I've heard that name. An assassin. Drawn from the ranks of the Immortals. It's said he had to kill one hundred other Immortals in single combat before he could be bestowed the honor."

Scout wasn't sure about the whole honor thing. She wasn't sure of much at all.

"You killed him?" Leonidas asked.

"We killed him together."

Leonidas pulled the blade back. "Why?"

Scout rubbed her neck. "He was going to kill us; well, me at least. Isn't that what people called Dagger do?"

Leonidas chuckled. "That is so. And I am impressed that two women could take out such an opponent."

"Oh, thanks." But then she looked to the east and saw the growing hint of red over the water.

Leonidas' humor vanished also. "It will soon be time." He turned from her and gazed over his men. Those who weren't on guard duty were gearing up, although few had actually slept. "Did Pandora go back to Xerxes?"

"I don't know."

"How could she after killing Xerxes Dagger?" Leonidas said, but his mind was already on what was to come. He shouted commands to his surviving officers.

"It is best if you leave," Leonidas said.

"Maybe we should both leave."

"Never."

"Take your men," Scout said. "Lead them away from here. The Persians will be defeated eventually."

"Is that another prophecy?" But Leonidas was already looking to where his Spartans were forming.

Scout wasn't sure he heard her reply, before he headed off to command the final defense. "No. It's a promise."

Newburgh, New York, 1783 A.D.

EAGLE HEARD VOICES RAISED IN ANGER. His ears were ringing, his head throbbing.

Déjà vu all over again. Much like after the IED; but at least he wasn't on fire.

He opened his eyes. He was on his back. A rough plank ceiling above. It was dusk outside the dirty window, indicating he'd been out for a little while. He turned his head and heard the shattered bones grind in his shoulder as the pain stunned him with its intensity. He groaned and Hercules' face appeared over his.

"Hush! Keep your voice down. Master ain't happy."

Eagle smelled something and it took a few moments to recognize it: axle grease. Eagle looked at his left shoulder: wrapped in not-so-clean linen.

"Did you get the bullet out?" Eagle asked.

"Went through," Hercules said. "Hole on both sides."

A door slammed open and Washington came into the room, Caldwell right behind him. "We don't have time for this, General. I told you. The nigra tried to attack me. Your own man said he isn't in the head. He needs to be put down like a mad dog. And you need to be on to Philadelphia."

Washington folded his arms, staring down at Eagle. "He's never given trouble before."

Being talked about like he was a pet that had strayed pained Eagle as much as the shoulder. Hercules was glaring at him, eyes imploring him not to say a word.

"He was going through your correspondence, General, sir," Eagle said.

Hercules grimaced.

"He's a liar," Caldwell snapped. "He attacked me."

"Did you attack him?" Washington asked Eagle.

A red vein bulged on Caldwell's forehead.

"No, General, sir," Eagle replied. "Simply told him he should not be going through your private papers."

"You're questioning my word by asking a nigra?" Caldwell had pushed up next to Washington. The General shifted away from the intrusion ever so slightly.

Eagle noted the lack of military formality in the words and he was sure Washington noted it also. In the short time he'd been around the General, Eagle appreciated he was a man who observed everything.

"I'm trying to ascertain what caused my property to be damaged," Washington said. "And how damaged it is, not just from your shot, but in the head. I will allow that he was acting strange in the barn earlier." He shifted his direction of questioning. "Hercules. Where was Samuel when you entered my office? Was he attacking Colonel Caldwell?"

Hercules stood straight and didn't answer right away.

Washington's right eyebrow arched ever so slightly. "Hercules?"

"Didn't look like it, Master. Looked like he was trying to get away. The Colonel was on the other side of the deck and Samuel was near the door and—"

"*My* side of the desk?" Washington asked.

"Yes, sir. But I don' know what happened before then, Master," Hercules added.

The General turned toward Caldwell. "An explanation, sir."

"I don't have to explain myself against the words of nigra, sir. This is out of line."

"A simple question," Washington said. "Were you on my side of the desk?"

"Yes, but I was at the window, looking out at the troops on the drill field. Concerned about your comment reference their demeanor. Then your boy here attacked me."

"Why?"

Caldwell was outraged. "How would I know, General? Even you said he isn't right in the head."

"You might well be right," Washington said.

Eagle opened his mouth to say something and was surprised to see the slightest shake of Washington's head.

"I will deal with the matter," Washington said in a cold, even voice. "I am distressed that you were put in such a position, Colonel. Please wait for me in my office, if you would." It was not phrased as a request.

"I should be addressing the officers," Caldwell said. "They've been gathered for a bit and you know how a crowd grows restless."

"We'll get to that matter," Washington said. "I need to instruct Hercules on what is to be done with Samuel."

"Should be hanged for attacking a white man," Caldwell said.

"It's a consideration," Washington said.

Eagle noted that Washington's tone was consistent, level, neither angry nor threatening. Not without affect, but affable. As if everything were no large trouble and could be dealt with. Eagle had experienced the same a few times before in his military career. Moms had it; Nada also.

A smart person, though, would hear the undertone of a command.

Several seconds of silence ticked off before Caldwell finally accepted the inevitable and left the room.

"How is the wound?" Washington asked Hercules.

"Shoulder done, Master. He won't be working the fields no more."

"You stand by your words, Hercules?"

The General's chef licked his lips, glanced at Eagle, then back at his master. "No, sir. I was wrong, sir. Never meant to speak against the Colonel. Sam, he was running. He might have gone after the Colonel for some crazy reason. Got the gun pulled on him and thought better of it."

Eagle half-lifted up, the pain in his shoulder sharp rocks of pain grinding. "Sir! My shirt pocket."

Eagle held the position despite the searing pain.

Washington reached down and slid two fingers into the pocket. He pulled out a piece of purple cloth with the word MERIT sewn on it, edged with lace. His eyes widened. Then he reached inside his blue frock coat.

"Hercules," Washington said without taking his eyes off Eagle. "Leave me with Samuel for a moment. Be right outside."

Hercules was trapped by his status, unable to protest. He slipped out the door.

"What is this?" Washington demanded, holding up the cloth.

Eagle didn't say anything, slumping back onto the cot.

Washington pulled his hand out from inside the coat. An exact replica of the badge was in his hand. He compared the two. "They are the same. Exactly. Down to the stitching. That is not possible."

This was a paradox. Eagle was suddenly aware of that. Because it was the same object. At the same time. In the same room.

What would Doc make of this? Roland? Eagle settled on somewhere in between; of interest, but not of importance at the moment.

"How did you get this?" Washington held up the one he'd taken from Eagle.

"A friend gave it to me, sir."

"This makes no sense," Washington said. "None at all. You have this, which you cannot. There was only the one made at my personal request."

"Sir, the only issue right now is the officer assembly. You must give the speech."

Washington would not have been a successful combat commander if he couldn't regroup and gather himself together in a chaotic situation.

"A slave telling me what to do," Washington said. "A slave trying to run off with some of my correspondence. The day is full of marvels." He clenched the Badge of Merits in his fists. "What was Colonel Caldwell looking for?"

"The letter from Mister Hamilton, sir." Eagle had to swallow to get enough moisture to talk. "Sir. He shouldn't be here. Colonel Caldwell."

Washington was still as a statue. "What do you mean Colonel Caldwell shouldn't be here?"

"Sir. He should have died when the sentry shot him last year."

"How do you know that?" Washington demanded. "We kept that quiet. You were back at Mount Vernon. The official report was that he was wounded by a British dragoon while returning to camp. Few know a sentry shot him. And we hung the man."

Eagle remained silent.

"You're not Samuel," Washington said. "You look like him. But you're not him. You don't speak like him. You don't act like him."

Eagle felt as if he were over a void, ready to fall in a bottomless pit. "I am what you see, sir."

Washington opened his left hand. He was running the piece of cloth through his fingers. "We haven't awarded one yet. Yet now I have two." He was almost speaking to himself.

Eagle felt faint. The wound. Being here. What was at stake. "'The road to glory in a patriot army and a free country is open to all'."

"My own words," Washington said. "It's forbidden for slaves to read. How did you know them? If you knew Caldwell was looking at Hamilton's letter, you can read. Who taught you?"

"That doesn't matter, sir. You must make the speech to the officers. Not Colonel Caldwell."

"Caldwell is popular with the men," Washington said. "An effective orator. And he will use his Bible as a final persuasion."

"The Bible?" Eagle couldn't hold it in, forgetting the situation, the mission, spurred by the pain and shame of his current situation. "The Bible helps keep my brothers and sisters in chains. Keeps them for trying for a better life *now*, not in the promise of a next life."

"Insurrection and sacrilege." Yet Washington didn't seem upset. "I can hear these words you speak and understand, but few can. I have had a higher cause for years now: this country."

"The same with your officers, sir," Eagle urged. "Appeal to their sense of duty. Honor. Their loyalty to the cause for which they have fought and suffered. If they are the men you believe them to be, that will be more than sufficient."

Washington held up the Badge of Military Merit which Edith Frobish had given Eagle. "You will have to explain this to me. How you have this. How you learned to read. How you know the things you do. There is not time now, though. You will do this on the 'morrow."

That would be a hell of a conversation, Eagle thought.

But it was never going to happen.

"Your officers are waiting, sir."

Washington stuffed both Badges of Merit into his pocket. "We *will* speak later."

Ravenna, Capitol of the Remains of the Western Roman Empire, 493 A.D.

THE WORD EXCRUCIATING comes from crucifixion.

Eagle probably knew that without a download, but it was news to Roland. He was allowing the download to supply him with information as he stared up at the man nailed to the wood. He'd always wondered why churches would take a symbol of torture and make it central to their belief system, but that was pretty low on his list of things to ponder.

It wasn't a very long list anyway.

Roland allowed the download space in his brain, interested in this. The Romans didn't invent crucifixion. That popped up next. Poor Edith; she'd been forced to input that no one really knew who was the first to get the sick idea to nail someone to an artificial tree. It must have bugged the heck out of her to input the data: *that no one really knew.*

Roland figured that it had happened after someone had been nailing people to real trees for a while and wanted to do the same thing in a place where there weren't trees? But where'd they get the wood then? Import it? Why? To make a show, that was obvious, since these crosses had been placed here to send a message. And it had to have been devised some time after nails were invented, right? Which begat which? Who was sitting around one day looking at a hammer and some long nails and a tree and some person they didn't like and went: Hey!

Roland crossed his arms across his chest, feeling the hardness of the armor. This cross wasn't like the one in churches and Mac had on his belt for his mission. It was shaped like a time-out was called in football. A *'Tau cross'* according to the download. Where the crossbeam rested on top of the vertical pole, forming a capital T.

Roland inspected the victim. The nails didn't go through the hands or wrists, but the forearms. Between the radius and ulna bones. A part of Roland wanted to hold on to those two words so he could toss them at Doc one day.

Roland wondered how long it took before it was figured out that a nail through the hand or wrist didn't hold very long before small bones and soft flesh gave way? But the two larger bones in the forearm? Much better.

Those first two nails were pounded in while the victim was prostrate on the ground. Easier leverage. A good team could get them both done in less than thirty seconds. Then the *patibulum* (bar) was lifted and fit into place at the top of the *stipes* (vertical pole).

While the condemned was being lifted, the shoulders and elbows usually dislocated, but what was a little extra helping of pain when the purpose was pain and eventual death?

Roland looked at the man's legs. They were twisted to one side. A single nail went through the heels, right foot fixed above left. Further up, a piece of wood, a *sedecula*, was in a notch just below the buttocks, helping to support the victim's weight. Which seemed contrary to the purpose of execution but fit right in with the concept of a slow, lingering death.

Regardless, death was inevitable.

Roland snatched a piece of the download that Edith hadn't apparently considered overly important; a footnote. The executioners were required to remain on duty until all the condemned they'd nailed to wood had died. He looked about, but didn't see any soldiers hanging around. The good old days of Duty, Honor and Empire, were over.

Roland drew his sword and tapped the crucified man on the side of his leg. "Hey."

"What do you want?" The man gasped after getting those four words out.

"What is the plan?" Roland asked.

The man was fighting for air. Despite the *sedecula*, and the nail through the heels, most of his weight was on his upward extended arms, compressing his chest and making his diaphragm struggle. This made breathing most difficult.

"The guards are gone," Roland said. "There's no one anxious to get off duty and get a drink or visit a whore, who will break your legs so you die faster. Or put a spear in your side." He shrugged. "The cross will do all the work. Eventually. You look pretty healthy. Well, you looked pretty healthy. Before this. You might last a few days." The download didn't give a world's record for lasting on the cross; seems Edith's interest didn't swing toward the morbid.

"What do—" the man couldn't finish the sentence.

"Told you. The plan. Your first group of assassins didn't get me. And the woman with the first four? Your friend? She hopped out of here back through a gate. And the ones you paid to attack me in case the first group failed? Those three idiots? Dead. So. I get it. Take me out before you were supposed to do whatever it was this evening. But doesn't look like you're going to get to do it. Are there any more of you?"

Roland realized he was asking too many questions of someone who could only get a few words strung together. "Tell you what. I'll get you down if you promise to tell me the truth."

The man was nodding vigorously which wasn't a surprise.

"Not so fast," Roland said. "If I get you down and you lie to me or don't tell me what I want, I'll put you back up, but with better support for your ass so you last even longer."

The man lifted up on the nail through his heels, gasping in pain, but allowing his diaphragm to work better. "You'll let me go?"

"What? Of course not. You're going to die here. In this pigsty. But it will be quick. See," Roland said in a perfectly reasonable tone, "I'm being honest with you. I expect the same in return."

The man, dressed in a brown tunic, black trousers and with a smoothly cut beard, stared at Roland, but it didn't take long for reality to make the decision for him. He nodded.

Roland walked behind the crucifix and studied the mechanics. He took his helmet off and placed it on the ground. Cracked his neck. Walked back to the front. "This is going to hurt a little."

Using his dagger, he got leverage on the nail through the heels. He ignored the screams, and rocked the nail back and forth until he was able to grip it and pull it out. Then he had to work fast as the man was suffocating.

As he went back around the cross, Roland realized no one passing by was paying any particular attention to what he was doing. They probably hadn't paid too much attention when the crosses were put up either. The average person, Roland knew, had a tremendous capacity to ignore really bad things, as long as it didn't affect them.

Roland jumped and missed the short piece of rope dangling down the back. He could hear the man gurgling, choking. Roland jumped again, grabbed it, his weight pulling it down. The beam, the *patibulum*, lifted out of its notch and it, with the man still nailed to it, fell to the ground.

The man was trying to scream, except he didn't have the oxygen to do it.

Roland knelt next to him. "That wasn't too bad, was it?"

The man was a newly landed fish, gasping for air, arms stretched above his head, still nailed to the *patibulum*.

"Anyone else here from your timeline?" Roland asked.

The guy was transitioning from fish to mammal. "How did you know?"

Roland pointed to the man's left arm. "Sun was just right as we rode by. Doubt anyone else in this era has a steel rod in his forearm; must have ripped open when they hoisted you up. But I imagine you didn't plan on getting crucified. Wasn't very visible, but there was a glint. Sort of like the tiny reflection from a sniper's scope. I'm sort of trained to spot things like that."

The man's eyes were closed in pain.

Roland doubled-down on that by wiggling the nail in the arm he'd indicated. What the man emitted couldn't quite be called a scream. More a whimper.

Roland realized this was a unique situation. Scout had run into the Shadow's agents, but killed them, pretty impressively, if he had to say so. But also quickly. No chance for questions.

"What's with you guys?" Roland asked. "Scout saw the contact lens in one of your agents. You've got a steel rod. Not very smart."

The man kept his eyes closed and didn't respond.

"Why are you messing with us?" Roland asked.

The man coughed. A trickle of blood leaked out of the corner of his mouth and Roland realized he was in worse shape than the bad shape he'd suspected.

"I don't know," he finally said.

"What?"

The man opened his eyes. He looked up at Roland, eyes locking. "I'm a soldier. I just follow orders."

"Oldest excuse in the book," Roland said. "And I get it. I follow orders too. But your people give the orders. You must have a clue why."

"Not my people giving the orders," he said.

"What?"

"We're soldiers. That's all we have in our timeline. Soldiers. That's all we can pay the Shadow with. To let us live. Survive. Not be destroyed. Our soldiers are our currency."

Roland sat back on his haunches as the implications sank in. "That's messed up."

"Better than being obliterated as if we never existed. We tried fighting and were almost extinguished. Can't fight the Shadow with just weapons. Takes something more."

"What's the something more?"

The man shook his head. "Don't know. We gave up a long time ago. Just trying to survive. Give our kids, those who aren't soldiers, a way to survive."

"What's your name?"

"Teleclus."

"Russian?"

The man mustered some pride. "I am Spartan. All soldiers from our world who are the tribute to the Shadow are Spartans. It is the price we pay for having been the most powerful nation when the Shadow attacked and we lost."

Roland sat back on his haunches. "Spartan? That's weird. Scout went—" he halted, realizing he was about to violate a rule. The first rule of Time Patrol: *You do not talk about the Time Patrol.*

Then again, the guy was dying.

Second rule of Time Patrol: *You do not talk about the Time Patrol.*
Roland believed in rules.

Back on task. "Who was the woman?"

"Our handler. Diana. *She* is from the Shadow. I think; we don't know much. She brought me here as her security. She paid those four and told them where to wait. Then had me recruit more as back up. Redundancy."

Yeah, they sent at least two for Scout, Roland thought.

"How'd you end up on this thing?"

"When I reported back to her. Told her I'd hired more killers. She had some of Theodoric's soldiers with her. Betrayed me. Turned me over." He took a deep breath. "I knew there was little chance of coming back. Few of our people come back when they get sent on a mission for the Shadow."

"But she'll be back right?" Roland asked. "Or she left someone else here to do what needs to be done?"

The man looked at Roland, confused. "What?"

"Who else is here to finish the mission?"

"'The mission'?" The man closed his eyes. "I'm very tired."

"The mission," Roland said. "Keep Odoacer from getting killed. Kill Theodoric. Whatever. Change our timeline."

The man shook his head. "Told you. No one else came with us. But she probably paid off other to do her bidding. Always the easiest way. Pay others to do the dirty work. But you don't understand."

Roland sighed. He got told that a lot. "What don't I understand?"

"The mission Diana gave me." The man looked to the left at the nail in his arm, then to the right. "I got that rod in my arm—" his voice faltered, his eyes growing unfocused. Shock was setting in. "On another op. Can't remember. Why can't I remember? I came back from that one. I was lucky."

"What don't I understand?" Roland asked, his voice gentle. "What was your mission?"

"You."

The Missions Phase IV

Rome, Roman Empire, 44 B.C.

"FRIENDS, ROMANS, COUNTRYMEN, give me your ears. I come—"

"No!" A woman's voice cut through Marc Antony's drunken words. "Do you want them to rip their ears off and toss them to you? *Lend* me your ears. *Lend* me your ears."

Antony stood on a wide bed, stark naked, swaying as if at sea. He laughed at the interruption. "I'll rip their ears off if need be to get them to listen."

Moms and Spurinna had been let in a back entry to Antony's house. Led by one of the Seer's slave contacts to this inner sanctum of Caesar's co-counsel. They stood behind a gauzy curtain, listening and watching. The woman who'd spoken wasn't in their field of vision.

"Friends, Romans, countrymen, *lend* me your ears." Antony burped. "I come to bury Caesar, not to praise him. I promise to return your ears when I am done speaking." He flopped back onto the bed, nearly falling on one of the four nude women sprawled around him. They immediately reached out, caressing, cooing.

Moms and Spurinna startled when at low voice right behind them. "He's an utter idiot, but idiots can be useful if correctly coached."

The same voice who'd corrected him. They both turned.

A slender woman, as tall as Moms, with pale skin and bright red hair flowing over her shoulders, smiled at them. "Do either of you recognize the words the great Antony speaks?"

Moms had the dagger she'd taken from Spurinna's chamber pressed into the soft spot, just under the woman's ribcage, pointed at her heart just scant inches away. "I do. And that's why you die."

"Hasty, hasty, hasty," the woman said. "We haven't even been properly introduced. I know of you," she nodded at Spurinna. "Who calls herself a Seer but is just a spy-master. And you are?" She nodded at Moms.

Moms knew Nada would not be happy she hadn't already killed the woman, but the damn vagaries of the variables as Dane liked to say, stilled her hand.

"It appears I must go first," the redhead said when there was no reply. "I am Pyrrha."

The download was fast: Pyrrha, daughter of Pandora.

"Perhaps you've heard of me?" She asked Moms. "My mother at least? She always seems to get the higher billing. It's really not fair considering I am, mythologically at least, the mother of all mankind after the Great Flood." She stepped back from the knife.

Moms let her hand drop.

"A widespread tale, is it not?" Pyrrha asked. "The Great Flood? The deluge Zeus sent to cleanse the earth? Leaving only two people, one man, one woman, to repopulate the world. My husband, poor Deucalion, and myself. We were at a loss how to proceed once the water receded. We were all that remained of the human race, standing on Mount Parnassus." Her voice held a hint of mocking her own story.

"The names change, the locations change, but the essence is there in all the myths and religions around the world. Ah yes, repopulate after a great flood. Why a God would want to kill everyone is the question no one seems to ponder too deeply in worshipping such an entity. And why one would want to *continue* worshipping the God that practically wiped everyone out, is another question worth pondering."

"What—" Moms began, but Pyrrha wasn't finished.

"So Deucalion and I threw stones over our shoulders. My husband's stones became our sons, while mine, our daughters. Really, seems it would have much easier to simply copulate. Speaking of which—" She inclined her head toward the bed where Antony was entwined with the women. It wasn't clear who was doing what to whom. "Men," she said sadly. "Such simple creatures. Why we let them control things is beyond me."

"What do you want?" Moms asked.

"You still haven't told me your name," Pyrrha said. "You're not Scout. She's younger."

Moms' skin went cold at the mention of her teammate's name. Her hand tightened around the hilt of the dagger.

"You must be Moms," Pyrrha finally said.

"I am."

"It is an honor to meet you," Pyrrha said.

"I don't think so," Moms said.

Antony's voice was muffled, drunk, distracted. "The evil that men do lives after them. The good is oft interfered with their bones. So let it be with Caesar."

The three turned toward the bed at the sudden change in Antony's voice when he said the name. He got to his knees. Shoved one of the women away, sending her sprawling off the bed. The others scooted away. Confused. Wary.

Antony got to his feet, steadier than he was before. "The good is often interred with their bones," he recited. "So let it be with Caesar. The noble Brutus—" Antony paused, looking about as if suddenly aware of his surroundings. He shook his head, trying to clear the fog. "The noble Brutus. For Brutus is an honorable man. So are they all, all honorable men."

The women scattered, running from the room as Antony leapt off the bed, snatching up a sword. "*Honorable* men?" He cursed. "Caesar was my *friend! Is* my friend. Faithful and just to me. But Brutus says Caesar is ambitious. And Brutus, oh yes, *he* is an honorable man. And he says Caesar is ambitious. Then why did Caesar turn down the crown I offered him at Lupercal? Three times I offered. And three times he refused. Is that ambition? He made me small with those refusals. If one should have a grudge, it should be I. And *Brutus* is an honorable man and *I* am not?"

Antony slashed with the sword. "But what do I know? You all love him. And not without cause." He lifted the sword once more, to kill the invisible demons surrounding him, but he let it go, clattering on the floor. "What do I know?" He fell to his knees and cried out. "Oh judgment! Thou have fled to brutish beasts. Men have lost their reason. I have lost mine."

Antony leaned over, forehead to marble, and sobbed. "My heart will be in the coffin with Caesar. It will be in there."

He crumpled to the floor, sobbing.

"He could have saved him, you know," Pyrrha said. "Antony's sword at Caesar's side. But now?" she indicated the wreck of a man curled up on the floor.

"What are you doing here?" Moms asked.

Pyrrha indicated Spurinna. "Fixing what your fool tried to do."

"Why would you want Caesar to die?" Moms was confused. "Why not have him live? Change our timeline?"

"I tried," Pyrrha said. "But there are things that cannot be changed. You'll learn this, if you get the time. The Fates have made this a higher law."

"The Fates? Who are they?"

"There is so much you don't know," Pyrrha said. A Gate opened behind her.

"Ah!" Pyrrha said, sensing Moms intention. "If you kill me now, then Scout will die the forever death."

"What do you mean?"

Pyrrha stepped close, put her mouth next to Moms ear. "Beware the Ides." Her lips brushed along Moms cheek and then she kissed her on the lips. Hard. Fierce.

Pyrrha stepped back and the Gate snapped out of existence.

Petrograd, Russia, 1917.

THE THREE MEN SPUN ABOUT from the small fire as Krylo opened the door. They drew pistols and aimed them at Doc.

"Easy." Doc held his hands up. "We come in peace."

"You are not Russian," the well-dressed man in the center said. He was obviously the Count, as the other two wore peasant garb. He was a tall man, over six feet, with a thick dark beard, streaked with white. He wore an expensive coat and a fur hat.

"I'm American," Doc said.

"Then we speak in English," the Count said, switching languages. "So only the two of us will understand. I assume you are the man I am here to meet?"

"What do you mean?"

"You are from—" he paused—"another time. Correct? Why else would an American be here? And now?" He didn't wait for an answer. He bowed slightly at the waist. "I am Count Pyotr Golovkin."

"Doc."

Golovkin didn't seem impressed with the name or the lack of title. "That is all?"

"That is all."

"Things must be different in your time," Golovkin said. "Is it short for Doctor?"

"It's a name I was given." Doc looked at the other two men. They had turned back to the fire, warming themselves. Krylo had joined them, and they were conversing in Russian in low voices, barely audible.

Golovkin rubbed his hands together. "So. Should we proceed?"

"With what?" Doc asked.

Golovkin cocked his head. "We are here for the same reason, are we not?"

"And that is?"

"To save the young Tsar, of course."

"And you know this how?" Doc asked.

Golovkin appeared surprised at the question. "What other outcome could there be here? Nicholas?" He shrugged. "The Tsar was done before he ever took the throne. He never had the strength to rule Mother Russia. He's already given up power. Today the Bolsheviks make it official. Put all the false stamps and signatures of the revolutionaries on the document. But young Alexei? He is the future of Russia. And we must get him out of here. The quiet in the streets is deceptive. Things are going to turn ugly very soon."

"You are here to help me, aren't you?" Doc asked.

"And you, me," Golovkin said. "My men are good shots, but I think we can get out of the palace and through the city to the harbor without trouble. If we move quickly. I have hired a boat that will take us to England. It awaits. But we will have to leave the Tsar. That is the agreement I have worked out with the Bolsheviks and it is what King George finds acceptable."

"But you don't know what's supposed to happen," Doc said.

"I know what *has* to happen," Golovkin said. "There can be no other path for Russia." He took a step closer to Doc and lowered his voice. "One of my spies has informed me that the Germans are giving that pig Lenin money to fuel the Bolsheviks and are helping him to return to Mother Russia. He is a traitor to not only the Tsar but to Russia. He will be here within the month. I know Lenin. I met him in France. He is a very dangerous man."

Doc knew what Golovkin was saying was true: Lenin *was* in Germany at the moment. He'd been exiled twice, once in 1900 after spending three years imprisoned in Siberia, and then again in 1907. He'd been against Russian involvement in World War I, for which Doc had to give him points: so far the Russians had lost more soldiers in the war than any country in any previous war. Ever.

The download further confirmed what Golovkin had just said: the Germans were going to return Lenin and his key men in a secret railway car in April. The German intent was to foster more anti-war fervor in Russia. In that, they would succeed. But Lenin would be forced to briefly flee once more, then return and finally depose the Provisional Government and proclaim Soviet rule in November. At which time he would make peace with Germany and the Russian Civil War between the Reds and the Whites would commence. And in the midst of all that, on 17 July 1918, Nicholas II, his wife, the four Duchesses, and Alexei, would be assassinated.

"You are to do what I tell you," Doc said.

Golovkin frowned. "And that is?"

"Nothing. I've already taken care of what needs to be done."

Golovkin took a step back and folded his arms across his chest. "What have you done? The Tsarina is trapped here with her children. The family has to get out. There is not much time. You say you've taken care of things, but as far as I can tell *nothing* has changed. Unless you can tell me differently."

Doc tried to muster some inner Nada: "I'm not just telling you to do nothing," he said. "I am ordering you."

Golovkin unfolded his arms, reached out, grabbed Doc by the elbow, and pulled him out of the small room, away from the others.

"What are you saying?" Golovkin demanded. "That we leave the family to the mob? They will not last long. Only that fool Krylo remains from the Imperial Guard. And he is only good for shoveling coal and hiding. The Bolsheviks come and go as they please. Soon it will please them to come here and take the family."

"They will be protected," Doc said.

"By who? The Bolsheviks?"

"Yes."

"Why would the Bolsheviks protect the very people they are overthrowing?"

Doc was relieved there was something he could answer honestly. "They will continue to protect them as they are already doing to keep the Russian people from turning against their revolution. If the Bolsheviks harm the Tsarina, and especially the children, think what will happen?"

Golovkin stroked his beard. "That is supposing many things. That the mob can be controlled. That the Bolsheviks continue to do as you say. Yes, it is the smart move for them, but they have done many things that are not smart. And they will hold the royal family prisoner, will they not?"

"Yes," Doc admitted.

"And when Lenin gets here? I do not think he will be as merciful."

"He will," Doc said. "He has to. He is as much a prisoner of events as they."

"But how will young Alexei regain the throne if he is a prisoner?" Golovkin didn't wait for an answer. "Many of the royalty will fight the Bolsheviks. Once he is safe in England Alexei can be an inspiration to them. Their hope for the future."

"They have to stay here," Doc said.

"Then you are telling me that the revolution will not prevail? The Bolsheviks will fail?"

"We do not get to chose what will unfold," Doc said.

"That is not acceptable," Golovkin said, pulling his heavy revolver out.

"I am ordering you—" Doc began, but all went black as the butt of the revolver hit him on the side of the head.

Palos de la Frontera, Spain, 1493 A.D.

"'GUILT'?" GEERT REPEATED. "What has de Cisneros done that he ought feel guilty?"

"It's not what he's done," Mac said. "It's what he's getting ready to do."

Night covered the town and the two ships. Dozens of lanterns illuminated the quay and both ships. Now that the Cente Suisse were gone, off with Columbus to La Rabida, Mac and Geert moved out from behind the building.

The Franciscan was greeting sailors coming ashore from both the *Pinta* and the *Nina*, blessing them as each rowboat load was discharged but he seemed distracted, constantly looking toward the *Pinta*.

"When I was a student in the Q-Course," Mac said, "they taught me—"

"Q what?"

Mac was having trouble controlling his mind; and his emotions. His dark past boiled inside of him as he stared at the priest. "A school for soldiers. My specialty was targeting things. Figuring out the most effective way to attack something. We used a formula, sort of systems engineering. It was called—" he realized he was speaking Latin and the acronym didn't carry over—"doesn't matter what it was called. There were six things to look at."

Geert was lost, but Mac didn't care. Talking it out crystallized it. He held up a single finger. "Criticality. How valuable is the target? For the Shadow, their target is our timeline. That's pretty valuable, especially to us." A second finger. "Accessibility. Can the Shadow get to what it wants to achieve? It can today." He indicated the ships and the priest.

"Friar de Cisneros is Shadow?" Geert asked.

"He's either from the Shadow or he's working for it." Mac held up the last three fingers. "Recuperability, vulnerability and effect. Can we fix whatever the Shadow is doing today? Are we vulnerable to what it's doing? How devastating will the effect to the timeline be of what it's doing?"

"So *what* is it doing? What is the priest doing?"

Mac gave a grim smile. He pointed at the *Pinta*. A stretcher was lowered into a rowboat. "Recognizability is the last factor."

Geert frowned. "One of the crew is sick? That is normal for a long voyage. Scurvy. There are many—"

"I'm not supposed to tell you of the future," Mac said. "But in this case, the truth will be known in a few years anyway. Those men on those ships, some of them, brought back syphilis," Mac said.

"They've brought back what?"

"A disease. One you get from sex."

Geert snorted. "Another reason to abstain. The clappan is something many sailors get."

Yes, Edith had that in there: an early word for gonorrhea. "No. This is something new."

"Is it deadly?"

"It can be."

"But if you know it was brought back," Geert pointed out, "then it *was* brought back. How is anything different?"

Mac pointed at the priest waiting for the boat carrying the stretcher to reach land. "Because of him." Mac stood. "It's time."

"What does de Cisneros have to do with some sickness? How do you know this?"

"Because I think he's a real priest, but he looks guilty. He doesn't like what he's about to do."

"You know this how, my friend?"

"I understand guilty priests. He reeks of it."

Mac drew his dagger as he slid through the welcoming crowd and came up behind the priest. The rowboat was almost to the quay.

"They are saying that's Martin Pinzon," Geert said in a low voice to Mac, indicating the man in the stretcher.

"Friar de Cisneros," he called out.

The priest turned. "Yes, brother?"

"I have something you need to hear."

The priest's eyes darted to the rowboat. "I must bless Captain Pinzon on his successful journey."

"You must hear my confession first," Mac said.

"We are of a different order," he said.

"I insist," Mac said.

"I would be glad to at another time," the priest said. "But—"

Mac surreptitiously pressed the point of the dagger against the priest's side. "I must confess now."

Geert was on the other side. "I feel a confession coming on also, brother."

Together they hustled him away from the crowd, out of the halo of light welcoming the sons of Palos de la Frontera home from their journey. The priest glanced over his shoulder as Captain Pinzon was lifted up and placed in the rear of a cart by members of his family. The group headed off, away from town.

Mac and Geert dragged the priest down a short bluff onto the pebbled beach, just above the high water mark. It was dark, only the starlight and a quarter moon for illumination.

"What were you going to do?" Mac demanded, letting go of the priest.

De Cisneros dropped to his knees, folded his hands and began praying rapidly in Latin.

Mac smacked him on the side of the head and he fell over, onto the beach. "You'll have time for praying later."

The priest got to his knees and went to fold his hands in prayers once more.

"Get up," Mac ordered, an edge that stopped the hands before they joined.

"You are Devotio Moderna," de Cisoneros said as he slowly stood up. "What are you doing here?"

"What were you going to do?" Mac demanded.

"Give the blessings to—"

Mac hit de Cisneros in the nose with a fist, a sucker punch that stunned the priest. The sound of the nose breaking was very clear and blood poured forth. While the priest was still stunned, Mac pulled the purse off his shoulder. He looped the strap over his shoulder, then searched de Cisneros' robe. He found a dagger and tucked it into his belt, just behind his cross.

Friar De Cisneros was blinking hard, trying to regain his wits. Blood dribbled from his nose and his eyes were full of tears from the punch.

Mac looked in the purse. A metal tin. Mac opened it. Resting on a bed of soft linen was a pewter syringe. The plunger was extended, indicating it was full. "What's in it, Friar?"

"I don't know."

"Who were you going to stick it in?"

"Captain Pinzon."

Mac closed the tin and dropped it back in the purse.

"Why?" Mac asked.

Geert had turned into a bystander, several steps behind what was developing in front of him.

Friar de Cisneros gathered himself. He pointed at the two ships anchored in the estuary. "Can you imagine what is going to happen now that they've brought word of their discovery? What Europeans will do to the people who already live on the other side of the ocean? Do you know what Columbus has written in his report?"

"I've got a good idea," Mac said. "How do *you* know what he wrote?"

"I was shown it."

"By who?"

"By an Angel of God."

"Not likely," Mac said. "An emissary of the Shadow."

"Ah!" Geert exclaimed, finally understanding.

The priest didn't care what Mac said. "Columbus writes that the natives are *fearful and timid*. And *guileless and honest*. As if those are negatives! He writes that they might become Christians and inclined to love our King and Queen and Princes."

"What's wrong with that?" Geert asked, obviously puzzled. "Seems you and your brethren would want them to become Christians."

"It will not be a choice," De Cisneros said. "I know how Rome works. The Inquisition? The natives will be forced to convert. Those who don't convert will be killed. They will be made into slaves. They will . . ."

"Die," Mac cut him off. "Almost all the natives will die. Mainly from diseases brought from here to the New World. Just as Pinzon and others in his crew are bringing their own disease back with them. And yes. The natives will be enslaved. Converted by force." He tapped the side of the purse. "But what is this syringe? What were you planning to do?"

"I was to inject Captain Pinzon with it," Friar De Cisneros said. "I was told it would prevent his death and the deaths of those across the sea. Save them from enslavement. Surely both of you, being men of God yourselves, understand why one with a pure heart would want to help others?"

Mac had to take a deep breath as he finally understood. He was facing the most dangerous person: someone who believed they were doing a good thing. Who didn't understand the means by which he was doing it.

"How do you think sticking Pinzon with this syringe will change that?"

"I was promised it would. I must trust the word of the Angel of the Lord who brought it to me."

A Valkyrie. Mac knew. Just as a Valkyrie with a prophecy had visited Raleigh, so had de Cisneros. He wasn't Shadow. He was what he appeared to be. A man of good faith.

Friar de Cisneros' eyes glinted in the starlight. "From what you say, you have seen an Angel, haven't you?"

"I have," Mac said.

"Did it give you God's mission?" de Cisneros asked.

"It tried to kill me," Mac said. "Because it wasn't an angel. You were lied to, Friar." He tapped the side of the purse. "I have a good idea what this is. Just as diseases from here are going to wipe out almost all the native inhabitants of the New World, that Angel wants to piggy-back something onto the syphilis virus with this to make it more deadly. Another Black Death at least. If not worse."

"I don't understand what you are saying," Friar de Cisneros said. "If an Angel tried to kill you, then you are not a man of faith."

Geert was thrown by that. "You saw an Angel?" He asked Mac.

De Cisneros dropped to his knees and clasped his hands together. He began reciting the Lord's prayer: "Pater Noster, qui es in caelis, sanctificetur nomen tuum. Adveniat regnum . . ."

"What do you mean you saw—" Geert began but then gave a strange grunt.

Mac looked up from the Friar. The point of a rapier protruded from Geert's chest. He looked surprised more than anything else.

"I don't—" Geert said, then the life faded from his eyes and he dropped as the rapier was pulled out.

The Swiss Guard who'd followed them into the tavern stood there, bloody blade in hand.

Mac drew his own rapier while taking an automatic step back to get some time and distance.

The Guard used that time to slam the dagger in his other hand into the base of Friar de Cisneros' skull, ending his prayer and his life. The Guard stepped over the two bodies, both weapons at the ready.

The download could supply information, but not the years of muscle and brain training to use these weapons. This was more Roland's gig, Mac thought as he took another step back.

"Why?" he yelled at the Guard.

Who seemed puzzled at the question. "Orders."

"Whose orders?"

"Told you. My sergeant's." The Guard took another step forward, raising the two weapons in what Mac assumed was the proper attack position. The download flickered a bunch of images of rapier/dagger defense positions and—Mac shut that down.

He was fighting the Swiss Guard's version of Roland. How best to do that?

Mac spun about and ran away.

Thermopylae, Greece, 480 B.C.

SCOUT SLIPPED OUT OF CAMP, heading south along the well-worn path that headed to southern Greece. She paused at one of the hot springs six hundred meters from the Spartan camp. The path was broader, and with the coming dawn, she could see the path below open up, descending to a wide plain. Once the Persians got past the Spartans, all of Greece lay before them.

Scout turned landward, closer to the mountain, searching, slowly moving along.

She reached a cleft in the side of the mountain. Inside it was the slightest trace of a path winding upward. Scout began to climb, the point of the Naga Staff leading. Up, up, scrambling on a path made for goats, not humans.

After five minutes the path briefly widened to a small, flat open space. Fifteen feet wide, ten feet deep. On the far side, the path curved up and to the right.

As good a place as any, Scout decided.

Just in time as Pandora appeared, coming down. The Sibyl paused, trying to hide her surprise at Scout's presence.

"You aren't as smart as you think," Scout said. "I may not have been educated in the Sight, but a friend taught me many things. He called them Nada Yada's. One was to never trust anyone who tries too hard and too fast to be your friend."

"I'm not your friend," Pandora. "I am your family."

"Yeah. Right. Then what are you doing here? And who's coming behind you?"

"The battle will play out as it did in this timeline's history," Pandora said. "I gave you a chance to save some lives and delay the inevitable. This is on you if you did not take advantage of the opportunity I presented you."

"You really think Leonidas would withdraw? Spartans retreat?"

"Of course not. Thus your history will play out according to script."

Scout took a step back as a dark mist crept down the path behind Pandora. Not a natural phenomenon. It slithered around her feet, slowly enveloping her.

"You are alone," Pandora said. "Your Nada Yada isn't here. No Spartan is here. That is what you can expect from men. They will always fail you. Join us. Your sisters."

Scout was barely listening. The mist was preceded by a wet, oily smell. One she'd experienced before, in the Space Between. The netherworld were various timelines met via Gates.

Something bad was coming.

She almost took another step back. But didn't. If she retreated, then Pandora won. Fear won.

"Hope," Scout said.

Pandora was confused. "What?"

"*Elpis*," Scout said. "Hope. It remained in your box. Your *pithos*. Why?"

"For men, hope is the worst plague of all," Pandora said. She pointed to the northeast. "Despite the reality, Leonidas and his men still have hope. They know what's going to happen to them, yet deep inside, there is some flicker of hope. It is the curse of men to never accept the inevitability of reality."

"Something is coming," Scout said, gripping the haft of the Naga tight.

"Can you tell me what it is?" Pandora said.

"Are you testing me?"

"Perhaps."

"It isn't human." Scout was certain of that. "It's evil."

Pandora stepped to the side. The mist reached Scout.

"You think you know things," Pandora said. "Your world is just one of many worlds. Many the same, many much different."

"Blah, blah," Scout said. "You really—" She stopped speaking as something bounded out of the path, past Pandora, into the open space. "Oh crap."

The creature had the body of a lion, the head of a serpent and the tail of a scorpion. The head darted back and forth, tongue flickering, searching. The barbed tail moved in concert with the head.

"Your pet?" Scout asked, Naga at the ready.

"A reality from another timeline," Pandora said. "A legend in your timeline."

The snakehead had stopped moving, aimed directly at Scout. Along with the tail.

"A chimera," Scout said. "'A thing of immortal make', according to Homer in the *Iliad*." Great, now she was turning into Eagle.

"You still have a choice," Pandora said.

"You don't know me at all," Scout said. "It was never a choice." She charged forward, swinging the Naga, trying to take the snakehead off. The head darted down, under her blow and she sensed more than saw, the scorpion tail striking downward.

Scout threw herself to the side, the barbed point hitting rock just inches from her. She rolled, coming to her knees, Naga ready.

The mist had now covered the entire open space. The stench was sickening.

The chimera faced her, as much as such a beast could face someone. Now the snakehead arced to the left, poised, while the scorpion tail went right, high.

"What now?" Pandora called out.

"Shut up," Scout yelled. She got to her feet. She focused on the slits in the snake eyes, the tail in her peripheral vision. "You're an ugly bastard."

Then she ignored both head and tail. Dove forward, rolled, and jabbed upward into the lion chest. She sensed both the snakehead and tail coming for her from either side as she shoved the Naga point deep into the creature. She twisted away from the tail as a sword sliced through the neck and the snakehead tumbled to the ground.

The chimera toppled over.

"Thank you," Scout said as she pulled the Naga out of the body.

Leonidas' face was in the shadows cast by the cheekpiece's of his helmet. He had his heavy shield in one hand, his *xiphos* in the other.

He stepped past Scout and struck once more, slicing off the still-twitching scorpion tail.

"I will be remembered as a coward," Leonidas said. "Deserting my men on the edge of battle."

"You're welcome," Scout said.

Trumpets blared in the distance, from the direction of the Gates of Fire. Leonidas turned, his body tense, listening. "The final assault begins. Assyrian horns. They will lead."

Scout pointed the bloody tip of her Naga at Pandora. "Are the Persians coming behind you?"

The body of the chimera slowly crumbled inward, turning to dust.

"Answer me," Scout demanded.

Pandora sighed. "Of course they come. The battle must play out as history dictates."

"Is there any reason we shouldn't kill you?" Scout asked.

The mist dissipated, the light of dawn piercing it. The smell of the nearby sea was masking the odor of the mist and the beast.

"Because *you've* won," Pandora said. "This time."

A dark circle appeared behind her. She took a step back and was gone. The gate snapped out of existence. As it did so, Scout staggered, fell to her knees, as a vision blossomed in her mind, blotting out everything, every other thought, every sound, sight, feel, smell. She'd have fallen forward onto her face if Leonidas had not grabbed her shoulders.

"What is wrong?"

The vision faded and Scout returned to the here and now. "They come."

"I hear," Leonidas said. Voices, the clatter and clank of armored men, trickled down the trail.

"We cannot hold this place for long," Leonidas said.

"We're not supposed to hold this place," Scout said. She grabbed his arm. "We hold the wall with your men. Come!"

Newburgh, New York, 1783 A.D.

"GENTLEMEN." WASHINGTON'S VOICE was level, soft, but it carried clearly through the 'Temple', which was what the largest open building in the Newburgh Cantonment had been dubbed since

Colonel Caldwell conducted services in it every morning. A forty by seventy foot building in the center of camp.

Sitting with his back against the sidewall, on the outside, just underneath an open window, Eagle accepted there was no position in which his shoulder would not be in agony. The wound was bleeding through the bandage. Eagle was uncertain how many more hours he had left here, but if Washington could just get through this speech, Eagle could get back to the cot, lie down, and just wait.

Then get some proper medical care, not a packing of axle grease.

Washington spoke: "By an anonymous summons, an attempt has been made to convene you together. How inconsistent with the rules of propriety, how unmilitary and how subversive of all order and discipline, let the good sense of the army decide. In the moment of this summons, another anonymous production was sent into circulation, addressed more to the feelings and passions than to the reason and judgment of the army. The author of this piece . . ."

Washington continued, but Eagle already knew the speech. Besides being a military leader, Washington was a superb orator.

After discussing the letter which had been circulating, Washington zeroed in. "This dreadful alternative of either deserting our country in the extremist hour of her distress, or turning our arms against it, which is the apparent object, unless Congress can be compelled into instant compliance, has something so shocking in it, that humanity revolts at the idea."

Washington's voice rose. "My God! What can this writer have in view, by recommending such measures? Can he be a friend to the army? Can he be a friend to this country? Rather is he not an insidious foe? Some emissary, plotting the ruin of both, by sowing the seeds of discord and separation between the civil and military powers of the continent? But, here, gentlemen—" There was a long pause. Eagle forced himself to turn toward the building and get to his knees, peering in one corner of the window.

Washington stood at the pulpit, both hands on the edge, looking out over his blue-clad audience. Eagle saw that he had something clenched in one of his hands and realized it was the Badge.

Washington repeated himself. "But, here, gentlemen, I will drop the curtain, because it would be as imprudent in me to assign my reasons for this opinion, as it would be insulting to your conception to suppose you stood in need of them. A moment's reflection will convince every dispassionate mind of the physical impossibility of carrying either proposal into execution.

Eagle could well imagine Roland's reaction listening to such a speech. His head would explode. Doc would probably deplore the run on sentences, but an edge was creeping into Washington's voice, indicating he was speaking from the heart, letting it lead to the words.

"By thus determining, and thus acting, you will pursue the plain and direct road to the attainment of your wishes; you will defeat the insidious designs of our enemies, who are compelled to resort from open force to secret artifice. You will give one more distinguished proof of unexampled patriotism and patient virtue, rising superior to the pressure of the most complicated sufferings: and you will, by the dignity of your conduct, afford occasion for posterity to say, when speaking of the glorious example you have exhibited to mankind— 'had this day been wanting, the world had never seen the last stage of perfection to which human nature is capable of attaining'."

Washington stopped and there was absolute stillness in the room. The General's shoulders slumped, perhaps from exhaustion, perhaps from despair. Eagle knew that was the end. Yet he didn't sense that the officers were swayed.

Washington held up a single finger, as if asking for a moment. He reached inside his coat and retrieved a letter. "I have here a letter from a friend in Congress I would like to read to you. To show that your cause is not futile and lying forgotten." He unfolded it. Peered at it, his hand visibly shaking. He gave a slight shake of his head. "Forgive me," he whispered. He pulled a pair of reading glasses out of a pocket. "Gentlemen, you will permit me to put on my new spectacles, for I have not only grown gray but almost blind in the service of my country."

That broke the officers. Eagle could see the ripple pass through the rows of benches at this simple movement. As Washington began reading, several men were crying, seeing that their commander had paid like they had; given his health, his years, his life to the cause.

Eagle blinked and realized he too was crying.

He didn't even listen to the letter and he knew few of the officers were listening either.

It was done.

Eagle turned and slid back to the ground, his back against the wall, blinking the tears out of his eyes. And when he could see, in front of him, outlined against the evening sky was Colonel Caldwell holding a saber, the point less than a foot from Eagle's chest.

"You think you've achieved something, don't you?" Caldwell smiled. "You've failed. And now you die."

Ravenna, Capitol of the Remains of the Western Roman Empire, 493 A.D.

ALONG WITH THE OTHER ELEVEN PROTECTORS, Roland stood behind Odoacer, King of Italy, destroyer of the Western Roman Empire, old man, and currently very drunk.

Odoacer slouched in his throne, a garish wooden thing, much too big, making the king seem that much smaller. It was at one end of a long wooden table. At the far end was Theodoric. Seated on a stool. A dozen Ostrogoth warriors were behind him, faces painted, armed to the teeth. They didn't look like they were here to talk peace, but Roland had a sense this is the way they looked all the time: for battle, at weddings, for birthday parties, taking a dump, whatever.

Most of the Protectors were veterans of the Roman Army. Like their King, some of the men next to Roland were a bit long in the tooth and looked less than inspired at the current situation. The odor of alcohol was thick; some must have been prepping for the meeting the age-old stupid way.

The benches on either side of the twenty-foot long table were empty except for one man in red vestments sitting in the center on the right side: John, Bishop of Ravenna, the download suggested. The priest who'd brokered the truce and potential joint leadership deal. Each king, and the bishop, had a plate heaped with food in front of them, but while neither King had partaken, the bishop, a portly man, was going at it quite greedily; not surprising after the three-year siege Ravenna had been under from Theodoric. Odoacer had a goblet in his hand, but Roland noticed that Theodoric had not lifted his. The bishop was on his third.

Roland's combat instincts were screaming 'Ambush', but any idiot would know that just from the way things were arranged. Odoacer didn't seem overly concerned as he drained the goblet and held it out. From one of the sally ports leading into the courtyard a boy dashed out, filled it and disappeared.

The two kings had yet to speak a word to each other since Theodoric and his entourage entered five minutes ago.

"Are you ready to finalize the treaty?" Odoacer broke the silence, which lost him points in Roland's opinion.

Theodoric confirmed that with a slight smile. "Of course."

"How will we do this?" Odoacer asked. "We can not both be King. Nor Emperor. We must use another term in order to rule together. I suggest we use the Roman term: consul."

"You would like to go back to being Roman," Theodoric said. "You fought for them long enough. Before you turned on your Emperor."

"The Roman way worked well enough," Odoacer said. "It will work again. And it will give us footing with the East."

"I know more about the Roman way than you," Theodoric said. "I spent many years in Constantinople."

"As a hostage," Odoacer said.

"I became a *magister militum*," Theodoric said. "A master of soldiers. And I have been a consul of Rome."

"Not this Rome."

"This Rome," Theodoric said, "exists at the whim of the East."

"We don't have to," Odoacer said.

"I disagree."

Roland saw movement up and to the right. Someone was on a balcony, overlooking the courtyard. A woman in a long black robe. Roland recognized her from the ambush. She turned her head and looked directly at him. She smiled and gave a slight nod.

Roland didn't know what to make of that, then again, he'd always exasperated Mac the few times they gone out together and women had given Roland the 'eye' and Roland had been oblivious to their come-on.

He did know, though, that this wasn't a come-on. The woman reminded him a bit of Neeley: tall, short dark hair, dark eyes. Age indeterminate. Her hands rested on the railing, no weapon visible.

Roland scanned the rest of the area, searching for potential assassins: targeted either at him or Theodoric.

Nothing.

Theodoric picked up his goblet and that must have been the signal, because eight of the eleven soldiers standing around Roland, and behind Odoacer, walked away, four to each side. They went halfway down, then turned, angling to face their former King.

Twenty to four. Despite what Mac said, Roland could do this kind of math very quickly.

He looked up at the woman once more. What did she have planned to change the inevitable? Right now it was heading down accepted history highway.

Theodoric drank slowly, eyeing his counterpart over the rim. He drained it and put it back on the table. Then he stood. "Bishop?"

John looked up, surprised to be interrupted, then quickly, as fast as someone as fat as him could do quickly, got to his feet. He grabbed a leg of some meat and took it with him, departing the scene.

"You barter in betrayal," Odoacer said. "How much did it cost you to suborn my Protectors?"

"Nothing," Theodoric said. "I appealed to their sense of survival. You have been losing for years. How long can you expect to keep men loyal in such circumstances?" He used his chair as a step up onto the table, drawing his sword. His Ostrogoths drew their weapons and the eight defectors took a step back, clearing the path on either side of the table.

Roland still waited for the fly in the ointment. Two of the men with him slid their swords out and flanked their king. They seemed ready to go down with the captain. The third, finally able to do math, walked away, joining the first eight. Leaving Roland alone behind Odoacer.

Roland looked up at the woman again. She was focused on Odoacer.

Expanding his basic math to speculative math, Roland wondered why the two were remaining loyal to Odoacer, given the current odds? Going down with the captain is one thing, but the ship was pretty leaky to start with, given the king's condition.

It was a suicidal move.

Unless it wasn't.

Theodoric paused halfway down the table and looked to his right, at the officer who'd shuffled Roland into line when he'd arrived at the palace. "You told me you had paid off all?"

"Three are new, sir," the officer responded.

Roland slammed the point of his *spatha* into the back of the soldier on the left, going directly through the heart and hitting the breastplate from the inside. He'd caught the man just as he was starting to leap onto the table. The other made it onto the table, but was surprised that his comrade wasn't at his side. Nevertheless, he went for Theodoric.

Odoacer shoved the wooden chair back, struggling to his feet, lifting the sword that had been on his lap. Roland easily knocked it out his feeble hand with the flat of his own sword, laid the sharp edge against Odoacer's throat, then watched the duel on the table-top.

The soldier was good. Very good. Theodoric was forced to give ground, barely able to stop the assault. If there'd been two? He'd have died already.

That's how quickly history would have changed.

With his free hand, Roland drew a dagger and threw it, hours and hours of practice becoming useful. It struck the soldier directly behind his left knee, buckling it, and that was all Theodoric needed to finish him off.

Roland looked up to the balcony and nodded at the woman. A ripple of anger crossed her face, gone so quickly another might have wondered if it had ever been there, but not Roland. She looked at him, gave a slight bow. Stepped back. And was gone.

Theodoric stalked down the table, sword raised with both hands high over his head.

Helpless, facing imminent death, Odoacer cried out in a surprisingly loud voice: "Where is God? Where is God?" He seemed genuinely surprised.

Theodoric struck a mighty blow straight down, smashing through Odoacer's helmet, splitting his head asunder.

Blood spurted and Odoacer collapsed forward onto the table at Theodoric's feet.

"He doesn't have a brave bone left in his wretched body," Theodoric declared as he struggled to pull his sword out of the skull. He looked back at his Ostrogoths. "Kill them all. His wife. His brother. Any of his soldiers who do not swear allegiance to me." He finally got his sword out and sheathed it without cleaning the blade. He gestured at one of his men, who handed him a large axe.

Theodoric lifted it over his head. He swung, muscles and gravity working together.

Roland was splattered with brain and blood as the axe-head finished splitting Odoacer's head in half.

Theodoric acknowledged Roland for the first time. "Shove it up on the table."

The download confirmed the command. This was the way it happened. Roland grabbed Odoacer's belt and threw the corpse onto the table. Theodoric resumed his grisly work, splitting Odoacer in half as the legend, and the history, recorded.

The Missions Phase V

Rome, Roman Empire, 44 B.C.

"HERE I WILL STAND TILL CAESAR PASS ALONG," Moms murmured.

Spurinna was next to her, quiet and subdued. Overwhelmed with the past few hours, the reverberations of her errors in judgment still echoing in her mind, along with Pyrrha, her words, and her disappearance. She'd asked no questions when Moms demanded to be led to the Senate. They'd left Antony passed out, absent from the moment that would write the future history.

They were outside the Senate. Waiting.

"My heart laments that virtue cannot live," Moms continued, speaking the words from the download out loud. *"O, Caesar, thou mayst live. If not, the Fates with traitors do contrive."* She glanced over at Spurinna. "Act Two, Scene Three."

"A play?"

"Yes. Written far in the future." Moms knew she shouldn't be talking like this. "That's a fatal secret, by the way."

"All I've witnessed today is a fatal secret," Spurinna said. "I am an old woman. There are few foolish old women in Rome." She pointed. "He's coming."

Surrounded by sycophants and no guards, Caesar strode toward the Senate. Hands were clutching at his robes. As he was about to pass, he saw Spurinna and halted. "You realize the Ides are here."

As Spurinna made to answer, Moms place a hand on her arm, responding in her place. "And they have not yet gone."

"Indeed, they have not." Caesar waved an imperious hand and the crowd stepped back as he moved within a few feet of the two women. "I have heard and seen all the warnings. Yours—" he nodded at Spurinna—" and then Calpurnia's dream. Cleopatra sent a servant with a warning; the fact she didn't come herself, message enough. Antony has not shown himself. Another message."

"Then why?" Moms asked. There was a shadow in the depth of Caesar's eyes, an awareness of the situation.

"'Why'?" Caesar repeated, taking the question seriously. "What you see before you? Is a man already dead."

"The strokes?" Moms asked. "The heart-mind sickness?"

Caesar was startled. "That. But more than that. They wait for me today. If I don't make the appointment they have arranged, will they not wait for me tomorrow? And every day? And if I never show up, will that not indicate a craven coward? And can a coward rule? Eventually they will not wait and they will come for me. It is inevitable."

"Fate," Moms said.

"Yes." He glanced toward the crowd waiting at the entrance to the Senate. "I do not fear death. We all die. I fear being forgotten. I would rather die as Caesar, than live and be forgotten."

"*A coward dies many times before their deaths,*" Moms quoted. "*The valiant taste of death but once.*"

A sad smile on Caesar's part. "Very well put."

"So it will be written," Moms said.

The crowd was edging closer, pushing the time.

"I do fear one thing," Caesar said. He leaned close so only Moms could hear. "Can you tell me: what of Brutus? I love him like a son. Will harm come to him when he tries to protect me?"

And Moms lied.

Petrograd, Russia, 1917.

DOC HEARD A DISTANT NOISE, a very irritating one. A fast-paced clattering, clacking noise. It took him a moment, but then he realized it was his own teeth. Doc forced them to stop chattering, but he couldn't control the shivering. He sat up into darkness, except for the dying embers of a fire. The fireplace at which Golovkin's guards and Krylo had been warming themselves.

Panic overwhelmed the shivering. How long had he been unconscious? How long for the fire to go out? To burn down to embers? How much of his time bubble was left?

Doc jumped to his feet and regretted it as he almost passed out. His head throbbed. He assumed he had a concussion and for a moment pondered how that would affect his ability to calculate and—

"Nada Yada!" Doc said the two words out loud. Focus on the mission. If he were pulled back now, who knew what that idiot Golovkin would do. Had done!

Doc opened the door and peered out. It was dark outside the Palace. How late?

Doc headed for the Tsarina's quarters, praying that she, and her children, were still there.

As he came to the corridor that ended in the main entrance to the Tsarina's quarters, Doc was relieved to see both of Golovkin's peasants guarding the door. Doc approached in what he hoped was a commanding manner.

He wasn't very good at it, as both men stepped in front, barring his way.

"I demand to see the Tsarina!" Doc yelled as loudly as he could. "By the spirit of Rasputin, and the Will of God, I must speak to her."

He heard arguing on the other side of the door, one of them a woman's voice. So he had not failed. Yet.

The door swung open. Count Golovkin filled the doorway. He glared at Doc.

"Why did you not tell me—" he began, but the Tsarina's voice cut him off.

"Out of the way!"

The Count finally followed an order, stepping aside.

"My Angel!" the Tsarina called out, seeing Doc. "Where have you been?"

Doc glanced at Golovkin and he shook his head.

"There were other matters to attend to," Doc said.

Golovkin spoke up. "If you had told me of your prophecy, I would have assisted you."

"The prophecy was for the Tsarina," Doc said.

But Golovkin's eye glittered with something Doc couldn't quite place.

"Might we speak privately?" Golovkin asked.

Doc was going to object, but the Tsarina answered for him. "Yes. You men discuss this. I must prepare the girls. We are almost ready to leave," she said to Golovkin, shutting the door.

Golovkin pushed Doc further into the corridor, out of earshot of the two guards. "We do not have much time. The only reason I do not shoot you down right now is because the Tsarina believes in you, like she believed in that fool Rasputin. And a shot would draw attention we don't want from the Bolsheviks. They are outside arguing among themselves what to do now that the abdication has been formalized. Many advocate coming in here and killing all of them immediately."

"Where do you propose taking the Tsarina and girls?" Doc argued. "There is nowhere for them but here."

"England. To their cousin, King George. He promised that he would provide haven for the family."

"And he revoked that promise," Doc said.

"They are family!"

"They are Royals," Doc said. "Do you understand what is happening here? This is an assault on the concept of the monarchy. Do you think King George wants that on his soil? In the midst of a war that all his people are growing weary of? And the Tsarina is from Germany! How do you think the British people will react to that? When their fathers, brothers, sons, are dying battling the Germans on the Western Front? He gives refuge to a German? Get in reality, man."

Golovkin was stricken. "But, where do I take them?"

"Nowhere. I told you. The Bolsheviks will guard them. It is not in their interests to harm the Royals. It is *against* their interests."

"Will Alexei become Tsar as you promised the Tsarina?"

Doc looked him in the eye. "Yes."

"In two years?"

"Less than two years."

Golovkin didn't seem convinced. "If it is true, that would be good."

It occurred to Doc to check the download. Count Pyotr Golovkin would join the White Army, along with most of the nobles. He would be dead just over a year from now, betrayed by his own soldiers when they defected to the Reds. The information was graphic: his eyes would be torn out, then he would be forced to run a gauntlet of drunken soldiers, jabbing their bayonets at him, until he finally collapsed and bled out. He would be just one of the approximately ten million who would die in the five years as Civil War following the Revolution.

This was all about death.

"What is it?" Golovkin asked, seeing the look on Doc's face.

"Nothing. Just a bad memory."

"Your memories are our future," Golovkin said. "What is looming that brings such distress to you?"

"There are many hardships ahead for everyone," Doc said, as vague a true statement as he could utter.

They both turned at the sound of a commotion echoing through the palace.

Golovkin pulled the big revolver out of his coat. "They're coming!"

"Put that away," Doc said. "If you fight, the Tsarina and the children are sure to be killed. I guarantee you that they will not be harmed!"

Golovkin didn't put the gun away, but he didn't raise it. His two men came up and flanked him.

A large group approached down the main hallway. Doc stiffened when he saw that the Tsar was among them, Krylo scurrying close behind him. The rest were revolutionaries. Doc sifted through the download, searching for information about who was who this day at Alexander Palace.

The group halted just a few paces away. The Tsar gestured and Krylo whispered something to him.

Tsar Nicholas II pointed at Doc. "That man."

The man to the right of Nicholas issued an order. "Take him."

Four soldiers with bayonets fixed on their rifles moved toward Doc.

Golovkin stepped forward, halting them. "Wait." He addressed the man who'd given the order. "Kerensky, we must keep the peace."

"That is what I am doing," Kerensky said. "The Tsar has informed me that this man speaks as Rasputin's ghost. He has effects from the priest's body. He has snuck into the Duchesses' rooms and stolen from them. We are removing him before he can cause any more trouble." Then Kerensky matched Golovkin's step forward. "And what are *you* doing here, Count?" He glanced at the Tsar. "Your Excellency, does he have your permission to be at your family's private quarters?"

Nicholas II, former Emperor and Autocrat of All the Russias, had deep bags under his eyes. His shoulders were slumped and his hair roughly combed. He barely shook his head, not saying anything.

"Take him and those two pigs also," Kerensky ordered. The two peasants were dragged away, of no consequence, not making a protest. Several soldiers pointed their rifles at Golovkin. A pair had their bayonets pressed into Doc's coat.

Golovkin started to raise the pistol when the Tsarina's voice interrupted. "What is going on?"

"We are ridding the palace of vermin, your Majesty," Kerensky said. One of the revolutionaries snatched the gun out of Golovkin's hand.

"He is an angel sent by Grigori from heaven!" the Tsarina cried out.

"My dearest," Nicholas murmured, moving past everyone to his wife.

"He is our angel!" Alexandra protested.

"He is the spawn of the devil," Kerensky said. "Just as Rasputin."

Nicholas put an arm around his wife's shoulder. "My dearest." He led her to the door. He turned and faced the group. He summoned some energy: "May the Lord God help Russia!"

Then he shut the door, the Tsarina still crying out for her angel.

"Come," Kerensky ordered.

Shots echoed in the distance, a ragged volley.

Prodded by bayonets, Golovkin and Doc were paraded down the main corridor, out into the freezing night air. *This isn't real,* Doc thought. He felt detached, as if this was happening to someone else.

This isn't happening.

He and Golovkin were marched down the wide stairs to the circular drive, then off to the side, where small trees had been cut down. They fueled a fire around which a dozen revolutionaries were passing a bottle.

Doc saw bullet marks in the stone wall. So did Golovkin. There were two bundles off to one side and Doc realized they were the two peasant guards.

"Kerensky," Golovkin protested. "I am a Count. You have no authority over me."

"I must keep the peace here," Kerensky said. He raised his hands, as if in surrender.

"I am chosen by the Tsarina," Doc cried out. He held up the icon.

"The wall!" one of the men by the fire yelled.

The bayonets pressed. Doc and Golovkin backed up until they could go no further.

"This is your fault," Golovkin said to Doc. "We should have escaped with the family when we had the chance."

This made no sense, Doc thought. "There is no need for this! Everything will happen as it did!"

"This is not how I die," Golovkin said. "This is not how I die," he repeated, as if he could convince someone. "I should die leading my troops. Not like this."

Doc reached out and grabbed Golovkin's hand, remembering the man's horrible fate from the download. "This is better."

For you, Doc thought. He looked up, desperately wishing he were a man of faith. He spotted a candle flickering in a second floor window to the right. In the halo of light he saw Anastasia's sad face, her dark eyes looking back at him.

A command was shouted, followed the sound of rifle bolts loading cartridges into chambers.

Doc smiled sadly at Anastasia and with his free hand gave a little wave.

She waved back.

This was penance.

Palos de la Frontera, Spain, 1493 A.D.

MAC HAD ALWAYS FINISHED well ahead of Roland on the two-mile run when they were taking their semi-annual physical fitness test. Not to say Roland was a slouch; the big man did pretty well moving his weight that far, but Mac was a runner.

Mac estimated he'd put about a half-mile's distance between him and the butchery on the beach. He'd heard no sound of pursuit and a few glances over his shoulder hadn't indicated any, but he doubted he was safe. Men like Roland, and this Swiss Guard, were single-minded once given an order and the guy was probably jogging along, figuring he'd eventually catch up.

Some people were just that way. They were finishers.

So Mac kept running along the beach, the Atlantic to his right. He'd dropped the rapier right from the start. And the dagger. Now, he paused for a few moments to tear off the monk's robe. He was naked except for sandals and the purse over his shoulder, bouncing against his hip.

His stomach revolted and he dropped to his knees. He vomited the ale from the tavern and the scant contents of his last meal, which he couldn't even remember.

Got to his feet. He felt a little better. He took off once more.

Mac kept running, feeling his pulse become steady, his breathing rhythmic. Then one of the sandals gave way. He kicked the other off and angled until he was running in the surf, sand underneath his feet.

He felt free. As if he could run forever and ever—

Thermopylae, Greece, 480 B.C.

"ASSYRIANS ARE IN THE LEAD," one of Leonidas' rangers informed him as he and Scout ran up to the Spartan camp. "Swordsmen."

"Archers?" Leonidas asked. More trumpets were blaring from the far side of the rampart. The Spartans, as was their way, had no trumpeters, drummers or any 'noise-makers'.

"Just infantry," the ranger reported.

Scout walked past the King as he received other reports. To the wall.

Scout's focus was to the left, at the side of mountain. She began to climb down the far side. A Spartan sentry grabbed her arm, but she shook him off. She reached the ground and made her way to a spot about twenty feet in front of the Spartan's wall. The mountain rose straight up, the stone face surprisingly smooth.

Scout placed her hand on the rock.

"What are you doing?" Leonidas joined her.

"This is the spot," Scout said.

"For?"

"Where the map will appear."

"And once you have it?" Leonidas asked. "Do you know where you take it?"

"I have seen a vision."

A ranger came running up, warning that the Assyrians were within assault range.

The king turned to Scout. "You must wait behind the wall. When your map appears. I will get you to it." He grimly smiled. "I trusted your promise. Trust mine."

Scout allowed him to lead her back to the other side of the wall as the first ranks of Assyrians appeared.

There were less than 150 Spartans left.

The Assyrians charged and the final battle began.

Scout waited. She had to wait. It wasn't time. Not yet.

The issue was how long could the Spartans hold? Despite the ongoing slaughter of the Persian army, every now and then a Spartan went down. A warrior who could not be replaced, while Xerxes had an almost infinite supply.

The carpet of dead grew deeper, the wall of rock and corpses higher.

Scout looked to the sea. The storm that had been lingering offshore almost all night and this morning was finally moving. Landward.

"Is it time?" Leonidas' left eye was covered in blood.

Scout reached up and wiped it clean with her cloak.

The air was riven with the screams of wounded, the clash and grunts of warriors locked in mortal combat. Thunder came closer.

Along the top of the wall, here and there, Assyrians reached the crest. Only to die. But it was happening more often. Time was running out.

"Soon," Scout said. "Very soon."

"May I use your weapon?" Leonidas asked, holding up his *xiphos*, the blade broken a foot from the tip.

Scout handed him the Naga.

With his other hand, Leonidas gestured. Ten Spartans whom he'd held back, his only reserve, charged up, eager to join the fray.

"There!" Scout pointed at the spot she'd indicated earlier. A black sphere was forming. Frightened Assyrians scuttled back from it, opening a hole in their front. Leonidas held up five fingers and pointed. Half of the ten Spartan reserves dashed into the gap, widening it.

"Come," Leonidas yelled at Scout, straining to be heard over the combined roar of battle and storm. He jumped over the wall, swinging the Naga in a large arc. Clearing space. The last five Spartans followed. They locked their shields, protecting Scout. Leonidas pressed forward.

Leonidas stepped off to the left, just short of the Gate. Scout's escorts turned to face the battle, but for now, the Assyrians were too frightened to press the assault in this direction.

"Go!" Leonidas yelled.

"Not yet," Scout shouted back, focused on the utter darkness. This Gate was not for her.

Out of the Gate came two hands holding a golden orb. The hands were blistered and raw, burned so deep, bone was exposed in places. But they were steady. The sphere was large, almost three feet.

The hands came further out, the arms as damaged as the hands.

Scout reached out and took hold of the sphere.

It was surprisingly light; yet heavy in a different way. Scout found it difficult to hold, as if were pushing back against her flesh in all directions.

The hands suddenly snapped back into the Gate and it abruptly closed.

Scout yelled. "To the wall!"

Leonidas took point, the five Spartans flanking him in a wedge. There was little resistance from the Assyrians, their ranks disjointed, but there was no sign of the five who'd charged the breach in their lines.

The rest of the Spartans had regained the wall and stood on top of it, the entire Assyrian front having pulled back for the moment. Scout followed Leonidas over the wall, holding the golden sphere in front of her. She could see that the surface wasn't smooth, woven with two-inch wide strands in a seemingly random pattern.

The entire thing was pulsing, as if alive.

"The next assault will be the last," Leonidas said to her once they were over the rampart. "We cannot hold any longer. They are bringing up archers to finish us. You must go."

Scout heard him as if he were far away. She could see something in the strands, realized they were moving, ever so slowly, as if she held a nest of golden snakes, but she felt no revulsion. They weren't snakes. They were something else. A map.

Leonidas' hand on her shoulder jolted her. "You must go. Now." He was looking past her, to the south. "They are coming over the mountains. We're surrounded."

Fifty Immortals were coming round the bend from that direction, weapons at the ready. And behind them was Pandora, Naga staff in hand.

"We have lost," Leonidas said. "I will kill Pandora. That, at least, will be something."

"I have the map," Scout said. "I can open a Gate. Here. Now." She had one hand underneath the sphere, holding it up. The other was sliding over the surface. "I see."

A golden glow suffused Scout from the sphere.

"What are you doing?" Leonidas had the Naga ready and was considering whether charging the Immortals or waiting would give him the best chance at Pandora. The Persians were less than fifty feet away. The handful of Spartans in defense behind them were slowly giving ground to the Assyrians.

Scout removed her top hand from the orb and pointed to the left. A line of gold flowed from her fingertips to a spot five feet away. Spread. Turning from gold to deep black. A Gate was forming.

"Stop!" Pandora's command cut through the screams and cacophony of battle. She was leading the Immortals in an all-out charge. Everything seemed to be slowing down.

The Gate stabilized.

"Come with me," Scout said to Leonidas, taking a step toward the Gate, sphere in one hand, the other toward the King. "Come."

Leonidas smiled. He flipped the Naga around, seven-headed snake hilt toward Scout. "You'll need this. My destiny is here."

Scout's fingers curled around the haft as Leonidas spun about, bringing up a sword he'd scavenged. Pandora's Naga blade hit it, sliced through, but that was enough of a delay.

Scout was gone, the Gate snapping shut behind her.

Newburgh, New York, 1783 A.D.

"WHAT DID I FAIL TO SEE?" Eagle was utterly confounded by Caldwell's statement. So much so that the sword pointed at him was almost a secondary consideration.

Almost.

"Doesn't matter now. You're done." Caldwell pulled his arm back to stab Eagle in the heart when there was a solid thud.

Hercules' frying pan slammed into the side of Caldwell's head, the food in it flying.

The officer dropped to the ground.

"Oh, my dear God," Hercules whispered. "I didn't mean to. I didn't mean to. Lord forgive me. I'm a dead man."

Eagle gritted his teeth, pushing the pain from his shoulder back as he got to his feet. He grabbed onto Caldwell's coat with his good arm. "Help me."

Hercules dropped the pan and took hold.

Together they dragged the body across the grass toward the dark tree line.

"What have you done?" A woman's voice asked as they pulled Caldwell into the cover of the trees.

Eagle let go of the body, half faint from the effort. He saw Nancy come forward, look at the body, then at Hercules who was in a state of shock. "What did you do old man? What did you do? You're gonna have to run with me now." She glanced at Eagle. "You're pure trouble. Pure trouble." Then another practicality hit her. "Where's my food?" she asked Hercules.

Which explained the frying pan, Eagle thought. *What had he missed?*

"I'm a dead man," Hercules sat down, burying his head in his hands.

"What are you doing out here?" Eagle asked Nancy as he knelt next to Caldwell's body.

"Finishing what I started," she said. "Getting out of here. Uncle Harkless bringing me some victuals from the dinner. Now we're *all* dead. You a storm of trouble."

She had the bag, which had been awaiting the contents of the frying pan. A small satchel, several scrolls of paper poking out.

"You still have those papers?" Eagle said. "Why—"

"These be new ones to buy my way out of this place," Nancy said. "All the way to England."

Eagle took a slow, deep breath. "Who gave them to you?"

"That man this fool just done killed," Nancy said.

"He gave you papers before, didn't he?"

"Yes."

Eagle's finger was on Caldwell's neck. "He isn't dead."

"Oh, no," Hercules said. "Oh, no. He'll be seeing us all hung."

Eagle reached toward Nancy. "Let me see what you have."

"Why?"

"'Cause you don't know what you're doing," Eagle said. "You bring the wrong papers to the British, *they'll* hang you."

"Why would they?" Nancy was confused, but passed the bag to him.

Eagle began to scan the documents.

"Since when do you read?" Nancy asked. Hercules was moaning something now, over and over.

Letters to Washington about various topics, military and political. Even a few pieces of personal correspondence. But from what Eagle could tell, nothing of history-changing proportions. The speech had been made. The coup averted. If Caldwell's real mission here was to get Nancy to bring this to the British, and the first attempt had been foiled even before Eagle arrived and those papers confiscated, why would he—

"Nancy," Eagle said, focusing on the one constant. He closed his eyes and accessed the download.

"What?"

Edith was thorough, very thorough. The records of every slave Washington had ever owned, laid out on a spreadsheet, much like prized cattle. Nancy was listed there. And then one year she wasn't there. But not this year. The records indicated that she was sold in 1785. Where? To whom?

"I need get going," Nancy said, grabbing her bag back. She kicked Hercules. "Come on, you fool. You got no choice now. Got to run. You too," she added, looking at Eagle. "Even the old General will hang you for hitting a white man. No black can ever do a thing against a white without paying in blood or life."

Eagle stood up. Nancy turned to leave and he grabbed her arm. "Nancy. Wait."

"What?" She jerked her arm out of his grip and he gasped in pain.

"You can't run away."

"I can't *not* run away now. This fool saw to that."

"Hercules," Eagle said. "Get up. Take Nancy back."

"You're crazy," Nancy said. "You see this?" She shoved her foot at Caldwell. "People gonna miss him. He wakes up, goes back then—"

"He won't be waking up," Eagle said.

That gave Nancy paused. "What you plan on doing?"

"Don't worry." Eagle said. "Both of you go back."

"I'm not going back," Nancy said. "I got my ticket and I'm going. My back is on fire. Not going to be a slave no more. Can't do it. Can't do it for another minute. No way for a person to live."

"It isn't," Eagle agreed. "That's why you have to stay."

Nancy looked at him, dark eyes glinting in the growing glow from the Cantonment as night began to close around them.

"You're talking foolish again."

Eagle put a hand on her shoulder. "You said I was crazy earlier, correct?"

"You're scrambled in the head," she said.

"I am. I have visions. You have to stay because of your son."

"My son? I got no son. Got no husband. I won't *ever* bring a child into this world to be a slave. That's the worst sin in the world. Worse than killing this piece of trash here." She kicked Caldwell's unconscious body, taking some satisfaction in finally getting to strike out against a white person.

"You'll have a husband and you'll have a son," Eagle said. "He'll be important. I've seen it. In a vision."

"How can a black boy, a slave, be important?" Nancy said.

"He won't be a slave all his life," Eagle said. "He'll be free. He'll write a book. An important book. I can't tell you any more than that. But you have to trust me."

"You want me to go back, put my chains back on for a book? You're crazier than Uncle Harkless."

"Both of you go back," Eagle said. "You try running, they'll catch you. Once they know Caldwell's dead and find his body, you won't get far. You know that. Every sheriff, every militia, every white man for a hundred miles around will be hunting you. And when they get you, and they will get you, they'll hang you."

Nancy looked down at Caldwell. "But he ain't dead."

"He will be," Eagle said, picking up Caldwell's sword.

"You're crazy," Nancy said. "You can't kill him."

"I can and I will. And then they'll come for me. You'll both be safe if you go back now." Eagle pressed it home. "Take Uncle Harkless back. Once they realize I'm gone and put that together with the confrontation between Caldwell and me earlier? They'll have no doubt I killed him. Give me the papers, too."

"How are you going to get away?" Nancy asked, her resolve weakening in the face of reality.

"Don't worry about that," Eagle said. "As you said. All of this is on me. I'll bear the burden."

Hercules stood, having listened, even through his horror, figuring the angles like a man who'd survived his entire life by seeing them. "You're taking care of this?" He indicated Caldwell.

"He's on me," Eagle said. "You saved me. Gave me my life. I'm giving you yours back."

Hercules turned to Nancy. "He right, Nancy. You won't make five miles before they run you down."

"Go." Eagle pointed with his good arm back to the Cantonment. "That meeting will be breaking up soon. Caldwell will be missed."

Nancy looked uncertain. Eagle got close to her, leaned over to whisper in her ear. "I'm giving you hope. Not for you. But for your son and millions of our brothers and sisters. Your son's book will help lead to freedom for all our people." He reached into her satchel and pulled Washington's papers out.

"How can one book do that?" Nancy asked.

"How can the Bible keep people in chains but also free them in their heads?" Eagle asked in return.

"You got that right," Nancy said. "But . . ." She turned her head, her eyes but inches from his. There were tears in them. "Only if the boy will be free one day. That's the only way. Only if he'll be free one day. You gotta promise me that."

"He will be," Eagle said. "I promise you. On my life."

Hercules tugged on her arm. "Come on."

They moved toward the light of camp, but Nancy paused just before they left the trees and looked back at Eagle. "What's your real name?"

It had been so long since he'd used it, giving it up when he joined the Nightstalkers that Eagle had to actually think for a moment. He smiled, all the pieces falling into place. "Josiah. My name is Josiah."

Eagle watched them scurry back to slavery, feeling the weight of the moment and the hope for the future. Then he looked at Caldwell. He almost wished the preacher would come back to consciousness, to know his fate.

But there was no time to wait on that satisfaction. Eagle placed the papers on top of the body.

Eagle killed him with a single thrust through the papers into heart. He left the sword in the body and stepped back. In just a few seconds the body collapsed on itself, to ash, and then to nothing. Leaving the sword standing in the dirt, Washington's paper pinned under it.

Eagle he turned about, away from the Cantonment. He began walking, cradling his bad arm with the other. Long strides at first. But as he covered more distance, the blood continued to seep out of the bullet wound, pushing past Hercules' axle grease. The shock of being shot, of all that had happened in such a short time span, began to take a toll. His strides became shorter and slower.

Eagle almost fell, half unconscious. He shook his head. Something had alerted him. Then he heard it. The distant bay of hounds on the scent.

How much longer? Eagle wondered. He moved faster, but the terrain grew steep. Storm King Mountain, Eagle realized. He was moving south and east and Storm King was that way. And over it? West Point. Where he'd—

The bloodhounds were closer.

Eagle tried to run and it jolted his mangled shoulder so painfully he almost passed out, falling to his knees.

A man can only take so much, Eagle thought, as he got back to his feet and staggered forward. So strange. So strange that this had turned out the way it had.

"Uncle Tom," Eagle whispered as he walked into a tree in the darkness and staggered back. "Uncle Tom."

He could only take so much. Only so—and then there was only darkness.

Ravenna, Capitol of the Remains of the Western Roman Empire, 493 A.D.

IN THE FOREST OUTSIDE OF THE CITY, away from any road or trail, Roland stood bare-chested between the two fresh graves wearing only a loincloth. He was caked with dried blood, brains, and dirt. Streaks of sweat had cut narrow lines through all of it. The sun had gone down a while ago and a full moon punched shafts of light through the bare branches overhead.

Eric was to the right. Teleclus to the left.

Warriors from two different timelines. Both dead and buried, today, here, in this bubble of time in order that nothing changed.

Except their deaths. Which meant, as every Time Patrol member had fundamentally understood when they signed on for the gig, that they didn't matter in the big scheme of things. Their deaths weren't even the tiniest ripple in the river of history, either in this timeline for Eric, or in another timeline for Teleclus.

How many people really did matter? Kings?

Apparently.

But in his last mission it had been a nun. Actually, the child that would have been if Roland had not stopped her rape. But she'd still been killed by the Time Patrol agent from that era. She'd only have mattered if Roland had failed.

It was hard for Roland to understand.

"Where was God?"

He couldn't tell from which direction the woman's voice came.

His sword was ten feet away, piled on top of his armor and the rest of his clothes. Nada would have bitched him out for leaving his weapon out of arms reach. A Ranger Instructor would have given him a minus spot report. He might die now because of the oversight.

He slowly turned in a circle, scanning the forest.

She was a tall, slim figure standing between two trees twenty feet away. No weapon as far as he could tell, although her hands were hidden under the cloak wrapped around her. Her breath was small puffs in the chill night air.

He could get to his sword before she could get to him. But he remembered Teleclus: weapons were not enough.

"It was actually a question," she said. "Where *was* God for King Odoacer?"

"I don't know."

"Do you think Odoacer really believed in God?"

"I don't know."

"Do you?"

"I believe in my sword."

She laughed. "Simplistic but realistic."

Roland hated being asked questions. "Who are you?"

"What did Teleclus tell you?"

"He told me he was screwed. His timeline was screwed."

She laughed again. "Elegantly put." She threw off her cloak. She wore a medium length tunic with hunting boots. Of more interest to Roland was the short bow and quiver over one shoulder.

"You're a hunter?" he asked.

"Of sorts. I've had different names in different places, in different times."

"How does Diana sound?"

"It sounds like Teleclus told you more that you admitted. What else did Teleclus say?"

"He said the Shadow's mission, your mission, was me."

"That was the first part of my plan," Diana allowed.

"But you still tried to have Theodoric killed."

"That was the second part of my plan. It would have succeeded if the first part of my plan had. But how do you know I'm from the Shadow? There are many timelines."

"Teleclus said you were."

"Maybe I'm from God," she said. "Maybe I *am* a God."

"Maybe you have a big head," Roland said. "If you're a God, I shouldn't have been able to stop your plan."

"But if Odoacer's God were real, why was the King abandoned at the end, to die by Theodoric's hand? Perhaps Gods have their limits?"

"Right," Roland said. He sprinted for his sword. In his peripheral vision he saw the woman pull the bow off her shoulder with one hand, snatching an arrow out of the quiver with the other and then . . .

The Return

MOMS WAS SLIDING THROUGH the tunnel of time, forward. To her own time. There were no images of possible timelines flickering outside of the tunnel. Just darkness so absolute, it blocked any possibility of something different having occurred on the Ides of March.

Caesar died.

Fate, Moms thought.

That is what fate is.

No other options.

An absolute.

*****

Doc was heading toward the light without any effort on his part or urging from his subconscious or an Angel.

Was there an afterlife? Doc wondered distantly, outside of himself, yet inside. Had he been wrong about God all his life? Was the light heaven or hell?

But then images began to flicker on either side. It took a few moments before Doc could make some sense of them and he realized he was still alive.

Instead of looking to the other timelines, he first checked his chest, half-afraid to see blood flowing from bullet wounds, but there was no blood. Only then did he cast his gaze about.

To the left, in another tunnel, King George V, with a young Alexei at his side. Abdicating in the face of virulent protests by the English people, ending the British monarchy. World War I sputtering on as Europe fell further apart. Bolsheviks joining sides with the Germans as the English withdrew from the continent. America staying an ocean away.

Germany winning the First World War, controlling France and Italy.

There were other tunnels, above, below, all around, but Doc was moving too fast to focus on more than one, and this one was the closest and clearest.

The Great Depression, which didn't seem so great based on the images. No sign of Hitler or Nazism at all. No World War II until the Soviet Union, in a desperate attempt to funnel a rising tide of discontent outwards, attacked Germany. England allying with Germany.

An image of an American fleet of battleships traversing the Pacific, heading toward Japan, and then the tunnel veered away, into the gray of multiple timelines.

That didn't look so bad, Doc thought.

Possibilities.

******

Mac allowed himself be taken forward in time, arms akimbo, floating. He was breathing hard, but not out of breath. Off to one side a possible timeline flared up, showing a plague spreading outward from Spain, burning across Europe. A virus with the perfect timing: enough incubation to not kill the host too quickly, but contagious enough to spread fast.

It left behind only a handful.

A flash of the North American continent, but things were no better there as different diseases left behind by Columbus' crew spread from the island to the mainland.

That time tunnel narrowed as Mac went further forward, until it simply snapped out of existence.

Mac closed his eyes.

At peace.

*****

Scout was sliding through space, not time. Through a gate, into the Space Between, the sphere in both hands. She was in a tunnel, just above the dark water of the Inner Sea, the smell distinctive. There were two people standing waist deep in the black water directly ahead. One of them had his hands up and as Scout went by, he snatched the sphere from her, but she knew it was all right to let go, it was the entire purpose of this journey.

She turned to look and could have sworn the man was Dane but then she was swept up into another the tunnel. Moving forward in time.

Heading to her own time.

What did I just do? Scout wondered.

She 'looked' about, at the boundaries of the time tunnel. Running in the same direction, moving forward in time, were innumerable tunnels, all threads of timelines. So many they were almost a solid mass. But the threads were pulsing, alive, radiating an array of colors, indicating time was a variable, not constant. That there were possibilities.

An infinite number of possibilities.

But as she sped forward, she saw more and more lines that simply ended. Sometimes fading out. Other times terminating a splash of red or black.

How many timelines were there?

How many had been destroyed? How many had destroyed themselves? How many were fighting the Shadow?

And then the most chilling possibility: *How many constituted the Shadow?*

*****

For Eagle there was nothing. Unconscious, bleeding out, he was pulled forward through the tunnel of time, life draining away.

*****

Roland was sliding forward through the tunnel of time. To his own time. There were images of possible timelines flickering off to his right.

A timeline where it was Theodoric who died and Odoacer who ruled, trying to keep his kingdom together, but being subsumed by competing tribes in just a few years.

Interestingly, it curved back into this timeline, snapping into place.

It would have made no difference.

There was another, further away.

Theodoric and Odoacer as co-consuls, ruling an amalgamation of the old Western Roman Empire and the Goths laying siege to Constantinople.

A new Roman Empire arising, east and west combined.

An Empire responding out of eastern Persia, uniting with a fledgling Islamic Caliphate.

The images were going by faster and faster as Roland got closer to his own time. Concentrations camps. Guard towers topped by a blue flag and a crucifix on it; planes with Arabic writing and strange symbols on the sides, attacking Rome, the Vatican fire-bombed. Flames.

But that was not a timeline the Shadow had tried to push.

Unless. Somehow? Roland shook off the frightening possibility that Telelcus' words had been accurate and somehow, Roland was the true target.

He couldn't be that important.

Roland turned away from it. Not real. Possible changes that hadn't occurred. Were they any worse than World War I? World War II?

Were they—

Off to the left all he saw were stars. Glittering. A brilliant nebula full of color.

There was God?

Debrief

DOC HELD A COMPRESS AGAINST the side of his head. Roland wore just a dirty loincloth and hadn't bothered to clean up. He was covered in blood, dirt and other material that defied easy defining; not that anyone wanted to try. He'd come back without sword, armor and a sense of humor.

"What happened to your shoulder?" Moms asked him, indicating a line of blood. She was intact, uninjured, appearing much the same as when she left, although she was no longer self-conscious in the Amata outfit.

Roland ran his finger along the cut. "Huh. Didn't feel it. Arrow. Guess it missed as I was getting pulled into the tunnel."

They all turned to Mac, who seemed very calm, wearing a pair of Time Patrol grey coveralls since he'd arrived buck-naked, with just the Friar's purse. Waiting for him to comment on Roland's surprise at having been wounded.

"Are you all right, Roland?" Mac asked, with real concern.

Roland blinked. "Yeah."

"Who shot at you?" Mac asked.

"Some chick," Roland said. "I think she was from the Shadow."

Scout looked up from her hands. The skin was burned from the map. The equivalent of a bad sunburn. She hadn't felt it until she arrived back. "What was her name?"

Roland shrugged. "Guy said her name was Diana. She was there when I arrived and there when I left. She had a bow and arrow and took a shot at me. I was lucky."

"We were all lucky," Moms said. "Except Eagle." She looked at one of the doors. "Dane said he'd let us know as soon as possible."

"He looked pretty bad," Roland said. "He's got to be okay." That was as close as Roland could come to prayer, but it was as surprising as Mac's lack of snark.

Moms reached out and picked up Doc's coat. She wiggled a finger through a hole. "What happened?"

"Firing squad," Doc said.

"But the bullets didn't hit you," Moms noted. "Just the coat."

"I don't pretend to understand this." Doc was staring at his hand, at the fingernail marks the Count's hand had made when it clinched just before the first rifle in the firing squad went off.

One of the four doors open and Dane walked in. "Eagle will make it," he said. "He's stabilized and will need shoulder surgery."

"Can we see him?" Moms asked.

"Not yet," Dane said. "There are some loose ends from your mission debriefs we need to cover."

"Really?" Doc said. "How about the fact my Time Patrol contact had his own plan for the future?"

"Mine too," Moms said.

Both of them briefly explained Golovkin and Spurinna.

"That's not good," Dane understated, when they finished. "But not unexpected. They're doing the best they can without any idea what the future is to be. Like we are right now with our own future. It's natural that some would try to be pro-active."

Doc stuck a finger through the hole in his coat. "This is what pro-active causes."

"But you made it," Dane said.

"I did," Doc admitted. "But the agent didn't. And the Tsarina and the Duchesses and Alexei and—" his voice broke.

"You knew their fate going in," Dane said. "It was their fate before you left and—"

"And Anastasia," Doc said, ignoring Dane. "I swear she knew what I was. And she knew that Rasputin wasn't of her time."

Dane's voice was firm: "I don't think Rasputin was from the Shadow or a time traveler. Like Mac's missions to Raleigh on Black

Tuesday, and with the Friar this time. I suspect Rasputin was visited by a Valkyrie and received messages he thought were sent by God. Give visions to a man who was most likely bipolar and you've got a dangerous mixture."

He shifted from Doc to Mac. "You were right in your suspicions. Analysis of the syringe reveals a recombinant virus that would merge with the syphilis. Make it much more virulent and contagious. It's an ingenious biological weapon."

"Not from that time period?" Mac asked.

"The syringe is time appropriate," Dane said. "But the top genetic scientists today would be hard pressed to come up with this virus. That's definitely not of that era. It's from the Shadow. Again, a Valkyrie most likely gave it to the Franciscan."

"Who else could it be from?" Scout demanded. "Who else do we need to be worried about on these missions?"

Roland spoke up. "There was someone from another timeline on my mission.".

"Diana?" Scout asked.

"No." Roland shook his head. "She was probably Shadow. There was someone else. *Another* timeline. A warrior. Said he was from Sparta, but in a timeline where Sparta ruled the world. But they owed tribute to the Shadow and sent warriors as payment. He said he was taking orders from Diana."

"We know there can be an infinite number of timelines," Dane said. "The Shadow has destroyed some. Conquered some and holds them as vassals. Some are moving forward, unaware of other timelines."

"You know," Moms said, ignoring Dane, "this Diana sounds a lot like the way her namesake is described in Roman mythology. Goddess of the hunt. In Greek mythology, she was called Artemis."

"How'd you make that connection to mythology?" Scout asked.

Moms turned to her and before she could say anything, Scout said: "I ran into Pandora."

"I met Pyrrha," Moms said. "Pandora's daughter. And she knew your name," she added. "And my name."

"And Pandora had the Sight," Scout added.

"I've got your report," Dane said.

"That's not an answer," Moms said. "What's going on?"

"This is something new," Dane replied. "We don't know what it means. We don't know if this Diana is even connected to Pandora and Pyrrha."

"But those two are *definitely* connected," Moms said. "Are they Shadow?"

Scout cut in. "I'm not sure they are. Pandora seemed to have a different agenda. And she killed a Valkyrie that was coming for me."

"We'll look into it," Dane promised vaguely, which caused Scout to roll her eyes.

"You don't know squat, do you?" Doc said. "You not only don't understand the science of the time travel we're playing with, you don't know who or what the Shadow is. You don't know—"

Dane angrily cut him off. "I know the Shadow wants to wipe this timeline out. Isn't that enough? It is for me. *My* timeline was annihilated by a Time Tsunami while I was in the Space Between. Everyone I knew, my family, every living being, gone. Nothing left. Just a dead Earth. My Earth." He glared at Doc. "I might not know 'squat' but I do know that."

There was a long silence.

Moms broke it. "Could you please take us to see Eagle?"

Dane looked as if he were going to protest, but the five team members were on their feet and he bowed to the inevitable. "Come on."

He led them out of the team room, along the spiral deck, to another of the numerous ubiquitous white doors. He opened it. An ascending staircase led outward, away from the pit of the Possibility Palace.

"The future?" Doc asked, his scientific curiosity punched through the morbid reminders of his mission.

"No," Dane said. "We're going to the outer rim of the Possibility Palace. There's more to Time Patrol headquarters then just the inside."

"Apparently," Scout said.

Dane briskly climbed the stairs, the team wearily following. They went up for several minutes, before reaching another door. Dane opened it and indicated they should pass through.

Dane shut the door behind them.

"To the left." He led them along a slightly curving corridor lined with doors on the right.

He paused at one door and knocked.

Eagle's voice replied. "Come in."

Moms shoved past Dane and led the way. The team piled into the room, Scout last in line, slamming the door in Dane's face. They all halted, not at the sight of a bandaged Eagle reclining in a hospital bed, a Kindle on the covers over his lap, but at the view through the bay window and the vista below and beyond: A wind swept undulating plain, covered with towering grasses. Almost as far as the eye could see, but in the distance, a mountain range soared into the sky above the prairie. It was impossible to discern how far away the mountains were, and thus, how high, but they were majestic. The sun was setting behind them, casting long shadows.

"Something, eh?" Eagle said. "I don't know where or when we are right now, but it's not populated as far as I can tell. Haven't seen a single contrail in the sky. There's no sign of civilization outside of here. Seen some birds at a distance but couldn't tell what they were. Haven't spotted anything on the ground yet, but sometimes the tall grass moves as if something is pushing through."

"The past." Doc walked to the window and put a hand on the glass. "The distant past. Has to be."

"Most likely," Eagle agreed.

"How are you?" Moms asked.

"Got some shoulder surgery coming up," Eagle said. "I'm tired. But otherwise, I'm good." He held up the Kindle. "I'm more than good." He put it back down on the covers.

"What are you reading?" Scout sat on the foot of the bed, as the rest of the team crowded round.

Eagle didn't have to look at the screen to tell them the title, even though it was long. "*The Life of Josiah Henson, Formerly a Slave, Now an Inhabitant of Canada, as Narrated by Himself.* Published in 1849."

"That was your mission?" Scout asked.

"Thought it was George Washington," Roland said.

Eagle smiled. "It was Washington. But it was much more than that." He thumped the Kindle with his good hand. "Harriet Beecher Stowe used this book and Henson's life story as the basis for *Uncle Tom's Cabin.* Which was the strongest contributing factor to the abolitionist movement in the North."

"Was he there? Where and when you went?" Moms asked. It was growing darker outside, the sun halfway down, behind the mountains, a single peak silhouetting it on the right side.

Eagle's smile disappeared. "I convinced Josiah Henson's mother, Nancy, not to escape, on the promise that her son, who hadn't been born yet, would be very, very important.." He tapped the Kindle. "This proves he was."

"Except she had to stay a slave," Doc noted. "And I let everyone who I met die. Including Anastasia. Maybe I could have saved her at least?"

"You not only couldn't have," Moms said, "it would have compromised the mission."

"'The Mission'?" Doc said. "People die because of—"

"Now you know why Dane sent you," Moms said. "You had to understand first-hand what this means. The implications of the Patrol."

"They would have died regardless," Eagle said. "We kept things as they were. Are. Good and bad."

"We're playing God," Doc argued.

Roland snorted. "God? Where is God?"

Everyone turned to him in surprise.

"What?" Moms asked.

"That's what the king asked," Roland said. "Odoacer. After I betrayed him and just before Theodoric killed him." He looked at his teammates. "Is there a God? Is there some being controlling all of this? Pulling our strings? Someone besides Dane?"

"I don't know about God," Scout said. "But I think there is something more."

"Fate," Moms said. "Or more appropriately, the Fates."

"What do you mean?" Scout asked.

"Pyrrha said the Fates were powerful," Moms said. "She said there are things that cannot be changed. Things that the Fates have made as part of a higher law." She glanced at Scout, not adding the part about the 'forever death' that had been threatened.

"Who are the Fates?" Roland asked. "Some sort of Gods?"

"Not Gods," Eagle said. "In a way, the Fates were the checks on the Gods. A principal of natural order being supreme."

"In other words, God, but not God," Roland said. "Nature." He turned from them and walked over to the window, where night now covered the land outside. "Look." He pointed up at the stars. "There is God. The Fates. Whatever you want to call it. Something bigger than us. Smarter than Dane. More powerful than the Shadow."

The rest of the team joined him, except Scout, who reached out and took Eagle's good hand and squeezed it tight. They all looked out at the stars.

"Pandora left one thing in her box," Scout said. "I believe it ties in to what Roland is saying. I believe it's the thing we have that will save us."

The four by the window turned to face her.

"What was that?" Moms asked.

"*Elpis*," Scout said. "Hope."

New York City: The Present

"THE NEEDLE'S FINE," Edith Frobish said.

The hieroglyphics were back. Edith, not trusting her eyes or Ivar's, had asked three different passerby's. All confirmed they saw what she and Ivar saw, then hurried away from the crazy couple standing next to Cleopatra's Needle.

"The team did it," Edith said.

"They did," Ivar agreed. "I hope everyone is all right."

Edith had her satchel and Ivar had a large backpack full of notes over one shoulder. They'd come back to the here and now do some research and had just met back up at the Needle.

"We'll know shortly," Edith said. "Let's get out of here before we run into another policeman wondering why we're wondering."

She had an extra bounce in her step now that all was in place in her world. She pushed open the metal door on the side of the Metropolitan Museum of Art labeled: 'Authorized Personnel Only'.

There was no security guard on duty.

"That's odd," Edith said.

Ivar shifted the heavy load he was carrying. "Let's go. I want to look at this data for—"

"No," Edith said. "This isn't right."

Ivar sighed as Edith led them down a corridor but turned left instead of right.

"Edith," Ivar began, but then she pushed open a door and stepped through. Having no choice, Ivar followed. They were on a balcony overlooking one of the exhibit halls. A throng of people were milling and moving below them taking in the paintings and sculptures.

"Everything's fine," Ivar said. "Can we—"

Edith gasped. She lifted a hand, finger trembling. "Look!"

Ivar stared where she was pointing. A row of paintings. "I don't—" he faltered as one of the paintings faded from sight.

No one in the crowd seemed to notice.

"I don't—" Ivar began, but then another painting was gone.

"Oh, dear!" Edith exclaimed. "Not the art."

"It's just some paintings," Ivar said.

Edith turned to him and grabbed him by the shirt. "Don't you understand? The art is the beginning of everything. If it all disappears, it's the end of everything."

THE END

Coming 23 May 2016
D-Day
The next installment in the Time Patrol Series
by Bob Mayer

The future is made by ordinary people doing extraordinary things.

The fact that history doesn't record the heroics of these people doesn't alter that.

The 6th of June is a day full of such events.

While history doesn't record the heroics, there are those who notice. And there are those who want to stop those ordinary people and change our history in order to create a time tsunami and wipe our present out.

It is up to the Time Patrol to send an agent back to each 6th of June and make sure that doesn't happen!

Order your copy now!
Amazon

For more on the following, I recommend these books:

Nightstalkers: Time Patrol. How the Nightstalkers became the Time Patrol

Time Patrol: Black Tuesday. The first mission run by the Time Patrol, to 29 October in six different years.

The Nightstalkers Series: The Fun in North Carolina. The Fun in the Desert. And a history of the Nightstalkers and how they dealt with the Rifts, a President who cannot tell a lie and more! Where the Nightstalkers first encounter Scout in a gated community in North Carolina.

The six book Atlantis Series: Tells the story of *another* Earth timeline that faced the Shadow and fought a battle against it covering centuries. We meet Tam Nok, Sin Fen, Foreman, Dane, Amelia Earhart, and more from another timeline that battled the Shadow. As well as: The Ones Before. Corpse Loddin. The Space Between, The Shadow, The Ones Before.

The books cover a battle in the present and great battles in the past such as Little Big Horn, Isandlwana, the 300 Spartans at Thermopylae, Gladiators in the shadow of Mount Vesuvius and more.

About Bob Mayer

Bob Mayer is a NY Times Bestselling author, graduate of West Point, former Green Beret (including commanding an A-Team) and the feeder of two Yellow Labs, most famously Cool Gus. He's had over 60 books published including the #1 series Area 51, Atlantis and The Green Berets. Born in the Bronx, having traveled the world (usually not tourist spots), he now lives peacefully with his wife, and said labs, at Write on the River, TN.

For more information check out COOLGUS.COM

31200356R00131

Made in the USA
Middletown, DE
23 April 2016